I0763373

THEY LOOKED WEST

GRADY SOUTHWICK

THEY LOOKED WEST
2nd Edition

In association with
Elite Online Publishing
Sandy, UT 84070
info@eliteonlinepublishing.com

ISBN-13:

DEDICATION

This book is dedicated to my beautiful wife, Patty, and my daughters, Shawnie, and Kallie. Without their efforts this work would not have been possible. They were the encouraging light in the tunnel that kept me working to the end. They are both a great blessing to me in my life, and I am grateful for their love and support.

CONTENTS

FORWARD

The setting for the novel is post Civil War America. The North had just defeated the South in one of the bloodiest wars ever fought on the American continent. During the war years, many American families were relocating to the rich and fertile valleys of the upper and central California regions and all along the Pacific coast from Oregon to Washington. Although, many traveled by ship around the farthest most point of South America, the majority had limited resources and funds and made the trek by foot, wagon, or horseback. Groups of families and neighbors would often form coalitions with mountain men and westerners who had made the crossing before while exploring the regions for fur animals. The trip usually consisted of a wagon train pulled along by large oxen at a lumbering pace. Most of the travelers made the trip by walking alongside their animals. These were hearty people who could take the rigors of the day and continue for months on end until their desired destinations were reached. Many were not so fortunate and the mortality rate along the trail was surprisingly 18%. Most of the victims perished due to sanitary conditions. The trails that most of the pioneers followed were drawn along water courses that intersected and flowed toward the Missouri River on the east side of the Rocky Mountains and toward the Pacific Ocean on the west side. In the spring, these tributaries would fill in with snowpack and melt during the early summer months, providing the pioneers with fresh water for their stock and personal needs. Unfortunately, the use of these slow moving meandering waterways meant death to many an unsuspecting human being. The animals were driven through the shallow parts and allowed to rest and replenish themselves in the cool streambeds and pools. This same water was taken and consumed by millions of travelers along the trails.

A hidden and deadly disease called cholera came on the scene in the late 1840s and was finally named and recognized by medical professionals around the time of the Civil War. Medical professionals of the time were baffled for a cure. Some of the local Indian tribes had small herbs and treatments for the symptoms of the disease, which would help if administered immediately, but these were not cures. A cure never developed until the early 19th century, and by that time most of the expansion of the United States had already taken place. Other deadly diseases that plagued the western travelers of the times were small pox, malaria, anthrax, and typhoid fever. Smallpox was a deadly disease especially for the Native American Indians, who had no immunities to its infectious lesions. Thousands of Indians were taken by the disease in the early part of the 1800s. The deadly disease found its way all along the Missouri River regions and clear up into Canada. The once proud and fearful Blackfoot tribe of Northern Montana was decimated by the pox and reduced in numbers never to be a warlike force again. The Missouri tribes, such as the Ponca and Osage, were hit hard by the disease, and their numbers reduced to a few hundred Indians just after the Civil War era. As the white man expanded his reach on the rich and vast lands of the West, he brought disease and unwanted turmoil to the nomadic lives of the Native American Indian.

During the Civil War years, the United States government could barely keep enough soldiers stationed on the frontier to patrol the paths for the civilian masses in route to the rich goldfields of California. Military forts were built along the Oregon Trail and Bozeman Trails. These two courses paved the way for the modern expansion of the era. The army sent what little manpower it could spare to meagerly supply and defend these small outposts along the frontier. The Native American Indians saw this move by the white man as an infringement on their territorial hunting grounds. They were determined to defend their rights with their lives. As the westward movement moved along, clashes between the Indians and settlers were inevitable. A massive amount of lives and bloodshed were the cause of encroachments upon the Indians' buffalo hunting grounds. The buffalo was a complete source of life to many of the nomadic and plains Indians of the era. Blazing several major trails through the middle of the buffalo domain infuriated the Plains Indian and threatened his way of life. The army's position of the time was to make whatever treaties it could until the war was over and more troops could be sent to the region. Many treaties were made, and all were broken by the government of United States as free elections changed the course of politics and ideas in the eastern civilized halls of Congress. All the army could do was wait around for new orders and try to carry them out as ordered. Meanwhile, the Indians became more dangerous and warlike. Depredations by the hundreds were made by raiding and hostile roving bands of Indians. The entire frontier was unsafe for unescorted travel. At one point, the entire Oregon Trail from Omaha, Nebraska, to Fort Laramie, Wyoming, was not safe to journey without a major military escort. Still, the expansion of the West continued. Groups of white emigrants would band together for defensive purposes and make the trek westward. These wagon trains provided safety in numbers and, for the most part, success to those who made the passage.

Just at the end of the Civil War, the United States government decided it would speed up the westward movement and elected to build a transcontinental railway from the Atlantic coast to the Pacific coast. This railway was constructed mostly by freed black slaves from the southern states and Chinese immigrants from the played-out goldfields of California. As this novel's setting is during this period, the author felt the need to mention the railroad. It would not be ready in time for Haley Johnson to make the safe and comfortable trip by train. She was forced to make the trek by wagon train. With the war having just ended, the eastern streets were full of wounded and tired soldiers. The war had taken its toll on all the civilians as well. The nation needed a time of healing, and it was during this period that Haley Johnson's mother and father were drawn to the Utah territories by the Mormon prophet Brigham Young. Haley's father was a renowned scholar and university professor. The Mormons were in desperate need of fresh minds with educational and teaching skills. A job was offered to the old Professor Johnson, and he and his wife accepted the Mormon leader's hand. The Mormons were a religious group. The religious movement was in its infancy, and the Mormons had migrated west to the unknown reaches of the Great Basin to escape condemnation from the rest of the United States. They had made a westward trek in 1847 and settled in the desert valleys of the Great Salt Lake. By the time Haley Johnson and her family converted to the Latter-day Saint religion, the Mormons were well settled in the Utah area and had become a wealthy, industrious people. She would finish her higher level of education, and upon graduation she would make the trek west to meet up with her parents.

Gabe Tanner was a single, young, white European-bred son. He had been brought west by his father and mother both of whom died at young ages. Gabe was tendered in the care of an old mountain man that had taught him the ways of the trail and the game animals that called it his home. He was too young for most of the Civil War, and by the time the army got around to conscript him, he was already serving with the Pawnee Battalion and Major North. It was decided by the war department that his services would be better spent in the frontier regions of the West than on the closing battlefields of the Civil War. Gabe found himself learning to track, trail, and engage the hostile Plains Indian in all manner of warfare. He had seen countless hours in the saddle, scouting and following the raiding parties of wild Indians as the Pawnee Battalion served the government of the United States during the years immediately following the surrender of the Confederacy of the Southern States. Few in numbers, the battalion fought a fierce three-year engagement with the warring nations of the Sioux, Cheyenne, and Kiowa tribes. Gabe remained unscathed throughout but had many close calls with death as he scouted the recesses and far outlying paths of the frontier.

Along with his closest friend (his big grey horse named Old Smoke), he carved out a reputation for himself as being a good scout and Indian fighter of the period. After his enlistment had run out, he found himself without employment and plenty of time on his hands. When the Mormons approached him at Omaha, the young scout had nothing going for himself, and the offer seemed liked a good one. Little did Gabe know of the events which he would find himself in and the course his life would travel. Meeting new and strange people, Gabe found himself immersed in a religious group of individuals. The Mormons were bound for the Utah territories and their chance to live in Zion. They were loaded up with all their families and possessions. The wagon master selected for the trip was an old seasoned teamster named Otis. He and his two adopted Choctaw Indian sons made the trip from Omaha to Salt Lake City and return. Otis kept the wagons in order and made sure the new Mormons made the trip with safety and care. The Choctaw Indians Davey and Tim would accompanied the wagons, foraged meat, and scouted the passageways with Gabe Tanner.

The route decided upon for the wagon train was the northerly direction along the Loup River chain. This helped the Mormons avoid the polluted streams to the south along the Oregon Trail following the Platte River and its tributaries. The plan was a good one, and the wagon train made slow progress getting underway and working to the usual hardships of the trail. All of the attitudes among the Mormons were high with anticipation, and they all looked forward to the trek before them. Haley Johnson traveled with a family she had met earlier. She travelled alone and taught the children of the Mormons as a way to earn her keep along the trail. Everything was going smoothly until the grip infected the wagon train. People fell ill and many died from the effects. A miracle was afforded the Saints in the manner of a small orphaned boy named Will. His rescue at the hands of the scouts, Gabe and Davey would spell blessings of the utmost for many who had fallen victim to the sickness.

The plains were full of marauding Indians and villains. The army had posted several new forts in the upper Wyoming Territories. One fort worth noting was a fort along the Wyoming-Montana border named Fort Sheridan. This fort would become famous for several Indian massacres that took place near its borders. The presence of the fort infuriated the local Indians, and a great war chief named Red Cloud declared war on all whites in retaliation for the military posts construction. The warring tribes of the Lakota Sioux and their allies, the Cheyenne, and Arapaho immediately started depredations upon any and all who dared to trespass their paths on the open prairie. The warring tribes showed no mercy and made raids from northern Montana all the way down through the plains into the Republican and Arkansas River regions of Oklahoma and Kansas. The massive war parties overran the 4th and 7th armies of the United States government and made non-discriminate raids on white settlements and old time rival reservation Indians of the territories. Their longtime rivals were Pawnee, Osage, Ponca, and all the Missouri tribes that they had been at war with over the buffalo hunting rights. These later Plains Indian tribes had become friendly with the

United States government and had been allotted reservations and support for their friendship. The Sioux saw this as a sign of weakness and vowed to kill their Indian cousins to the south. Bloody raids were made on the unsuspecting reservation Indians, and the army had its hands full just protecting the travel routes that stretched for miles through Nebraska and Kansas.

Many warriors, such as Black Tongue and Yellow Hand, took up the war trail. This was the way of the warrior and all they had been taught from the time they were babies. This was their moment in the sun, and they would take every opportunity that passed in front of them to further their stature among their families and friends. They were wild and dangerous young men with no laws and miles of prairie before them in which they could enact whatever form of madness they perceived without retribution or consequences. The army of the day was barely getting accustomed to Indian fighting, and most of the ranks were comprised of young immigrants from European countries. They were conscripted in return for citizenship in the United States. They were ill-trained and badly outnumbered by the Plains Indians of the time. It is in this time period of confusion, war, and expansionism by the United States and its citizens that we find our story evolving.

MAP

N
E
S
W
Council Bluffs
Omaha
Nebraska City
Fort Kearny
Choctaw Indians
Pawnee Indians
North Trail
Old Indian Trail
Ponca Indians
Elkhorn River
North Loup River
Middle Loup River
South Loup River
Platte River
Oregon Trail
Dakota Territories
Niobrara River
Sioux Indians
Nebraska
Kansas
Badlands
Black Hills
Traders Creek
Cheyenne Indians
Wyoming Territories
Fort Laramie
Fort Caspar
Fort Bridger
Arapaho Indians
Colorado
A
B
C
D
E
A: Conner Massacre
B: Indian Raid on Mormons
C: Medicine Tree
D: Traders Creek
E: Frenchie's Cabin

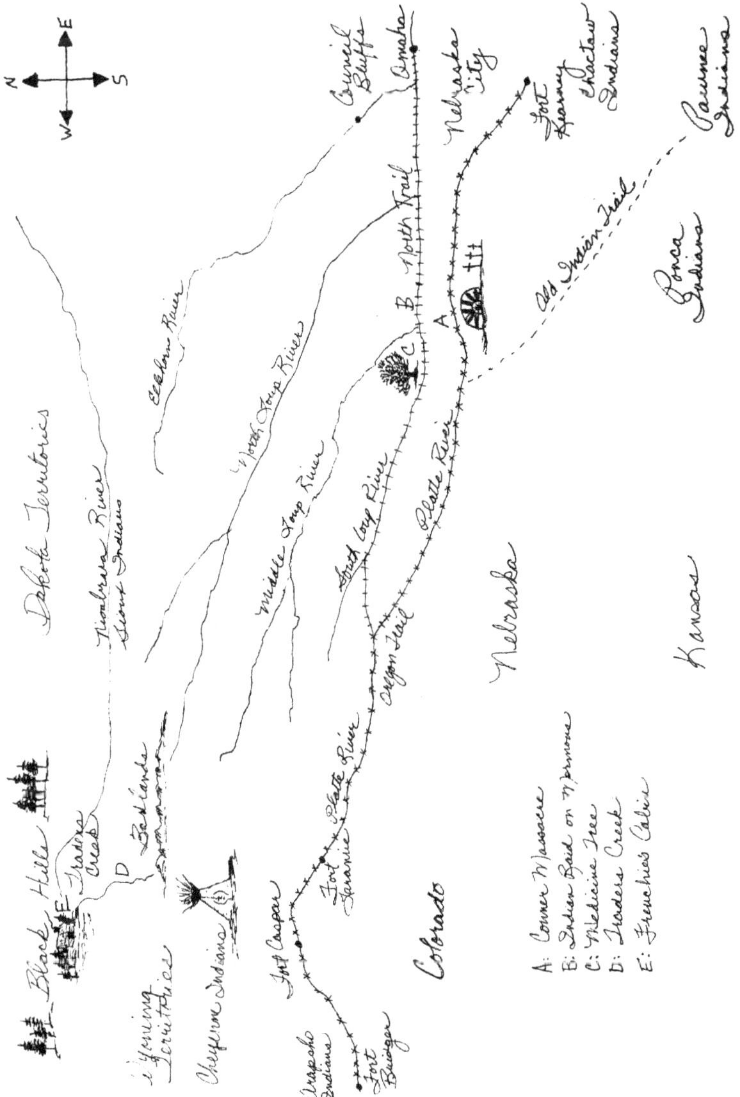

**Although the events in this story are based on real historical facts, any correlations between actual human characters or names are strictly unintended by the author.*

CHAPTER 1 - THE SCOUT

As the morning sun started to lighten the sky, the scout heard a faint familiar sound of northern geese, cackling on their way south for the winter. The days were getting shorter, and the frost lingered in the shadows until mid-morning. The morning sky had a hint of rain, and he saw some distant clouds that looked heavy and billowy. As he inspected his surroundings, he noticed the grey standing relaxed with one hind partially lifted to take his weight off. Old Smoke, as he named him, stared off into the distance with ears pointing to the sound from the sky. Last night's fire was nothing more than a small smoldering ember but still enough for a renewed flame, as he reached down and blew the ashes away to find the embers. There, just enough to get the small kindling started. He'd have a hot one brewing in no time. This small fire will take the edge off the frosty morning air the scout thought to himself.

As he took in the morning and the warmth of the flame, his thoughts brought in the world around him. Here he was on a scout for a wagon train company of Mormons heading west. The company was two weeks behind his traveling schedule, and each day brought more dangers than the last. It wasn't enough that the company was running low on supplies, but they were dealing with a different summer sky than he was used to. The frost came earlier than other years, and there had been rain in the air every three or four days for a month now. Combined with the new sign the scout had picked up yesterday just before sunset, it was a disaster waiting to happen.

Just yesterday the scout had spotted, along the neck outline of Old Smoke his horse, some distant figures that he perceived to be a herd of elk. While engaged in this endeavor he happened to looked down a ravine to his right side and saw a small disturbance in the far bank. Faint as it was, it still showed human travel. Now, what kind of human would be clear out in the great open traveling in a predatory fashion? There could only be two choices, and neither was good. It was either the worst kind of white man or Mister Indian. As the scout slid quietly from the saddle, his eyes never left the horizon. He dropped the reins on Old Smoke and walked to the nearest bank, looking for clues. Once through the dry wash to the other side, there it was, no mistaking; it was a partially defined moccasin track. Whoever left this track was a cunning foe, to say the least. He walked down through the wash and up the other side like he was floating in the air. There could only be one reason for this unseen foe being in this location: he was scouting for a group of others or he had eyes on the scout. How many others were in the vicinity? The scout needed to find out quickly so a plan could be made.

The scout had decided to stay out last night and act as if nothing was noticed so if he was being observed he would not alarm the observer. This was the reason for the fire and the usual morning offerings. He knew his smoke was known, and his location would give the scout some confidence that he had the unseen foe under control. The company wouldn't be alarmed at the scout staying out all night since many times in the previous weeks he would leave and hunt game several days out, returning at some point along the route to wait for the wagons with fresh meat. This time would be no different, except he needed to alarm the company without really being noticed. The last thing the wagon company needed was a different look to their natural progression along the trail. This might change ol' Mister Savage and provoke an attack of some kind, and the company would not be ready. The scout wanted the terms of the trail in their favor so they might prevail and onslaught if necessary.

As he sat there on a log that had been blown out by lightning, drinking the brew and chewing on a piece of soaked hardtack, he studied his situation. His mind was racing for a solution. The company was a full day's ride--give or take--to the east of him. If he waited there, they would not arrive until tomorrow afternoon. That would be too much time for them, not being aware of the danger he had found. Also, his position would undoubtedly be relayed to the other Indians if there were more in the party. He needed to somehow slip past the scouting Indian and travel undetected towards the company hopefully meeting up with them sometime this afternoon. This might seem easier than it appeared, but one problem was he wasn't sure where the Indian was located. He needed to find him first before the Indian made a move in the wagon's direction.

He decided to go it on foot and leave his camp just as it was, giving the impression he knew nothing of the Indian's presence. This might be a big mistake because maybe this was a lone Indian looking for some horse hair or his hair. And leaving Old Smoke hobbled and standing in a white man's camp with smoke in the air might be inviting a small hide war. Indians prided themselves on getting as close to an enemy as they could and would either take some booty or leave a man on foot without putting themselves in real danger. Sometimes this could work to your advantage if you played the game right, and you could beat ol' Mister Indian at his own trade.

Many years ago the scout had learned some mighty good lessons about Indians and their ways from an old mountain man that had lived among them for many years. He took the young scout in when he was orphaned and taught him the wild ways when he was in his youth. The lessons he learned have kept his hair on his head to this day. Yes, he had had many a close call, and some real hair-lifting experiences, but the old mountain man taught him one thing, and that was to stay cool and keep his wits about him no matter how ugly the situation got. Now sitting there this morning, he was in a situation that he needed to find a remedy before it got ugly.

The scout slowly looked over the area around him, trying to make out any visible sign that might be Indian. He moved around his makeshift camp, cleaning up his brew and fire, acting like he was enjoying the great open, tending to his morning chores, rubbing down the grey, and cutting him some buffalo grass for forage. He decided to tie his hind foot so he had a three-way hobble. He did this with a piece of rawhide string he had in the saddle pouch. He made it look like he was examining his feet for soreness or stones so he wouldn't look suspicious. The scout knew if he tied the horse’s head that would be a signal that he knew of the Indian's presence, so instead he used the hobble system.

Now, the scout’s routine would usually make for the creek to fill canteens and maybe wash up a bit, but he thought he could make his observer think he was going after some breakfast meat. So he pulled the Henry from the scabbard and checked the breach. One shell in the chamber and fourteen to go if needed. Very slowly he started down the game trail that led to the creek bottom. There was a set of old buffalo trails worn deep by the passing herds to and from the water's edge. When he hit the bank of the stream, he kneeled slightly and took a handful of water to his mouth. As he did this, the scout was scanning the far distant horizon in front of him, looking for every detail he could to detect any danger. There was nothing. The fact that he was still alive from the previous night's dangers had his mind doing cartwheels. He had been up without sleep since he discovered the moccasin track, listening nonstop to the night wind and waiting for an attack or approach but nothing came. There he was with an unknown enemy somewhere in the vicinity. The unknown Indian knew all about the scout, but the scout didn't have a clue about him. So the scout determined to change methods that morning and level the odds just a bit.

As he crossed the stream and got up the far bank, the scout still had the grey horse in sight. His head was down, and he was busy nosing through the buffalo grass the scout had laid at his feet. A lone crow came winging down the valley and made several caw sounds that broke the morning silence. As he crested the bank, the land flattened out before him. The scout saw a vista of old trails winding back and forth through buffalo grass, birch trees, and pine flowing through the valley with rolling hills and small valleys as far as the eye can see in any direction. A member of the company had once mentioned to him upon seeing a vast, beautiful landscape like this, "God was having a real good day when he created all this."

The buffalo trails were worn so deep in places that they would hide a small child from view walking through them. This weighed heavily on his mind, for an unseen enemy would have concealment within several yards of him if he ventured out into the plain. He moved across to a higher hillside that gave him some view into the internal maze of trails, grass, and woodland.

He was just beginning to enjoy the scene when a small movement caught his eye to his left and disappeared quickly into the brush. He dropped to one knee and leveled the

Henry in one swift motion. As he tried to make out the movement, his eyes focused on the spot that had been his attention when another quick movement about twenty yards farther to the right brought his gun sight up to a position. With all his might, he tried to make out any form that he could identify. There it was, moving swiftly through the brush and finally into his sights in the open. Briefly, he made out the half outline of a deer. It appeared to be alone and moving along the stream valley to the north. He would normally take the shot and have a welcome venison meal strapped on Old Smoke for the company's arrival, but today was different.

Just in case he wasn't being watched at that moment, he didn't want to give his location away with a gunshot. From this kneeling position, the scout took the opportunity to look completely around himself and take notice of all things pertaining to the forest. He was nearly concealed from everything this low to the ground. So he decided to move slowly on his belly up the valley floor and another half mile from his camp. His goal was to get far enough out that he could make a big swing around to his left and maybe pick up a sign. If he didn't find anything there, then he would continue in this fashion farther south of his camp putting himself downstream of this position by a mile or so.

As the scout moved along, it was tiresome work on his belly with a long barreled Henry and his provisions, knife, and extra bullets belted to him. However, he made good time, and upon reaching his first point, he found nothing of interest on the valley floor. So he continued around to the south. Reaching this point he had covered three-quarters of the area that was in front of his camp. Now he was really concerned, for this had given the enemy plenty of time to steal the grey or set up some kind of ambush near his camp. This could be done without him detecting the enemy's position. Finally, the scout decided to walk cautiously back to camp and try something else.

When he came in view of his camp, his heart was happy to see the grey standing in the same position, finishing the buffalo grass. He quickly took off the hobbles and put on the tack and saddle. The scout had made up his mind to make a fast exit from the area to the rear of his camp and backtrack to the track he had discovered the night before and try to follow the sign from there with full daylight. Just as he was getting ready to stirrup, a horror before him unfolded and a chill went up his spine, thoroughly jolting his senses. In the hard-soiled underbrush, not two feet from the grey, was a faint moccasin track. It was just barely visible to the naked eye. He knelt and examined it and saw that it looked the same size as the other one he found the night before. He was now in a position of real danger. Why didn't the Indian take the grey? What was the motive here? Indians prided themselves on stolen horse hide. The grey was his for the taking, and an Indian on horseback was the most dangerous enemy in the country. This would have put the scout afoot in the big open and made him easy prey to a hostile band of Indians looking for his provisions and the rifle. Yes, the rifle is the grand prize in this chess match of wits and cunning. For an Indian with a repeating rifle, such as the Henry, would be tall man on the plains, equaled by none other.

The scout was in great peril and he knew it. As quickly as this all unfolded, he determined to make a mad dash for the open valley floor on the other side of the stream. That would, at least, get him out where an enemy could be seen approaching him. Here in this timbered camp setting, he was a sitting duck for any hidden archer looking to score big. He jumped into the stirrup and hit the grey on the flank with the Henry barrel, and away they went at a run down through the bogs and into the stream.

In two bounds the horse and rider were free from the water and pulling to the top far bank. Without looking back, the only thought the scout had was taking one in the back ribs from some unseen Indian ready with an arrow. As they hit the top bank, the valley opened up, and the scout and his horse put a good distance between them and the campsite. The grey was a tall, stout, gelding measuring sixteen hands and weighing a half ton or better. He was what some people would call a buffalo horse. He came from north Texas, out of a Spanish mustang mare and a Barb stud. The scout had traded four buffalo skins for him when the horse was just three years old. Old Smoke was what they call a flea ticked grey. He was mostly an off-white smoke color with small dark grey ticking spots all throughout his hide. He was very intelligent and had alerted the scout to more than one hidden danger on occasion.

The horse could run for an hour straight at a three-quarter effort. At full effort, he could do maybe four miles before winding out and needing a breather. So after about two miles, the scout slowed him down to a short lope, and they made five miles out in real good time. The scout checked the horse up when he felt safe and turned him to face anything that might be following. He didn't see anything moving, so the scout figured the immediate threat was over for the time being. In the distance, he heard the sound of faint thunder, and after looking over his situation, he decided it best to get back along the wooded foothills for some shelter and to make a new plan.

The grey moved strong and sure-footed as the pair loped toward the foothills in the distance. It took them about an hour, but finally they made the first stand of timber that followed the watercourse back south to the little Platte River. Determined to find a nice, secure spot from which he could see any threat coming, the scout moved the horse along the cottonwoods and aspen forest until he found a good vantage point with some grass and timber for shelter. The problem in all this was the scout had moved another half day farther west than the company's anticipated position in the fleeting moment earlier in the day. Now he needed another plan and one that would put him in touch with the company some time after mid-morning the next day. Should he risk a night venture or would this put him to an end? Or should he try and sneak back through in broad daylight? Should he wait out the situation? These thoughts raced through his mind as the hobbled grey browsed through the buffalo grass surrounding him. He sat there cross-legged with the Henry across his lap and realized for the first time just how tired he was. He desperately fought the feeling, but after some thought of convincing himself that he was not in danger, the scout laid on his side with the rifle between his legs and fell into a deep sleep.

Sometime later the scout was awakened by the sound of the grey horse chomping on some grass as he ate mouthful after mouthful of the dry but nutritious grass. The buffalo grass had not had enough frost to completely lose all its nutrient power. The big horse had learned over the years that when the gettin' was good to put it down fast and keep eating. The pair had been out on several scouting parties for the army, and the big horse had been without good forage for two or three days, only getting what he could when he and the scout stopped for a short rest. One winter the horse had foraged on cottonwood bark all winter long that the scout had stripped off the tree trunks up on the Snake River drainage. Old Smoke was an easy keeper, as horses go, and seemed to retain his weight regardless of his efforts to secure meager portions of prairie grass.

As the scout watched his horse putting down the grass, he came back to his senses and made an effort to check his surroundings one more time. He climbed up an old dead birch tree to get a better view of things. Once again the plains to the south of him were quiet. It was about three hours before sundown. If he was going to make a move, now was the time to get started. He had no doubt that he could ride the grey at a quick pace through the moonlight and be near the company at dawn. The problem being was what danger existed between the wagon train and the scout.

The scout had only seen two footprints, and that might not have amounted to much except the Indian had been in his camp and didn't take the grey horse. This had him wondering what the Indian's motives were and what his next move would be, and when. After contemplating the situation, the scout decided to make the night ride, so he climbed down from the lookout and started to prepare a small eat. The grey was not the only one going to need some nourishment. The saddle packs consisted of some hardtack and jerky with some coffee grinds and sugar. The hard tack and supplies he had purchased in Omaha a month prior, and the elk jerky had been handmade by the tame Indians that had been encamped near the settlement. The hardtack must be soaked in brew or water to soften it up for consumption. He was no stranger to the meal as he had survived on much less. Serving as a scout for Major North in 1866, with the Pawnee battalion down on the Republican River campaign, he was used to such grand vittles.

This little meal was just what the man ordered under the circumstances. There would be no fires now until they were out of danger, so the meal was a cold, quick one. The scout decided about sundown that it was time to have a light sleep. He relaxed under a tree with shed pine needles, making for a most comfortable mountain mattress. He looked to the northwest and could see rain off in the distance in several different areas. This would make for a most interesting night.

Sitting there the scout couldn't help think about the status of the company. He remembered the events that led him to accept the scouting job. He had been in Omaha and had just been mustered out, or discharged, as chief of scouts with the Pawnee Battalion. The battalion had been disbanded for the coming winter so the members could go back to their families and harvest their crops for the fall season. Indians do very little fighting in the winter months and mostly hunker down and "teepee up," as the saying goes. The Pawnee Battalion was formed by General Sam Curtis out of necessity to patrol the western route from eastern Nebraska along the Oregon Trail to Fort Laramie. The marauding Plains Indians at that time consisted of the Sioux tribes, Cheyenne, and Arapaho. They were at war with the United States government for encroachment and broken treaties that they felt were an underhanded move by the government to displace them from their hunting lands. The intrusion of the railroad at that time only gave the Indian more resolve to fight. The entire western plains, from Nebraska through Utah and beyond, were one big Indian war in the making. The Pawnee Indians, for the most part, had been friendly to the white man and were graven enemies of the fore-mentioned tribes. A lot of blood had been exchanged between these tribes long before the white man had made his presence.

So a campaign to enlist about 350 Pawnee scouts and Indian fighters had been designed by General Curtis and Major Frank North. The scout had enlisted as a civilian scout under his Christian name Gabriel (Gabe) Tanner in the year 1865, serving on the plains during the Civil War. His mother was a devout Protestant and raised him until her early death from cholera in a kind and loving way. He never really knew his father because he was killed in the Mexican War when he was very young. It was there in Omaha that the scout found himself in the process of making arrangements to travel up the Missouri river to winter out on the Yellowstone with a group of free trappers and hunt buffalo for hide money in the year 1867 when he had a change of plans.

CHAPTER 2 - THE COMPANY

While preparing for a buffalo hunting venture in Omaha, Nebraska, Gabe Tanner ran into a man named Stone who was with a party of Mormons. They were traveling to Salt Lake in the Mexico territories to unite with other Mormons. Mr. Stone had heard of Gabe Tanner's experience with scouting in the great open and was looking to employ a man that had made the crossing to Fort Bridger. Gabe had made the trip twice while in the enlistment of the army. One trip was made with a company of trappers and surveyors, the other trip with Colonel Patrick E. Conners of the 4th cavalry. Both times he encountered numerous Indian depredations and had several engagements with the hostiles. Although a young scout, Gabe was what you might call an experienced Indian fighter of the times.

Mr. Stone approached Gabe with a very generous offer of six hundred dollars to be paid half up front and the balance when the company arrived at Ft. Bridger. This was far more than he would receive from hide hunting at a dollar a hide, not to mention the hide business was never a sure deal. So Gabe decided to take the offer and told his buffalo hunting companions that he would meet them up on the Yellowstone sometime in the spring. The hunting party agreed as they left Gabe behind, and made their way out by boat towards the Yellowstone country a few days later. While the company of Mormons was getting ready to leave, Gabe used the time to prepare his small unit. It consisted of Old Smoke, a jenny mule named Sally, and a john mule named Oscar. He had a poke of money from his enlisted days, and the upfront money from the Mormons, so he felt he had enough to go well provisioned. He purchased a new Henry repeater chambered in .44 caliber, also a new colt navy pistol in .44 caliber. This, along with his 10" bowie knife should see him through some rough country. The Mormons consisted of 24 wagons and about 160 head of livestock, mostly mule teams and pack mules with about 15 head of beef stock. The Mormons were not necessarily well armed, for they believed God would protect them from the ravages of the trip. To this idea Gabe sternly argued until finally a council was formed, and the message was put to a vote. Mr. Stone was the spokesman for the group and all concerned called him bishop. He relented and asked the scout to advise them on a few weapons they might purchase for the trip. With their limited funds their purchases amounted to mostly worn out Civil War muzzleloaders with a few black powder pistols. After Gabe inspected the lot, he felt ill inside and had to hit the tavern for some liquid courage. These pilgrims were hard to understand. Here they had left their homes, some from Europe and some from the eastern states. Nearly all had a story of persecution and wrongful treatment by the Americans. They were traveling to the wilderness to seek asylum from the persecutors and to live their religion in peace. To that end Gabe's hat was off to them, for they were a sorry lot to a pair of eyes that had experienced the hardships to come first hand. Several times before they departed Gabe tried to envision them on the many troubles awaiting them even to the point of refunding their money and calling the whole thing off. They would hear none of it, and his stories seemed to give them more resolve.

Just before their departure, an inspection was made by the wagon master, a mister Otis Greer. His job would be to lead the company on a path Gabe would show them. He would take the day-to-day operations and make sure everyone would conform to the company's instructions. He was the law of the wagons, and his word was gold among the party. This was agreed to by everyone in writing on a legal document prior to the start.

Mr. Greer was not a Mormon but had made the trip as a teamster many times to Fort Laramie under wild and treacherous circumstances. He knew his business and was the best wagon master for hire on the prairie at that time. He had a pleasant demeanor that made the Mormons comfortable around him. He would be traveling with a pair of Choctaw Indians that he had raised from childhood. They were orphaned at a young age, and he found them on the prairie and took them in. They were in their mid-teens and were excellent at hunting and preparing camp. They were also expert packers, which would be a major asset on this excursion. Otis gave them white man names when they were little and taught them English. They were proficient in sign language and could speak several native tongues. Gabe got along very well with both of them, and they were good company on this trip. The taller of the two was named Tim, and the other one was named Davey. They would prove to be a great asset on this adventure.

The Mormons were a prayerful bunch of people. Gabe had never seen people praying over everything, including the weather, like they did. It was as if they couldn't make a decision without a group prayer. They would hold some strange meetings where they sang hymns and prayed and eat pieces of bread and drank water. They would go without food sometimes for several days while praying individually. They were led by Mr. Stone, and he made all final decisions for the group concerning their actions. He was the spokesman for them with their God, and he prayed for the whole group on many occasion. Gabe even heard his name mentioned on occasion in prayers, and it kind of hit him strange.

An agreement was made with Mr. Greer that the company would shut down completely on Sunday mornings and would not travel on that day. Actually, this wasn't a bad idea for it gave Gabe and the Greer boys an extra day for scouting and hunting without having to keep an eye on the company's progress. It also rested the stock, and Gabe figured that the wagon train made more miles than other trains he had been accustomed to in the past. Unlike other caravans traveling west, the Mormons would not leave anyone behind, regardless of circumstances. They would all pitch in and help with broken down wagons, sick families, or whatever would be the cause of the problem. They jumped right in and worked together to solve it and get back traveling again. On other caravans if you couldn't keep up, then you were on your own and left behind. This was when many of the depredations on the prairie took place from marauding war parties of Indians. The Indians very rarely attacked a company in force, unless it was to run off some stock. But a small three to four wagon affair would probably be wiped out and all of the occupants killed and scalped. The women would be taken off and made prisoners. This was a far--gone conclusion on the western prairies.

These Mormons were a hardy bunch and seemed to take to the task of rough life more so than others Gabe had been involved with. They complained less and seemed to be quite happy within their miseries. This was very strange to the scout. Even Mr. Greer, or Otis as Gabe called him, said he had never seen a less tiring group of people in all his days on the prairie. They seemed to have energy to perform the most difficult tasks. Their dreams of the Utah territories and what awaited them seemed to push them to the very limits of their souls. Several times on this expedition, Gabe witnessed things that were very coincidental, and his approach to this, was nothing is coincidental. Events happen because of causes from other events, be it human or natural. But in the scout's opinion, nothing just happens because we will it so for the better. But these Mormons didn't agree. They figured they had an edge on the rest of humanity with their relationship with God. They have him do their bidding for them by asking him to bless them and their surroundings for the good of all concerned. This was mighty strange to the scout.

They were getting a later start than normal on this trip, and it would cause them a lot of misery. The Oregon Trail had been used since the late 1830s, and the route had remained nearly the same as it was back in those days. Problems arose if you started too early. There was never enough grazing for the stock early in the spring, and the streams were swollen and some impassable. So the majority of the crossings took place from mid-May through mid-June. This company was waiting for others to arrive and assemble, so they never really got going until late August. Their plan was to travel as fast as possible and see how the fall weather treated them about the time they arrived at Fort Laramie. If good weather prevailed, they would trek to Fort Bridger and see what conditions were there. If they didn't like the outlook, then they would winter up the best they could at one of the forts and continue in the next spring.

It seemed like they would do anything they could to escape the persecutions and hatred that prevailed around them in present eastern cities and surrounding towns. They were not liked by many, and the law didn't side with them in any fashion. To Gabe, their money was as good as the next man's. He could not find fault with these people, and their religious style was of no concern to him. As long as they followed the travel plan and did as they were instructed they would all get along like mules and oats. As they started the trek, Gabe had concerns along with Otis. The grazing would be thin along the trail from the numerous wagon trains that had crossed previously that spring and summer. Combine that with the polluted waters, and it meant they would be traveling parallel to the main trail but several miles to the north for better foraging. The streams were low that time of year, and with the hundreds of head of stock crossing and the occupants of the wagons, the streams and rivers and seeps would be contaminated and not useful for human consumption. They would need travel to the north along the South Loup River and try to stay out of this trouble. As they traveled the company was instructed by Otis to have walking women to the left of the train and men to the right. This would afford the women with some privacy for their personal needs. They would gather together in a circle with their long dresses and bonnets and conceal one another from prying eyes as nature would take its course. The men were nothing short of animals when it comes to hygiene or manners. The only time Gabe saw discretion was when the women took them to task for their behavior, then some of them would be more discreet. All in all, the women ran the show, but the men liked to think they were in charge. It made for good entertainment for the scout and others that were less inclined to take up wagon living with the opposite sex.

CHAPTER 3 - ON TO ZION

As the Mormons started out like most wagon trains Gabe had experience with, the company pulled out of Winter Quarters with vigor. After three days on the trail, the trials of the trek started to take effect. The company slowed to a ten-mile-per-day pace, and everyone settled into the task. The wagons were extremely heavy, and although the Saints were warned that they needed to travel light, parting with their cherished belongings was difficult for all. Otis had the distasteful task of telling the wagon masters to lighten the loads. Constantly he would bark out the orders as he would get the look of death from would be patrons as they cried and begged for some sort of relief from the burden. Cabinets, tables, dressers, and the like were strung out across the prairie as far as the eye could see. Chests with belongings that were so heavy that a mule couldn't drag one after it fell from the wagons could be seen here and there along the trail. All the leftover baggage would bring a king's ransom on the open markets of the world, but out here in the great open it was fodder. Each wagon had several cooking pots. Some would hang from under the wagons while others would occupy the side of the wagon along with several water barrels and grain sacks for the stock. The wagons contents consisted of bedding materials and clothing necessities. For the stock's sake, only one person would be up on the buck driving the team while all others would walk along side. Some wagons had elderly, and concessions were made to ride up front. The consequence of this action was smaller quantities of belongings were allowed to offset the extra weight of the person riding.

Everyone was instructed to keep all firearms close to their person and be charged and primed for immediate use. This was necessary to all and resulted in several accidental shootings. Twice in the beginning rifles were discharged, and the results were catastrophic to the innocent mules receiving the brunt of the charge. Luckily no one was harmed in these mishaps. The mules were quickly dispatched and quartered for the meat. This was not met with welcome smiles, but the company had to adjust to mule meat. It required a lot of salt, but was quite filling with sourdough bread and beans. The Mormon women would take to the task of cooking the meat, and after a few attempts they got fairly good at boiling the meat and incorporating it into the various stews and soups they would prepare for the lot. Gabe had subsisted on mule meat on many occasions in the pursuit of the Indians and found it to be palatable when all else was barren.

At night, the company would circle the wagons and put the stock in the center to form a makeshift corral. This would protect them from all the predators on the prairie looking for an easy meal. Also, this would form a sort of breastwork in the event of an attack from the company's Indian neighbors. The rules of the trail were enforced morning and night. No one person was to wander out alone from the wagons for any reason whatever. Permission had to be obtained from Mr. Stone with the final say going to Otis. Armed groups of Saints were allowed to roam around doing hunting chores and gathering wood and food along the path. These were usually planned out by the men when everyone would know the location of the party for the most part. Several times the parties would become confused about their locations, and Gabe would be called upon to straighten them out and get them back on the right path. With the help of the Choctaws, this was fairly easy. Those boys could track a lizard across the prairie if they so desired. And they were good camp company for Gabe when he would go out on a hunt for meat.

As the company travelled farther west, the country became very wild and threatening. On average one in ten pioneers would perish on these wagon trains. Disease was the most prevalent, and accidents would claim their share of souls. Traveling this far north from the main trail would pose several added risks, and the company would be forever on guard. The Indian troubles were a very real threat along this path because the wagon train was far to the north from the normal route that was used for wagon travel. The Mormons would make for easy pickings if the moment was right and the Indians felt sure in a raid. But this was all agreed to, and all the members of the company knew of the dangers prior to departure. Gabe had instructed the Choctaws to keep a keen eye out for trouble along the way, and they would show him signs along the path as they discovered them. Gabe would investigate and determine as to what sort of danger it might present. It was one of these times when Davey found a small boot track that did not belong in this setting. As the scouts looked the sign over that day, they noticed a large dust cloud hanging on the horizon. Tim pointed to the sign and told those gathered there that buffalo were the cause of the disturbance. They expected to be within sight of them in another day of travel.

The boot track looked to be that of a young person traveling light without much direction. The track was wandering, and the sign showed confusion. It was decided by all concerned that Gabe should investigate this poor soul and find out the circumstances of the sign. The Mormons were bleeding hearts when it came to saving souls. They would take many risks that would endanger their lives just to help out a fellow neighbor. They would stare death in the face and still be concerned about someone else's welfare. It was mighty strange indeed.

So Gabe took up the grey, and with Davey the two of them moved their horses along the track to see what would become of it. The track was about a day old, and Gabe felt certain that they could overtake this person within a half day's ride. The sign tracked toward the horizon so the pair of scouts would be traveling southwest a little and parallel to the company. Between the main immigrant trail to the south of them and their position at that time was nearly twenty miles or so. Gabe didn't think it strange that someone might have wandered north from the main trail and crossed their path, especially if that person was lost in the great open. The only bearing an uneducated non-trail wise person might have is the setting sun. Most immigrants had the knowledge of the west to the horizon, and traveling that route was the way they were bound.

As Davey and Gabe rode along, they took their lunch out of the saddle packs and started chewing. The sourdough biscuits made by the Mormon women were delicious, and they nearly bit into their fingers gobbling them down with one hand on the reins and the other up to their mouths, shoveling the small morsels down dry throats. Washing them down with trail water from their canteens, they had the feast of the prairie riding along right in their saddles. About four hours into the ride, Davey slowed his horse from a trot to a walk and pulled up on the reins and dismounted. He observed the surrounding sign and mentioned that they were close, no more than an hour behind the track.

He was convinced it was one smaller human, maybe a hundred pounds and all alone. He was not sure whether it was female or male. About five hundred yards in front of them was a small butte, which the pair determined would give them some elevation for a scout. They headed for this point and left the track trail. Upon reaching the highest point, they were suddenly caught up in a grandeur the mind could not forget. Stretching out before them were dark figures on the prairie grass as far as the eye could see. They were the buffalo that Tim had told them they would encounter. The scouts dismounted and started to watch as the roving herds came within several hundred yards of their position only to continue moving along on some unknown course. It seemed as though they didn't have a plan only to follow the one in front to somewhere other than here. They would stop to graze for few moments then run to catch up with those in front of them, only to repeat the process over and over.

Gabe looked at Davey, and it was apparent that their thoughts were the same. They would be dining on fresh buffalo meat at sundown. This herd would make the track trail almost impossible to locate with all the animals crossing the track, so the two men decided a course northwest would be their best bet. Then they would cut back south at the tail end of the herd.

As Gabe slid back into the saddle, he reached down and checked the Henry. Pulling it from the boot, he levered one in the chamber and told Davey to give him a few minutes to prepare supper. As he leveled the Henry across the saddle horn, Gabe put his heel into the grey. The big horse took to it like he had been born for this kind of adventure. With his ears pinned back along his head, he broke into a full run within several yards. Horse and rider pulled down from the butte at an enormous pace and set a path straight for the nearest herd. At the sight of the horse running full on towards the beasts, they made a mad dash along the prairie in every direction. The grey cut to the south and started his pursuit without any encouragement from Gabe. He narrowed the gap between them and the herd in a matter of seconds. The pair chose a quick running young cow and steadily gained on her until they were nearly even in stride alongside the wild-eyed critter. Gabe pulled up on the Henry, and with one arm outstretched and the rifle butt against his forearm, the pistol shot into the side of the buffalo. She immediately pulled her front legs up under herself and slid twenty feet on her side.

The big grey horse was already pulling himself up with the sound of the shot. Gabe nudged him with his right knee, and he turned away from the pressure and slowed down, coming in a full circle. Horse and rider were face to face about thirty feet from the kicking beast. Slowly they approached as countless buffalo raced past their position and across the plains into the dust and chaos the shot had made. As Gabe got within ten feet, he levered the Henry again and pointed at the beast's head and fired. He had hardly dismounted when Davey came up and made the Indian sign of a good hunt.

The Choctaws were no stranger to the buffalo, and Davey made short work out of the cow with his blade. Handing Gabe a fistful of liver, the scout readily put out his hand and slammed the fresh bloody treat to his mouth. As they stood there relishing the prize, their faces were a combination of prairie dust and crimson blood. Their teeth looked like ravenous wolves on a kill. And the pair laughed at their pitiful sight.

The sun stood about mid-afternoon, and the scouts knew they had better get going if they were to have any success on this scout. The scouts filled out packs with as much meat as they could carry and started off to the north trying to cut some kind of track. As Davey worked the sign, Gabe kept watch on their surrounding position. The pair of scouts knew they could never be too cautious in Indian country. The plains were full of war parties, hunting parties, and all manner of traveling Indians. Some would be following the buffalo herds with their families, while others would be following the white man's traveling caravans. Some Indians were good, while others were not. It's the latter they didn't want to run into out in the great open. As they crested the first hill to their front, the two men were pleased to see a vast view of the plains and surrounding country. The valleys before them were full of small streams and tributaries from the larger rivers running to the north of their position. These small parcels of water were host to life on the prairie. Every type of critter followed the streams, for they were life's blood to the animals and their ways. All types of bushes, shrubs, and trees would spring up and thrive along the water route, only to die and fall over to become part of the earth again. This cycle was never ending and made for a grand venture to all who came across it.

CHAPTER 4 - ORPHANED

The scouts travelled along the first creek they came too, and it wasn't soon until the Choctaw found what he was looking for. He pulled up, dismounted, and pointed to the tracks in the soft dirt. The pair was close, real close. Gabe looked to their right and decided to put the grey up a small hilly ridge to give him a better view of the area to their front. Davey would stay with the track.

As Gabe reached the small ridge, he could see nearly ten miles in any direction. He slowly slid from the saddle while pulling his spy glass from its sheath under the horn. The scout started to survey the country. He could see Davey making his way along the creek bed. He would stop from time to time and dismount. Then he would remount and proceed in this fashion. As Gabe turned to face the horizon, he spotted the scene before them. There, in a small bunch of junipers and buck brush, at about two miles out, was a figure sitting on one of the limbs of a tree. The person was about eight feet off the ground. Gabe put a mirror signal on the Choctaw, and he immediately rode up to meet Gabe on the hill. The scouts rode toward the grove of juniper trees at a slow pace. They were not sure what was happening until they reached earshot of the area and realized this person was under attack from marauding wolves that were following the buffalo herds. From the sounds of it, they thought they had dinner all but in the pot.

As the two scouts closed within a hundred yards, they could see a small boy hanging on a limb as the wolves tried in vain to climb the tree. Gabe counted six live wolves and one dead one. He motioned for Davey to get ready, and the two men ran their horses into the scene with a frightening yell and hoop. Ammunition was too precious to waste on a mangy wolf. Gabe raised the reins on the grey and nudged him forward at the gallop. As the big horse came to a full run Gabe let out a howl that would scare the hair off of anything on the prairie. The Choctaw let out his battle yell, and the two of them went pounding down on the scene with vigor. At first the wolves were preoccupied, but once they saw the devil and his comrade headed straight for them, they decided it was best to vacate the premises. They lit out like their tails were on fire and cleared the valley floor in a matter of seconds. Gabe pulled up on the grey and came to a stop just twenty feet from the juniper trees. Davey was on the other side for safety purposes.

There in the tree, like a hounded-up coon, sat a small young man, scared out of his wits. Gabe put up his hand in a friendship manner and told him they meant him no harm. He was crying out of control and seemed frozen in place. Gabe guessed the scene was a bit much. The two scouts had fun with the charge, but at the boy's expense. They should have been ashamed of themselves, but that's how it was out there on the lonesome prairie. The two young scouts were wild, crazy, and full of adventure. Gabe rode over to the tree for a better look. The boy looked to be about ten years old, maybe eleven, and with all the dirt on the boy’s face. Gabe wasn't sure of his color. Gabe dismounted and told the young boy he could get down. Now that the wolves were gone it was safe. He was still shaking and crying uncontrollably. The scouts noticed the dead wolf at the base of the tree and a war musket lying on the ground nearby. The boy had made his stand and survived the ordeal.

Finally, the two scouts persuaded the scared little boy to climb down from the cedar. He stood before the scouts still shaking, dirty from head to toe. Gabe gave him his canteen and he drank hard, coughing and spitting until Gabe took it away and told him to slow down. The Choctaw was making a small fire and makeshift camp as Gabe tried to determine who and what this small boy was doing out here all alone. He had a small satchel around his neck and down one side, his blue eyes stood out through the dirt on his face, and he looked frightened out of his mind. Gabe asked him his name, and he said he was Will Conner and he was twelve years old.

Gabe asked where his company was, and he said he had run away in the night several days previous. Will told the scouts he would not go back there. He told a story that his parents had started west with a wagon train out of St. Louis. Some members of the party had gotten sick and the train had left them behind. His father was a doctor and had volunteered to stay behind and help the sick. The plan was that when the sick were better they would try to catch up with the main train. The main train would wait near courthouse rock for five days. After the train left, his father and mother were attending the sick when the train was attacked by Indians and everyone was killed. He had tried to bury his parents, but the ground was too hard for him to dig, so he covered them with rocks and left in the night. He was down by a stream when the Indian attack started. He had hidden himself in the stream bank bushes. It was obvious that he had endured a great deal for such a young person.

Gabe asked what was in his satchel, and Will told him it was his father's doctoring journal and notes. Gabe asked where he got the rifle. He said the Indians didn't take it because it was under the wagon boot in a box. He had taken it with a powder horn and a bag of shot. It was all he could do to put that rifle to his shoulder, let alone fire it with a full charge. Gabe took his hat off to this little warrior from that day forward.

Will said the wolves came on him in the morning and he had shot one and climbed the tree when the scouts came along. He had not had any food for three days, but he had drunk from the stream before the wolves came. Davey gave him some water soaked hardtack, and he went to work on it like a famished wolf pup. The scouts cooked some of the buffalo meat on sticks, and they all ate until everyone was full. Gabe took the boy down to the creek and cleaned him up as best he could. The young boy asked what would become of him, and Gabe told him of the company of Mormons coming up the trail behind us. The two scouts would take him to them and decide what to do later.

The scouts decided to wait out the night there in a small encampment and make for the wagon company at first light. Davey made the boy a nice soft place to lie down with soft dirt and leaves from the stream bushes that were abundant along the creek side. The boy was out in minutes after he lay down, so Gabe covered him with a raincoat and everyone hunkered down waiting for the evening to come. As the sun set, the two scouts took precautions with the horses and tied them to their saddles on the ground, then they put themselves onto the saddles for head supports and stared at the evening sky. The pair dowsed the fire out and settled in. The night around them was full of moaning wolves, and sometimes here and there they could hear a distant clap of thunder way off to the north of them. As Gabe lay there, he couldn't help thinking of the plight that this small boy Will had taken in the past few days and what might become of him in the future.

The plains were full of stories just like his from past excursions through this country. There were graves all along the Oregon trails, some with names and others only known to themselves. What concerned Gabe most that night was that there was a war party close by. They might have gone back to the scene of the massacre and noticed the boy's track and be in pursuit, or they might just run into the scout's trail coming from the wagons. If they travelled north from the scene, they would run into the scouts trail for certain. Either way it made for great concern and a sleepless night. Gabe kept the Henry between his knees and made sure he and Davey took turns throughout the night on guard.

About midnight it was Gabe's turn at guard, and he made the best of it with a piece of hardtack and cold coffee. This would keep him occupied and alert until his shift was over. Several times Gabe thought he heard a noise he couldn't identify out on the prairie, but it would drift in and out with the soft night winds that are common out on the great open. Finally Gabe decided to move to the direction of the sound out away from the camp and the horse noises, so he grabbed the Henry and softly walked out south about one hundred yards or so and sat down at the base of a large willow tree. With the tree as a back support, he put his head and ears out toward the sounds he thought he had previously heard. There in the distance was a faint sound and this time Gabe identified it as human voices. He immediately stood up and returned to the camp. Quietly he tapped on Davey's leg and motioned for the danger signal with sign talk. He arose and gathered his war bag and rifle, and without talk or instructions he moved out away from camp and into the darkness.

Gabe had no doubt that he was sizing up the situation, and his Indian instincts would reason out the dangers that the trio were facing. Gabe tried to cover up as much of the camp sign as possible while Davey read the trail to the south. He came back from the night as quietly as a slithering snake, his natural Indian ways and movements would defying logic. He signed for Gabe to kneel with him for council. Gabe knelt and the two men discussed the trouble. Nothing making voice talk at this time of night would be afraid of anything in the great open. That meant a large detachment of cavalry soldiers or Indians. A wagon train would be hunkered down and damn quiet at this time of night. Davey agreed with Gabe that only a large well protected camp would have no fear of being discovered and would feel quite at ease out on the open prairie.

Since Gabe was in charge of this little scouting expedition, he told Davey that he thought it best for him to take the boy along their back trail toward the company, while Gabe sized up the noise and made for him as soon as he could. The scouts woke the boy from his dreams and put him on Davey's horse. Davey held onto the side of the saddle and trotted along with the horse. Gabe had seen him and his brother do this for an entire day without tiring. They would make good time doing this as well. The farther they could get from here the better they all would be. As they rode off into the dark night, Gabe took one last look around the camp area and made a last swipe with a piece of creek brush to erase any sign as best he could.

Gabe mounted Old Smoke and rode toward the sound of voices. It took him nearly an hour of moving slowly and cautiously before he got the smell of wood smoke. Gabe decided to pull up and part with the grey so he wouldn't call out to the other horses and give them away. The scout tied his horse down in an arroyo and made his way south along a small ridge that followed the arroyo back to his horse. From here he would have a slight elevation of the camp and a quick getaway back to the waiting horse. The night had a slight breeze that carried the sound of voices, and they were getting louder as Gabe moved in that direction. The wary scout took the breeze in his face and quartered the camp until he could get a count of the horses. This would give him an idea of the size of the party he was scouting.

Finally, Gabe could see a distant fire glow. It led him right to the camp as the breeze stayed north and into his face. Gabe had put on his moccasins when he left the grey horse so he could sneak Indian style upon the camp. As he got within fifty yards or so, he knelt and surveyed the surroundings. The horse herd was to his left and the camp to the scout's right side. They looked about thirty or forty yards apart. Gabe crawled to the horses until he had a good view. Quietly he looked the horses over. There was no doubt in his mind this was an Indian camp. There were about eighteen Indian ponies and twelve to fifteen mules. No doubt taken on a raid from the white man. Were these the same Indians that had attacked Will's mother and father's camp or were they just raiding stock settlements on their way through? Now Gabe's movements had to be stealthy as a mountain cat. The Indians would have lookouts posted over the herd, and he did not want to be discovered by them. He crawled silently away from the horse herd and toward the camp for a better look at the Indians. Finally, Gabe moved into a position that gave him a good view of the camp. There were about sixteen Indians moving around the fire in all manner of Indian ways. Dancing, yelling, pushing one another, and making one hell of a sound. Gabe had known enough about Indians to know they were celebrating a successful raid. They had found some whiskey and were in the process of getting mowed down by the effects.

At first Gabe thought they had two white women with them but soon discovered that it was two braves wearing white women's dresses and bonnets. They must have taken them in the raid. The Indians looked like Sioux to Gabe with a couple of Cheyenne mixed in. From the camp, it looked like a lot of booty had been stolen from the white man. This made for a wild hair rising scene before Gabe. As the scout inspected the site, he noticed one smaller Indian sitting cross legged on the ground who appeared to be tied up. Focusing on the figure it appeared to be a young Indian girl. Probably taken in a raid somewhere and would no doubt be someone's rights to marry and have ownership over.

Gabe decided he had seen enough and would get as far away from this bunch as he could before his scalp was on one of those dancing spears. He felt fairly safe in escape since the Indians were well on their way to the big head basher that awaited them in the morning. They would be in no condition for war after the whiskey took its effects. Gabe slipped away as slick as he came in and found the grey waiting patiently where he had left him. The scout swung into the saddle and the pair made tracks to the north and away from the camp.

Horse and rider moved along at a good gait and made about eight miles from the Indian camp when Gabe decided to slow down some and move to the south again. Just in case the Indians did find his trail, he didn't want them to discover the company, so he led a track straight south, then he would cross the small tributary that flows into the lower south Platte and back across it once again. This would confuse anyone and would help the scout evade detection.

As the sun started to glow in the eastern sky, Gabe was already across the stream to the south. He entered the land where the main Oregon route was travelled. He could see most of the grass had been fed off, and the land looked barren compared to the route the Mormons were on. He turned east on the morning light and put the grey into a lope. The pair made their way northeast and found the stream once more. Here Gabe put the horse in the stream and walked him for almost a mile along the water's edge. Finally, he rode out of the stream and turned him due north. At this rate of travel, Gabe felt like he could be back to the Mormons about sundown.

About midmorning, Gabe cut a small older boot track on the trail. It was the track Will had made several days previous as he wandered the plains. Upon finding this, Gabe determined to follow it out and inspect the wagons and camp he had been with. Gabe still had an obligation to the post commander at Fort Laramie to report any Indian troubles he encountered. All civilized peoples were in this together as the nation reached out and expanded westward. Indian troubles were a matter to be taken very seriously. As traveling citizens, all travelers bound together for the common cause, and the Indian plight became everyone's cause. It didn't matter whether you were homesteading the frontier or just passing through on your way to the Pacific coast; you were bound and determined to run into the Indian. Some were passive and friendly toward the whites, while others would make a point of it to see you suffer in the most gruesome manners devised.

Gabe's thoughts kept going back to Will and the scene the young boy must have witnessed. Watching the war party the night before, Gabe noticed they were all painted for war. They had crimson-and yellow-painted faces with fresh scalps hanging on their lances. As they did their scalp dance, he could see the murder and delight in their eyes and faces. They were a blood-thirsty bunch and as dangerous as you would find on the prairie. Gabe would have to do what he could to prepare the Mormons for trouble if it came their way. Right now he needed to get the whole story about Will and his parents, and find out if others had survived the raid.

Following the back trail Will had made in the previous days, Gabe made good time. About midday, he came over a small hill where before him lay the ruins of the camp. Gabe carefully glassed the area for about twenty minutes to make sure there was nothing stirring around. Then he made his way down off the hill and towards the camp. Noticing the pony tracks in the dirt around him, the sign showed the Indians must have used the hill to their concealment and advantage. They had gotten to within several hundred yards before they were discovered. Here and there were remains of the raid. It appeared to be over in a matter of minutes. Gabe dismounted and surveyed the scene before him. It appeared as though five wagons with about twelve adults were in camped when the raid began. He could see where some had tried to flee out into the prairie, only to be ridden down and killed on the spot. Looting and pillage were the Redman's way on this raid, and they spared no one. No prisoners were taken, just scalps and wealth to the victors. The raid was fast and furious. It was probably over in less than five minutes. The bodies of the victims had been pulled out onto the plains and devoured by the wolves after the raid was over. Hardly a morsel was missed by the ravenous lot as they cleaned up the remains of the day. Gabe moved over to the stream bed and read the sign as told to him earlier by Will. The young man had a grandstand view of the whole mess. What a scene to witness and live through, especially at his young age. There was nothing for the scout to do here; the Indians had taken everything of value, and the day was getting on. Gabe made one last look for tracks and sign around the camp in a circle fashion. Finally he satisfied himself that all had perished, so he mounted and rode north toward the Mormons.

CHAPTER 5 - THE HIDDEN ENEMY

Making good time Gabe decided to cut a little northwest. That way he would be out in front of the Mormons traveling west and could scout the country in front of the wagons and make sure the Indian war party was still to the south of them. The scout estimated how far they might have traveled the past two days, and that was his course. Gabe suspected the wagon train to be somewhere in the vicinity of the large buffalo herd that Davey and Gabe had seen on the first day out following the small foot tracks. Gabe figured to make that area sometime around early evening. He started the grey into a soft consuming lope, and horse and rider began to cover the ground quickly. Gabe kept his eye on the western horizon since that was the area he suspected trouble if there would be any. The Indians were off in that direction, and if they hadn't discovered his trail or Davey's, then they might move on out of the country and to the north where their winter grounds would be. The fall buffalo hunting would be in full swing for the Northern Plains Indian in a few weeks, and most of the men would be engaged in this endeavor. Gabe suspected that this small war party was on a scout for the buffalo herds when they ran into Will's parent's wagons and decided to plunder what lay before them. They looked to be opportunists at will, instead of planning out the raid. The wagons just happened to be in their path.

Riding along in this fashion, Gabe stayed along the tree line so as not to profile himself. This would also offer him some sort of concealment if needs be. As the pair came to the first small tributary, Gabe pulled up the grey and walked slowly into the stream. He gave him his head, and he drank several long draws from the slow moving water. Suddenly the big horse raised his head and looked to the west. Gabe followed his line of sight and thought he saw a single figure along the ridgeline. Gabe could feel the horse's heart beating between his legs, so he knew the animal had a nose full of scent. The pair stood motionless for some time in the middle of the stream. This was not a good place to make a fight, so Gabe eased the horse to the far bank and over into the trees that dotted the waterway. Once inside the cover of the leaves, the scout dismounted and pulled the spyglass out to have a look. Far off in the direction, Gabe could see a single rider on a horse silhouetted against the skyline. Surely whoever it might be had Gabe pegged, since the lone rider was there before Gabe and old Smoke arrived. The big, light-colored horse would have stood out against the backdrop of trees making for easy detection. The stranger just sat there not moving, well out of range for a shot from the Henry. The stranger sat the horse Indian style. Gabe was convinced this person was up to no good. Maybe he was sizing up the situation and Gabe's horse, or the stranger was on a scout from the war party. *That must be the reason he is sitting there,* thought Gabe. Others could arrive any minute, and then they would have the advantage on the scout.

No doubt they would have Gabe's trail now. The only thing he could do was put the miles between him and them. Hopefully, he could continue north and then pick up the trail to the Mormons. This seemed to be the best thought in the scouts mind. Gabe called these instincts, and they had not failed him to date. He took one last look and then pulled up on the saddle horn and swung the grey to the right. The pair made a good trot through the trees and up the slope to a point Gabe could see. Turning around he was surprised to see the lone Indian still in the same spot. *What does this mean? Are others already surrounding me as I move along? Is he really all alone out here? Does he think the effort to lift my hair is not worth the risk?* All of these questions ran through Gabe's mind as he topped out on the ridge. As the horse and scout made it up from the valley floor, Gabe took one last look before coming out onto the open plains. Nothing could be seen in any direction. The Indian sat his horse facing Gabe and never moved at all. Gabe knew then that the lone Indian could not catch up to him with the open ground ahead of him and the speed of the grey horse beneath him. The scout nudged the grey into a run and made tracks out of there at a blazing gate. Gabe would look back from time to time but nothing followed him.

Just as the sun set on the horizon, Gabe slowed the grey to a walk and let the big horse cool out. The day's events were puzzling to him as the pair rode along. One thing was for certain; there were a lot of Indians in the immediate area, and the Mormons needed to be warned. A man could ride a horse through this country and never see a single live Indian. Then other times they were as thick as fleas on a hound. The latter brings nothing but trouble and will make a man old before his time with the effects of stress. Gabe had seen many a man go out of his mind with Indian worry on the plains and run off into the open prairie, only to be consumed by the elements. Fear and stress would eat away at some men and make them do things they would not do ordinarily. Gabe had seen a lot of this in the army while in the Indian campaigns. Sometimes there would be a complete breakdown in the ranks when men faced death at the hands of the Redman. And contrary to that, you would see gallant bravery from some of the most common of men as they fought the Indian and prevailed. Gabe had nothing but Indian thoughts as he and his horse walked along, while his puzzled mind raced for answers and a solution to the threat.

Around early night, the shadows were reaching out long and fast. Gabe and Smoke had made good time, and he anticipated the Mormon wagons within a few miles from their position. Coming up on the northern stream, which the train was following, Gabe noticed that he had not cut a trail of wagons. This made him feel anxious, and a small fear started in his mind. *They should have been this far west by now,* he thought to himself. The night made for difficult tracking, but even a novice woodsman, would be able to see the wagon trail as it had been made by that many travelers. But it was not there. The wagon train had not passed Gabe, he was sure of this fact, and he didn't think they would have turned farther north than the stream. Otis knew this trail, and Tim would have kept them on the path they had determined. They were far too large for a company to be besieged by the Indian party that Gabe had seen. So where were they?

Gabe dismounted and tied the grey to the bank willows. He took the Henry and decided he would make a scout on foot for the tracks of Davey and Will. The two of them would have come this way earlier had they not hooked up with the wagons. Being on foot would make it easier for Gabe to spot the tracks of a single horse with rider and runner. He moved out on the north side of the stream and had not gone twenty yards when he hit their day old trail. The trail showed that Davey and Will were moving east as they had previously planned. Gabe thought to himself that something must have slowed the Mormons down. It appeared the only thing for him to do was ride east until he met up with the wagons.

Gabe did not know the condition of the wagon train and how far he would have to travel to reach them. He was exhausted from being up the previous night and riding all day. Several times during his retreat from the lone Indian, Gabe had dozed off in the saddle, and when he awoke, it startled him with a jolt. Gabe was in enemy country, and sleeping in the saddle was for tender-footed easterners. The scout was a seasoned plainsman with a whole train of immigrants depending on Gabe's experience to get them through the rough country in one piece. The scout needed sleep, or he was not going to be any good to anyone.

Gabe rode down the stream bed to the east for about a mile in the dark. Here he found a small swale in the watershed bank and decided it offered him protection and a small campsite. Gabe hobbled the grey horse and pulled some buffalo grass for him to munch on and set the tired horse up as comfortable as possible. Gabe didn't dare take off the saddle, but he loosened the cinch so the horses belly could expand with the grasses he would eat. Gabe took out his canteen and soaked some hardtack until it became soft in his fire cup. The scout ate this with a piece of the buffalo meat that he had in his saddle bag. It was raw and smelly, but it filled the tired scout up. Gabe had not had time to jerk the meat, so it was used as was for the time being. A little salt and the morsel went down with only one belch. Gabe slid down into the bank recess and covered himself with willow branches. His mind raced with thoughts about all the things he was concerned with, and then as if someone blew out a candle, his mind went blank.

A small noise brought Gabe to his senses. What was it? Gabe could see the grey, not two feet from him with his head tilted to the west. The horse's ears were forward as he stood motionless in the dark sky night. His white form stood out against the landscape, and he obviously was hearing the noise that woke the scout. Gabe slid out of his hole and put a hand to the horse's nose to calm him. Gabe didn't want him calling out in the darkness to some unknown enemy horse. The noise the scout had heard was coming closer. It was the sound of a horse. Only trouble would be traveling at this time of the night, so Gabe checked the lever on the rifle and held tight to the reins. The scout decided his best course of action was to stand his ground there on the stream bank. It was the best position he could have found. Whoever it was that was coming through the darkness would have to step on Gabe, and then it would be too late for whoever it was to have the upper part of a night war.

The sounds were moving right in Gabe's direction, almost as if someone were following his trail. Gabe could only think of the lone Indian, and he reasoned that this lone Indian must be the hound on this hunt. Gabe stepped to one side of the grey and pulled the rifle up to his shoulder and pointed it at the sound. The scout heard a voice as he reached to pull the trigger on his rifle. A familiar voice, one Gabe recognized as one of the Choctaws, was quietly calling out to him. Gabe lowered the rifle and answered, "Over here." The form approached, and in the dark skylight, Gabe could make out the form of Davey.

The young Choctaw Indian dismounted and signed for Gabe to be quiet, that others were out on the night wind, and all was not safe. He motioned for Gabe to follow him on foot, leading their horses into the night. Gabe followed him for what seemed to be an hour or so without talking or stopping. Finally, Davey turned and motioned that he thought the threat was behind them. Gabe walked up on him and whispered his questions one at a time to Davey until Gabe had asked all that the scout needed to know. Davey told Gabe that he was looking for the scout and that he had reached the Mormons with Will safely.

The Mormons had moved several miles from when Gabe and Davey had left them three days previous. Davey said that the Mormons were in a bad way and that most of them were sick with the grip. The ones that could stand were caring for the others. Some were bad sick, as well as Otis and Tim. Davey had left Will with a man named Winslow who was on his feet. Mr. Winslow said he would care for the boy while Davey was away looking for Gabe. The bishop had instructed Davey to find Gabe and bring him into the camp.

While following his back trail to where he cut Gabe's trail, Davey had also come across tracks from six Indian ponies. This group of Indians were following the stream bed trail left by himself and Will, two days prior, as they headed back to the Mormons. Davey had gotten within several hundred yards of them just before dark and confirmed they were Sioux, and painted for war. He figured they were from the same bunch Gabe had scouted out on the prairie several nights before.

As Gabe stood there listening to the Choctaw, his mind was sorting out the events and calculating their next move. The two of them would need to move fast and as quiet as possible to the location of the Mormons and hopefully get there before the scouts or the Mormons were discovered by the Sioux scouting party. Gabe was confident that they would not attack such a large group of white travelers, but that they might try to steal as much of the stock as possible. With the Mormons in a state of sickness and off their guard, this might be easy pickings along the trail for the Indians. When the immigrants along the trails lost stock to the Indians thievery, all sorts of death and mayhem were concocted by those heathen devils. While innocent men went looking for their animals, they became scalp prey themselves, along with others that might venture out into the great open wandering about or left unguarded. All of these small little scalp wars would take place while the men were off hunting down their stolen animals. It made for a weakness in the wagon trains, and this is when the savage Indian was at his best. They were like wolves following the wagons. They were just waiting for the unprepared to slip up, and then swiftly they would pounce on the prey. These thoughts and many others came into Gabe's mind as he made the sign for Davey to mount up and trail the two of them back to the wagon train.

The pair of scouts rode slowly and cautiously. The last thing they wanted to do was to run into the war party in the darkness. Gabe and Davey already knew they were outnumbered, and that the enemy was hell bent on blood and booty. Traveling along the stream bed for a while, Davey decided to move away from the watershed and up onto the plain. The two scouts would be able to make faster travel that way, and if they ran into anything, the two men supposed they might be able to hear it coming and avoid it. Once out in the open plain, the scouts picked up their pace and made good time across the open prairie. Twice they thought they heard riders, but when the pair slowed down and listened, the noise seemed to be gone.

It was a long night. Gabe was glad he had taken the opportunity to sleep earlier. He would not have been able to make this ride without the rest he had received. When the body shuts down, you're good for nothing until it charges up again. Gabe knew the two scouts were out in front of the tracking Indians, the only problem he was concerned about was the location of the rest of the group. There were at least sixteen in the war party, maybe more. Davey had located six. And what about the lone Indian Gabe had run into? Was he part of the war party or something else? What was his part in all of this? Or was he just passing through? He didn't seem too interested in a fight earlier that day. Maybe he was just scouting the buffalo herds for his people. The Indians always had a scout out on the edge of the herds letting them know of the buffalo path. When the herds were within traveling distance, the whole tribe would move out on the open prairie and close the gap. Warriors to the front, pursuing the buffalo, with the women and children bringing up the rear trail for the blade work. This was the plains Indian's sole source of subsistence. The buffalo was everything to them. They would store up enough buffalo meat to last the entire winter and use all of the animal parts for their ways of life. Gabe had realized long ago when scouting for the army, that as long as the buffalo roamed the plains and valleys west of the big river, the Indian and all that was his, would continue to rule the great open plains and mountains. The white man was merely a temporary trespasser, traveling through this big country on his way to the west coast's fertile valleys.

As the eastern sky started to lighten up, the two traveling scouts could see a fire glow off in the distance. The two men had been riding long and hard all night long. Both of them were hungry and tired. They knew that the glow would be the morning cook fires of the Mormons as they stirred around the camp doing breakfast chores. It had been a long trip in the saddle since Gabe had bid the bishop goodbye three days earlier, and he was feeling the effects.

The two men came alongside the camp, and it seemed somewhat deserted. The wagons were in several groups strung out along the stream bank. The stock animals were scattered about with only a few souls watching over them. If ever there were an Indian raid made for the taking, this would be it. The Indians could make short work out of this bunch of immigrants very quickly. Gabe hoped the two scouts had arrived in time to help secure up the camp.

Riding through the wagons, Gabe asked one member of the group where the bishop might be found. The man showed Gabe the wagon, and the scout walked the grey over to the back of it. Gabe asked if the bishop was home, and a hand parted the rear cover on the wagon. As Gabe looked into the face of Mr. Stone, it reminded him of a skeletal head the scout had once found out on the prairie. The bishop was nothing but bulging eyes and bone. The man was in the extreme stages of the grip. Gabe had seen it before several times while in the Indian campaigns. Some would die on this trip from the disease. It was nature's way of thinning the ranks. Others would live to tell the story, but right now the Mormons had more pressing matters than just this sickness. If the group didn't shore themselves up and their livestock, they wouldn't need to worry about the grip because ol' Mister Injun would bleach their bones long before the sickness could put them in the grave. Gabe told the bishop of his travels and the Indian dangers that were present. The poor sick man felt helpless and had given up on the defenses of the camp when he had taken ill. Gabe assured him that he and Davey would gather together some of the men who were not as sick, and they would put the camp in a better position to withstand an attack.

Gabe instructed Davey to find every able bodied man and have them meet the scout at the Bishop's wagon within the hour. Meanwhile, Gabe rode the outskirts of the camp and planned out a course of defensive action.

As the men gathered about the bishop's wagon, Gabe instructed each one of his duties and made the necessary assignments to all concerned. The group of men would pull the wagons together tightly and put the stock into the center for protection. Gabe felt that if there were to be a raid, the animals would be the Indians desire. Some of the men went to cutting buffalo grass for hay forage while others cut cottonwood along the stream bed. All of the men were made aware of the dangers about, and for each party there was one among them that would be a look out for trouble. All the men were instructed to arm themselves and their loved ones as best they could. No one was allowed outside the wagon circle for anything whatsoever.

The water barrels were filled, and the Mormons settled into the task at hand. Gabe checked on Will, and he was doing fine. The boy had not become sick like the others and seemed to be in good spirits as he played around with three other boys his same age. Gabe thanked Mr. Winslow and asked him what might become of the young boy. He told Gabe that he and his wife would take him in and care for him as one of their own. They had another boy just a bit older and felt like the two could get along fine. Mr. Winslow kept saying something that puzzled Gabe for a long time. The man told Gabe that he and the boys were brothers and that it was his duty to care for them. Will was not Mr. Winslow's brother, and Gabe failed to see the connection. Gabe thought that these Mormons could be mighty query when it comes to their relationships with others.

At the start of this trip, one of them had told the scout that all of the Indians on the plains were brothers to one another and the white man. Well, Gabe couldn't believe that tall tale. Gabe asked him if he had been sipping on the fermented grains, and the Mormon man told Gabe that Mormons didn't partake of liquor. The scout nearly fell off his seat upon hearing that statement. It was tough enough to get through this ol' life, Gabe thought, but having to do so without partaking of the great relaxer was just plain anti-American.

As the men prepared the camp, Gabe sent Davey out on a scout to see if the two men had been followed by the Indian war party back to the Mormons' camp. Gabe rode out and scouted some himself. He didn't see anything, and he felt like the men had secured the camp in time. Several hours later Davey rode in and informed Gabe that he had not seen anything to be worried about while scouting the area. Nothing was found on the two scouts' back trail, and all seemed quiet. That's just what worried Gabe. When things go quietly in Indian country, that's when you better worry the most. Gabe rode over to the bishop's wagon and gave him a report. The man could barely raise his head, and Gabe thought that the Mormons might be putting the bishop into the ground before evening. The grip had run through nearly three-quarters of the camp. Many were very sick, and others were managing.

In the past, Gabe had seen the disease kill some within hours, while others would suffer for days, only to succumb to the disease after much suffering. Some would make a full recovery and the reasons why would baffle the smartest of surgeons and caretakers. Entire companies of soldiers had come down with the sickness during the war between the north and the south. Many deaths on both sides were attributed to the disease. It would ravage cities and towns without prejudice to race or sex. The scholars had termed the disease cholera. It was unknown to its causes, and a cure had not been found. It had infected the entire Cherokee Indian nation on the Trail of Tears and wiped out a good many of those souls. The only remedy was time. If a person made the first several days, then your chances were pretty good for recovery.

The Mormon men that were upon their feet were a busy lot. After the chores and securities were in place, they would tend to their families and each other. They were peculiar in their ways as Gabe watched from a distance in the camp surroundings. They would gather together in groups of two's and sometimes more, around a sick person, and put their hands on the head of that person and bow their heads and mumble some type of prayer. They would put something on the forehead of the sick person and say some words. The Mormon elders would move from one wagon and sick person to another, and they kept this up all throughout the day. As they would pass by Gabe, they would nod or smile as if this was just another day to them. How they could be pleasant in these circumstances was a mystery to the scout. Gabe had never heard so much praying in his entire life. The whole encampment seemed to be in constant solemn prayer.

Gabe decided it was time to pay Otis a visit, so he rode over to his wagon and made himself known. Tim came out of the wagon tent and greeted Gabe first. Otis seemed to have weathered the sickness and was doing better. He was still bent over somewhat and looked as though he had looked death in the eye and came out the other side. Davey was kneeling in the back of the wagon and wiping the forehead of Otis as the man lay there in a makeshift bed. The young Indian seemed very concerned about his white father's welfare. Gabe asked Tim how Otis was doing, and the young man replied that he thought his father's medicine was weak, that the Great Spirit was waiting nearby to take Otis up to his lodge in the sky. Gabe told him of his experience with the disease and that some would survive the ordeal. Gabe could see that this gave the confused Young Indian some hope in his eyes and facial expression as he looked at Gabe in wonder. Gabe told him that the only thing they could do was to wait out the hidden enemy in his body and keep Otis as comfortable as possible while the battle went on.

The Choctaws had some herbs in their medicine bags, and they were administering that to Otis as well. The disease was no stranger to them, as they told a story to Gabe that they had lost loved ones when they were small boys to the white man's sickness. Why they claimed it was a white man's disease Gabe didn't know. The scout guessed that they were taught at a young age that everything bad in their lives came from the white man. Truth be known, The white man was responsible for a lot of the misery the Indian had been subject too. White ways were not theirs, and the more the civilized whites tried to put on them, the more they seemed to dwindle in size and strength. The Indian nations were only a small token of what they had been when Captain Lewis and Captain Clark had made the first journey into their midst. Disease and war had run them into the ground, and only the strongest had survived to this point in time. Gabe turned and walked away from the Choctaws, as his thoughts had made him ashamed of the whole story.

As Gabe looked around the camp, he noticed how many people had fear in their eyes. Everywhere he looked he saw misery and sickness. The grip was taking its toll on the Saints, and only time would be their friend. One of the elders informed Gabe that seven members of the company had succumbed the previous night, and at least, a half dozen were not expected to survive the day. As Gabe walked through the camp to his horse, he could hear the cries of the people as they laid their loved ones into the ground. A small area out away from the camp had been designated as a graveyard. It sat among some beautiful cottonwoods and grassland that made for a peaceful retreat.

Gabe had asked one of the men earlier to care for his horse, and when he returned he found Old Smoke rubbed down and quite satisfied with his surroundings. The big horse was eating with his head down and didn't seem to notice all the suffering around him. As Gabe tended to his horse, one of the Mormon women came up to him with a plate full of food and some water. The scout thanked her as she walked away, and then he sat down near the grey and tried to manage the meal. It was hard going down with all the death hanging in the air that morning. Gabe had placed a guard system in the camp with the men, and they were as prepared, as a sick bunch could be under the circumstances. Now if the scout only knew the intentions of the war party. And that lone Indians intentions, he might be able to rest easier.

Later in the day Gabe awoke from a small nap with a terrible pain in his head, and his stomach felt like he would leave the Mormon lady's meal all over the prairie. He was knotted up in the fetal position and could not straighten out. His body ached all over, and he was sweating from every pore. What was this? he asked himself. What was wrong? Could it be that maybe the food didn't agree with him? These thoughts went through Gabe's mind as he tried to get on his feet. Oh, the pain was almost more than he could muster. He looked at the nearest set of bushes and ran as fast as he could in that direction. The scout had barely reached the secluded spot when the whole of himself came bursting out from both ends. He had one hand on the branches holding himself upright and the other on his guts. Nothing in his life had taken hold of Gabe this fast. He finally realized in his misery that he was in the beginning stages of the grip. But how could he have gotten the disease? He had not been in contact with anyone. As Gabe hung on to the limbs, the earth started to sway back and forth through his eyes. He became dizzy, and finally fell over onto his side and just curled up into a small ball of sickness.

The disease took the young scout so fast that he knew he was on his way to the other side. At least, Gabe hoped there was another side to go to. Would they take fellers like him? What was the price you had to pay to get in that glorious place called heaven? All these thoughts raced through his mind as he felt the life sap out of him, lying there in the mud and brush. Gabe was in so much pain that even the hair on his head ached. Every muscle in his young body racked with pain. He was so hot that he thought he was lying next to a furnace. Gabe slipped in and out of consciousness as he lay there. Is this how it would be? All alone out in a bunch of creek brush, lying there waiting to die. The scout was so thirsty; his mouth was bone dry, and he had a hard time swallowing what moisture he could muster in his mouth. Finally, the sun beating down on his face was blackened, and Gabriel the young scout and Indian fighter of the plains went to another place.

An angel was looking into my eyes, and she had a concerned look on her face. She was comforting me and singing a hymn while she cooled off my head. She was the most beautiful woman I had ever seen. She had long, flowing yellow hair and blue eyes. Her touch was so soft that it felt like a feather touching my skin. All the while she kept singing this hymn. I didn't recognize the words to the song, but it was most comforting. She would appear and disappear. One moment she was there softly singing and the next she was gone and everything was dark and dismal. *Is this heaven and now I'm back in hell? Why can't I see her all the time? Where is she? I want to be with her. Darkness is all I can see now. I must have made a mistake while I was living on the earth, and this hell is where I was sent. I didn't think they would let a man like me in heaven. I had fought men and raised all kinds of hell on the earth when the whiskey had its hold on me. I had killed many Indians and carved the hair from their heads. I was a loner and never let anyone befriend me. I was a bad person, so why would I expect anything more than this darkness and a portion of hell? Who are these people standing over me and what do they want? I think they want to kill me, but I am already dead.*

They are holding me down with their hands on me. I can't resist; I have no strength or will to live anymore. Oh, I am so thirsty. Do we need water in hell? This place is terrible. I can only see shadows and darkness. Someone is giving me a drink of water. It is the angel lady, and she is smiling at me as she holds a cup to my lips. I can see her features, and she is absolutely perfect. Maybe God has changed his mind, and I am allowed out of this hell. Everything is bright and peaceful once again. I want to stay here. I will not leave, no matter what.

As Gabe opened his eyes, he realized that he was still in the stages of the grip. He had not died. He was looking at the inside of a wagon tent and lying on his back. The scout's head ached something fierce, and his stomach had a pain from one side to the other. All the way across his guts he hurt. Whew, he was alive, and his thoughts were racing back into his mind.

Gabe looked at the bottom of the wagon tent and saw Davey standing just outside the flap cover. He could see him talking to someone just out of view. Gabe moaned out a small noise, and Davey immediately pulled the flap back and looked Gabe up and down. He climbed into the wagon and put a cup of warm water to Gabe's lips.

"This is warm water," Gabe said as he pushed the cup away from his face.

Davey put the cup back to the scout's mouth and said, "This drink will make you well."

Gabe looked at him and finally decided to trust his wisdom in this thing. Gabe drank the liquid; it had a faint flavor that he was familiar with but could not identify right off. As Gabe finished the drink, he smacked his lips together to try and figure out what the flavor was. It was some sort of berry drink. Gabe asked Davey what the drink consisted of and he said that it had come from Will's father's journal. He told Gabe that after Gabe had gone down with the grip it looked like twenty or more of the Mormons would die from the sickness. He said he felt like Gabe would be with them along with Otis. About that time Mr. Winslow was talking to Will about the disease and the situation the Mormons faced, when Will mentioned that his father had treated some sick people while in St. Louis. They had all gotten better. The young boy did not know if it was the grip or not. Mr. Winslow asked if he could see the journal the boy had carried off with his father's notes. Will gave it to him, and he started to read the pages.

The journal contained many notes on sickness and diseases the doctor had treated in the past. After looking through the text, Mr. Winslow was surprised to see notes concerning cholera. It showed a treatment for the disease that was quite successful. It was not a cure, but a way to increase a person's body to fight the disease. It consisted of raspberry leaves made into a tea, with sage leaves and white oak bark. This compilation of herbs was to be boiled for five minutes before administering it to the sick person. This tea was given in large quantities to the victims of the disease. It appeared to flush the body and replace the fluids that were lost during the dehydration period of the disease. This dehydration of the body is what would kill most victims. He also had notes on his theory of how the disease was spread. He stated that he thought it came from the water sources that were contaminated with animal and human waste. This made sense to Mr. Winslow since the company was trailing far north from the usual Oregon Trail, just to avoid the bad water pools that existed along the main route. The doctor's biggest discovery had been in the process of boiling water before consumption. He had good results in the past, using this method. This would help others from becoming sick, after the outbreak of the grip had started.

After reading these notes, the bishop was told of the information in the journal, and the whole camp proceeded to treat the sick with these methods. The Choctaws went out and brought in the herbs while the men and women boiled the water. This is the warm solution Gabe had been forced to drink. It would bring him back from the depths of hell.

As Gabe tried to climb out of the wagon tent, it was rough going. He was still weak. His strength would take several days to return to normal. But he was glad to be alive. The scout looked up at the sky and thanked God for his reversal decision. He had decided to spare Gabe from that awful place he had encountered. His grace on Gabe was humbling, and the scout bowed his head in thanks. The early fall air felt good on Gabe's skin as he looked outward towards the horizon. Gabe asked Davey how long he had been near dead. He looked at Gabe kind of strange and said he had been sick for three days. Davey said Gabe's medicine was powerful and that he had defeated the great death maker in a terrible war. He told me that Otis was up and around tending to the mules and other chores. His medicine was strong as well. The camp seemed to be alive with people in motion. Gabe's senses were starting to come back and the thought came to him about the previous dangers the Mormons faced from the Indians. Gabe asked Davey if anyone had been on the scout since he had been out, and he told Gabe that he and his brother Tim had shared the responsibility. They had not seen any sign of Indians. This made Gabe feel better. The scout took another cup from Davey and slugged the liquid down as fast as he could. The sooner this disease runs its course with Gabe, the better he would like it. Slowly Gabe walked around the encampment and surveyed the Mormons defenses. He was confident that the Indian war party he had encountered would not try to make a war on this group. The Indians liked the odds in their favor, and dead braves made for bad medicine. The Mormons were ready.

Gabe worked his way over to his horse and thought he might take a small ride out on the plains and make a quick scout of the area to the west. It was midmorning, and he felt like he could slip out and return before the afternoon shadows closed in. The scout saddled the grey with some effort. Gabe was still pretty weak, but he needed to go and satisfy himself that all was safe. After he got his gear together, he took some food from a sack that he had in the back of one of the supply wagons. As Gabe mounted his horse, he told Davey where he was headed. He said he would find the scout if he did not return by nightfall.

As Gabe rode through the camp, he could hear a soft voice in the back of his mind humming the hymn the beautiful angel had sung over him. The sound became louder as he moved through the wagons until he was next to a wagon that the sound came from. Gabe was amazed and just sat there on his horse, staring at the wagon cover as he listened to the soft voice that permeated the air around him. *Am I dreaming? Is this real? How can this be the same song that I heard in heaven?*

Gabe pulled the grey up alongside the wagon and sat motionless, asking himself these questions in his mind. It was the same beautiful voice of the angel he had encountered. Just as Gabe was about to be carried away into the clouds, a hand touched his leg and he came back to his senses. The scout looked down from his horse, and there was Davey looking at him.

"What's wrong?" he asked.

Gabe told him about the angel in his trip to the other side, and Davey just smiled at the scout. Gabe asked him why he smiled, and Davey said he wanted to show Gabe something. He pulled up on the wagon flap and spoke to someone inside. A figure climbed out of the wagon as Gabe turned his horse around to face them. There, in front of Gabe, was the angel that had sung to him in heaven.

Gabe didn't know what to do. He just stared as though someone had just walked across his heart. She was more beautiful than he could remember. Her hair was yellow gold, and her face was breathtaking. Her blue eyes pierced right through Gabe's soul. She stood there smiling at him the whole time. Gabe reached down and pulled his lower jaw up off from the prairie floor as he tried to dismount his horse. The startled scout nearly fell out of the saddle while trying not to take his eyes off of her. She flushed a little as Gabe stammered about like a dumbstruck mule. Gabe nearly tripped over his own feet as he moved three steps toward her. She just stood there smiling the whole time. Gabe started to speak, but the words would not come out. Finally, after what seemed like a lifetime, she told Gabe that she was glad to see him up and around. Gabe couldn't believe he was having this conversation with the angel.

As he started to babble like a sick duck, Davey introduced her. Her name was Haley Johnson. He told Gabe that she had cared for him while he was sick. Gabe was dumbfounded with all this information. He kept staring at her, trying to see if she was real. Gabe finally reached out and touched her face; she felt soft and warm. It was starting to come back to him in bits and pieces as they talked about his ordeal. But there was one thing Gabe was confused about now that he was back on his feet. "Why did some men hold me down and try to kill me while I was sick? he asked Haley. "Who were they?"

Haley laughed and told Gabe that they were the Mormon elders. They had placed their hands on his head and administered a blessing to him while he was sick and delirious.

This was too much information all at once for the confused scout. He was very nervous and confused, so he decided to leave. Gabe quickly thanked her for taking care of him while he was sick. He told her he was indebted to her. Then Gabe mounted his horse and rode off. As he cleared the campsite, the scout's mind was on overload. He was not aware of his surroundings. He just looked straight ahead, dumbfounded by all the information he had just received.

The grey moved swiftly along like he had a mission in mind. Gabe was just about to look back at the camp when he heard the sound of horse hooves behind him. He turned and watched as Davey rode up to him. He asked if Gabe was all right. Gabe told him that he was a little shaken up by all the information he had just received. Davey's concern for Gabe was warming, and Gabe had enjoyed his company out on the trails. Davey was studying Gabe, trying to get a feel for his mood. Gabe figured that his near death experience had worried the young Choctaw and confused his mind as well as Gabe's. Davey told Gabe that he would like to ride along with him for several miles and then he would return to the wagons before dark. Gabe told him to come along if he wanted too. The two men would be riding along the same trail they had taken when they had killed the buffalo days earlier. Gabe's stomach was still not right. He would have to bend over now and again from cramps. This made for a very uncomfortable ride.

About an hour out from the wagons, Gabe decided to dismount and see if walking would improve his strength. He told Davey that he had previously seen a spot along the stream that was thick with grouse, Gabe suggested that the two men try and procure some for their afternoon meal and if any birds were left over they could take them back to Otis for his delight. As the men came to the area of the grouse they tied their horses in a small depression near the stream so they would not be discovered. Gabe pulled the Henry from the leather scabbard, and Davey took his bow. As the scouts hunted down through the stream willows, the grouse would flush from their concealments and make a spectacular sight in the sky. Gabe let Davey shoot them from the ground if he could. Gabe had brought his rifle for defense purposes and dared not risk a shot to warn others of the two men's location. Even so, Davey managed fourteen birds and two cottontail rabbits. This would make for some fine eating.

As Gabe prepared a small fire in a makeshift camp with the horses, Davey prepared the day's catch. Both men cooked one rabbit and one grouse. The others birds and rabbits were prepared for the trip back to the wagons. As the savory meat seared, the two scouts began eating like two hungry vultures. Not a trace of meat was left to waste. The salt Gabe packed in his saddle bags gave the meat a succulent flavor. Gabe was starting to feel better all over from the ravages of the disease. His strength was coming back, and his mind was starting to clear up. Gabe removed himself from the fireside and went down to the stream to wash the sickness from his body. After a good soaping, he was refreshed and ready for the trail. Gabe told Davey to start the trail back to the wagons and report his plans to Otis and the bishop. Meanwhile, Gabe would scout out to the west for several days. Gabe would meet them near the Great Medicine

Tree[1] in four or five days. Davey agreed, and the scouts mounted their horses and said their goodbye's.

The Mormon wagon company would be traveling right past the mighty tree in several days from where they were currently encamped. This would be a good spot for Gabe to report back. By then he might have some fresh meat for their campfire stories.

---

[1] The Great Medicine Tree was a famous landmark along the Nebraska trail. It was a Giant cottonwood tree that was nearly twelve feet in diameter at its base, and hundreds of feet tall. It stood out all by itself on the lone prairie. There was not another tree around it for fifty miles in any direction. The Indians were superstitious about the tree, and some tribes would ride miles out of their way just to have a council and smoke their pipes under the shady leaves in the summer months. It was an icon of the plains, and many traveling souls would pass by it on their way to the west coast and marvel at its monstrous size. The mighty tree had withstood the elements for hundreds of years. It was a symbol of the mighty prairie it belonged to. This lone tree was sacred medicine to the Native Americans who witnessed the tree through many years of seasons.

CHAPTER 6 - BLUECOATS AND FEATHERS

It was scouting for sign and meat the last several days that had left Gabe in this situation. He was sitting under the tree, waiting for the darkness to cover his movements. An unknown enemy was out of his sight, and he needed to get back to the company and make sure things were alright with them. Gabe had left Davey and moved farther westward only to find himself in a match of wits with an unseen foe. The moccasin track he had found and the danger it presented were the beginning of several events that were about to take place that would change Gabe's life forever. Gabe had no idea of the dangers that surrounded not only him but the Mormons. At this time, he was only concerned with the person who left the moccasin track in his camp and had passed on the opportunity to take the grey horse off Gabe's hands. As the scout sat there on his mattress of pine needles, Gabe wondered if the track could possibly be from the lone Indian on the ridge he had seen several days earlier. What would be his mission out here on the plains, and why didn't he take the scout's horse if it was indeed the lone Indian? He wondered. The horse was his for the taking. Gabe's scalp was also up for grabs. He could have taken the scout several times as he had the advantage of stealth. All these thoughts were boggled up in Gabe's mind as he waited for the sun to set out on the horizon.

Gabe's horse seemed content eating his fill of buffalo grass. Little did he know the pair of them had a tough march ahead of them. Gabe checked his guns and made sure they were ready. He grabbed one last piece of hardtack and munched it down. As he made the grey ready for the trip, the last shadows of the evening started to turn dark. Gabe mounted his horse, and they made their way to the stream bank. The pair paused as Smoke bent his head and slurped up some cold prairie water. Gabe dismounted and took a knee. With his hand, he pulled several washes of the water to his lips and satisfied his thirst. The horse and rider were as ready as they could be. Gabe swung into the stirrup and pulled his revolver out of its holster. If they ran into anything in the darkness, it would be close up and the colt would be the best defense.

The night quickly fell on the scout and his horse as they made their way out onto the flat plain. Gabe figured this open area offered him the best chance of success. If the two of them did run into the lone Indian out there, they might have a running fight. Gabe was gambling that the grey could outrun the Indian's pony or others if he was not alone. The night sounds came all around the pair as they walked through the prairie grasses. Here and there Gabe could faintly make out buffalo trails in the dark. They would follow one of these until it went faint, then the horse and rider would see another one and follow it. All this time they kept the distant horizon to their backs. Gabe studied the stars as they came out and got his bearings and traveled west to east. The man and horse were going slowly but surely. The scout didn't want to run into anything if he could help it.

Far off in the distance, Gabe heard an elk bugle. His majestic call brought the ears forward on the grey. Old Smoke's instincts were fully alert as he walked through the night air. Several times Gabe thought he heard sounds that he couldn't quite identify. The pair would stop and listen until Gabe was satisfied that all was safe. They would continue in this fashion on and off most of the night. As they traveled along, the smell of rain permeated the night air.

Gabe would catch glimpses of lightning out into the distant night sky. It looked like man and animal might be in for some weather as they cautiously moved along. Finally Gabe stopped the horse and dismounted so he could put on a rain cape. As he was engaged in this operation, a blast from the sky hit the prairie floor not fifty feet from where Gabe and Smoke stood. The lightning explosion hit the earth with such ferocity that Gabe jumped about five feet to his left just to get out of the way of the bolt. As he did this, the grey horse left his tracks in the dust. Old Smoke's only resign was putting as much distance as he could between that thunderbolt and himself. Gabe lunged forward in a desperate attempt to grab the reins, but it was useless. Smoke ran off into the darkness faster than a scared coyote.

As Gabe's senses came back to him, he realized that he had placed the revolver on the saddle seat as he was draping his cape over his shoulders. If he could only find that pistol he would not be so helpless after all. Gabe could not afford a torch or light out there all alone on the dark prairie, so he had to resort to the hands and knees method of recovery. After what seemed like an eternity of scrounging around in the dark, the scout found the pistol exactly where it had fallen. *Now where is that jug headed horse?* He wondered. There couldn't be a worst time to be out on the big lonesome than this night, Gabe thought to himself. Here he was without his horse and on foot. He was at least thirty or more miles from the Mormon wagon party, and there was Indian sign on the wind. If any mounted enemy should fall on the scout, he might as well save the last ball for himself. Gabe didn't want to be captured alive and tortured by the savages. These were his thoughts as he swiftly walked in the direction of his last sighting of Old Smoke.

Walking along Gabe could see the faint outline of the horse's hoof prints as he had run wild through the buffalo wallows. He had stayed mostly on the hard dirt, which helped Gabe spot the sign in the darkness. Now and then he would gallop out onto the buffalo grass, which would make the trail much harder to follow. Gabe's only hope would be that the horse decided his belly was much more important than his fright and that he stopped to graze on the abundant grass.

As the scout walked along, he was very aware of his surroundings and his movements were calculated before he made them. The revolver was at half-cock, and he was ready for whatever the night wind might bring. Gabe couldn't fault Old Smoke for his behavior: he was doing what he was bred to do. Smoke was a flight animal, and all his instincts told him to run from danger. Gabe's only regret was that the big horse picked this time to remember all of his breeding and utilize it to his utmost advantage.

As the weary scout walked through the night, he wondered how far Smoke might run on a night like this. The grey horse might head into the water at some point, which would likely put him in the path of the Mormons. Or he might end up the new ownership of one lucky Indian brave. Either way, he was on his own until Gabe found him. The Henry was on his side in the scabbard. What a beautiful find this might make some lucky fellow that happened upon him. Gabe could only hope it might be a white man. This night had turned into a devil's puzzle, and Gabe was caught in the middle of the maze.

A light rain had started around midnight, and as the early morning sky started to lighten the plains, the scout took notice of his surroundings with the new light. The horse's trail was still visible for now, but if much more rain started falling, then Gabe would be without tracks. Following this track trail, Gabe was leaving a real good sign for any opportunist to follow if there might be any that wandered onto his back trail. He was wearing his knee high boots as supplied by his army service. Gabe usually rode with those on and carried a pair of moccasins in his saddle bags for light sneaking work. The boots would leave a defined heel impression and any tracker worth his salt could figure out the scout was afoot and trailing his horse instead of leading him. If the Indians spotted Gabe out here on the prairie before he saw them coming, the scout was as good as dead. His only hope at this point was that the horse might follow the water course, leaving Gabe with some type of cover to conceal himself if trouble came.

Gabe checked the colt to make sure it was dry, and then he kept walking along the trail. The rain was starting to increase as the prairie morning came to life. Sounds of thunder could be heard in the distance. Gabe was walking as fast as he could while keeping eyes on his surroundings. Twice he had to stop and survey a new valley as the trail took him farther east. Gabe would search out the valleys ahead and then proceed through them after he was sure nothing was about. This was the course he was on all morning long.

Gabe had just stopped to look at the area to his rear when he caught sight of movement about two miles behind him. The scout immediately dropped to his knees and started crawling toward the creek bank some forty yards to his left. If he could reach the stream area, it would provide some protection. Gabe had crawled close to the stream when he decided to glance up. There were three riders coming slowly and surely. They were working his back trail, and from their movements he perceived them to be Indians. At that distance, he could not make out for certain. Gabe decided to slide off the prairie bank and onto the creek bed. At this position, only his upper body would be exposed. The scout pulled the colt from the holster and checked it again for moisture. It looked dry and ready. He pulled half cock on the hammer and put his left-hand sleeve over the action to protect it from the falling rain. The horsemen were pressing the trail hard. They were out about one mile and now moving swiftly. The boot tracks Gabe had made were easy to follow, and it made the Indians' trail a quick one to figure out. They followed like a pack of wolves on the trail of a wounded elk. Gabe could make out their ponies now. They were definitely Indians. Now the only thing left for the scout was to determine which tribe they belonged to and how friendly they might be.

As they started into the valley area where Gabe was concealed, they stopped for a long while and were discussing the trail. They appeared to be Cheyenne or Sioux from the markings on the horses and the way they displayed their hair with feathers. If they moved another hundred yards along the trail, they would have the scout's position figured out. Gabe would have no choice but to fight. He was not about to come forward for a parley. Gabe could make out yellow paint on one of the braves. This meant that they were on a war trail. Any person they came in contact with would be considered an enemy.

The Indians moved along the trail very cautiously. They were looking all over the valley as they walked their horses forward. One Indian riding a pinto horse seemed to be the leader of the group. He would jester with his war club, pointing out impressions in the trail. Now they were at the spot Gabe had started to crawl towards the creek bank. If only he had the Henry, Gabe thought. He could probably stand them off. But with just a pistol it would be close-up fighting.

The leader of the group climbed off his horse and knelt down over the track. He motioned with his arm, and the other Indians looked directly at Gabe's position. Now they had the scout pegged. They knew Gabe had spotted them and crawled to cover. The Indians were intently looking at the creek bank, deciding a course of action. The leader mounted his horse and motioned for one of the Indians to circle back along the trail and try to cut around behind the scout's position. The other Indian rode out to the east, very slowly trying to get on Gabe's left side. The leader kept staring at Gabe's position, trying to bring up his nerve to push the enemy's concealment. Gabe kept his eye on him. The Indian leader was not sure if Gabe was armed. The Indian might suppose that Gabe's horse ran off with all of his weapons. The Indians were trying to exact the scout's location with this pincer move. One of them would flush the foe from the cover and the others would move in for the kill.

The leader started to move his horse directly at Gabe. The scout pulled the hammer back full on the colt and laid the barrel on his forearm for leverage. He was probably fifty yards away when he pushed his horse into a full run straight at the scouts position. Gabe quickly checked to his right and left to make sure the others were not within range of the colt. They were unseen to the scout, which made for a bad situation.

The leader came at a full run right for Gabe. The scout was below the charging Indian in the creek bank, so his sight position was from under the charging horse looking up. Gabe pulled up the barrel on the pistol and covered the horse's head with the front sight and pulled the trigger. The smoke blocked some of Gabe's view, but he managed to see the horse pull its front legs up under itself and tumble end over from head to tail. The rider was pitched about twelve feet out in front of the horse hard to the ground. The Indian started to rise to his feet in a weakened condition. He partially stumbled to his right side to gain his balance. As he did this, Gabe pulled the hammer back on the pistol and lined up the front sight on his torso. As the gun bucked, the Indian lunged to the left and dropped to the ground where he had stood. Through the smoke, Gabe could see the Indian was finished.

Gabe quickly turned and ran to the left from his old position. He needed to get out of the spot he had been in. The smoke from the pistol would give him away to the other two Indians. As Gabe was running down the creek bed, he heard the sound of hoofbeats coming down the water's edge. Quickly the scout jumped into a clump of serviceberries and hunkered down low. As the rider came into full view, Gabe pulled the hammer back again and prepared for a shot. This time, the Indian was on the opposite side of his horse hanging from the side. As he galloped past Gabe's position, the Indian pulled under the horse's neck and shot his pistol towards the scout. The ball cut through Gabe's left sleeve at the wrist and burned a path along his arm to the elbow. Gabe threw his right hand with the gun and all towards the pain and tried to manage it. The Indian wheeled his horse around and started toward Gabe for the kill. The motion was so fast that Gabe hardly had time to gather his senses. The Indian pushed the horse straight at Gabe on the run. The Indian's hand showed the pistol aimed and ready to fire. Gabe rolled to his side, making the Indian posture his horse's movement to counter Gabe's move. As the Indian did this, Gabe leveled the colt from his crouched position and fired directly at the horse. The ball struck the horse in the chest, and it peeled over on its side. The Indian fell with his mount and struck the creek water with a splash. Quickly Gabe pulled the hammer and fired. The ball hit the Indian in the back of his waist as he tried to rise up. He slid back into the water and went face down. Gabe went to the wounded horse and lay down behind it. This would give the scout some protection from the other Indian.

As Gabe lay there, the scene got real quiet except for the heavy gasping of the wounded horse. Finally, Gabe pulled the bowie knife from his belted sheath and cut the jugular on the dying horse. Nothing was moving now, the sounds of morning mulled by the rain drizzling down. Gabe had no idea where the other Indian was. Surely he knew his brothers were in peril. There had been four shots with two riders and horses down. Gabe wanted to reload the colt, but he dared not move. Time went by slowly, and after about an hour or so Gabe slowly crawled over to the bank's edge and peered out into the open plain. He expected to see a dozen Indians converging on his position. But all the scout could see was one lone Indian horse standing near its dead rider. The pinto was on his feet grazing on the prairie grass near the spot where he had tumbled.

Gabe looked around the area to see if he might be set up for a trap. If he made a move for the pinto, the other Indian might pick the scout off easy. So Gabe stayed where he was for the present time and reloaded his pistol. Gabe's forearm burned like he had been laid into with a branding iron. The scout wrapped his neck scarf around the wound and tried to ease the bleeding. The wound would not kill him if he could get some medicine on it and prevent infection. If only Gabe could find the grey; he had a medicine pouch in his saddle bags that Davey had prepared for him on the trail.

Now the scout was starting to think about survival and thoughts of killing were fading away. Gabe had been lucky so far. If he could wait out the day, he might be able to walk out of there in the dark. The Indian pinto didn't look hurt. Gabe might be able to catch him at dusk and then make tracks out of the situation he was in. These were the thoughts in the wounded scout's mind as he caught a glimpse of the first rider on the edge of the valley.

Two more riders were working his trail just like the previous Indians had. Gabe was in a real bad situation. He had one Indian out there somewhere that knew his exact location, and now it appeared two more were on the scene. Gabe wondered just how his luck might be running out when he noticed movement to his right along the same creek bank he was positioned on. It was a horse and rider turning off the creek area and running back behind Gabe and into the wooded area of the forest floor. Gabe could only make out glimpses here and there, but he was certain it was the other Indian that had shown up with the two the scout had killed.

He had been waiting for Gabe to show himself then he could pick the scout off with his rifle.

Why was the Indian turning and running away? Gabe asked himself as he looked back at the other two Indians following his boot trail coming up on the meadow's edge. Then it finally dawned on Gabe as the two Indians came closer: they were wearing army blue jackets. The same ones as issued to the soldiers of the 4th cavalry that were patrolling the plains. Gabe could see their markings. Their heads were shaven, and they appeared to be Pawnee scouts. Gabe could not have been more surprised than if he'd seen a prairie ghost. Cautiously Gabe stood from his position, giving his location away. The two Indians froze in their tracks. They were studying the scene out. They were about one hundred yards from Gabe.

As he stood out of his concealment, Gabe walked over to the dead Indian's pinto horse and examined him for wounds. The scout's shot had hit him in the upper neck. He had quit bleeding and seemed to be no worse for the wear. The bullet had just grazed him. The horse stood still as Gabe gathered the reins. By this time the Pawnee scouts had split up and one rode back along the trail and out of the valley. The other one just sat on his horse and stared at Gabe. The Indian was not sure what to make of all this, so he kept his distance. Finally, Gabe spotted a column of soldiers coming along the trail and toward him. The scout counted twenty-two, not including the Indian scouts. They were riding at a gallop. As they came within thirty yards the command was given to hold up. The troopers were at the ready with carbines drawn. The formation was split into two groups. Both deployed in opposite directions and moved out to about forty yards west and east. Three rode directly to Gabe's position with the scouts following behind.

Gabe holstered the colt and took his hat off to ensure they knew he was a white man. Gabe had enough trail dirt on him that he might be mistaken for a renegade Indian or army deserter. Gabe didn't want any surprises for his new prairie companions. The officer in charge rode up to within several feet of Gabe and inspected his situation. He looked at the scout and introduced himself. "I am second lieutenant Nathan Bryant of C Company 10th Cavalry detached from a main column south of this position. We are on a scout for a group of hostiles that we are pursuing." Who are you and what is your business out here on the plains?"

Gabe informed him of his name and business. Gabe explained how his misfortune with the lightning strike and Old Smoke had placed him out there afoot. The officer pulled his canteen from his saddle and threw it in Gabe's direction.

Gabe took a long and slow drink as he eyeballed the lieutenant. As Gabe handed the officer back his canteen, he told Gabe that the Indians they were following had raided several wagon trains and a surveying party for the railroad. It had been a bloody affair. The marauding Indians had taken female hostages from the wagon trains and numerous horses and mules. The main column was two days behind following their trail. The troops' orders were to locate the hostiles and slow their process until the main column was in a position to strike. They were on the trail of the hostiles when the Pawnee scouts had cut Gabe's trail.

The main group of hostiles, which consisted of sixty or more, had turned northeast earlier that morning, but a smaller group had followed Gabe's trail, and that led the cavalry to Gabe. Hearing this information made Gabe shudder. He would have been a dead man walking if the main group had come upon him. The lieutenant climbed down from his horse and ordered a makeshift camp set up until the Pawnees could scout the surrounding area for other Indians and sign. Several parties of soldiers and scouts rode out in different directions at the gallop. Gabe was asked to eat with the soldiers, and a medical officer was instructed to tend to the scout's wounds. Gabe told the medical officer that he would be back in a few minutes. He had some unfinished business to attend to.

Gabe immediately went to the fallen Indians and inspected each one. He pulled out his bowie knife and cut the scalps off of each one. The scout had been taught this trade many moons ago. It was expected out on the plains from Indian fighters. Gabe tied the bloody scalps to the Indian pinto's mane. Then he took the dead Indians' weapons of war. They consisted of two war clubs, a black powder revolver, and a Winchester Yellow Boy rifle. The rifle was in new condition. No doubt it had been stolen recently from raids that these Indians were involved in. Gabe gathered in all the ammunitions and several knives. There was also a nice medicine pipe on the dead horse. This would make for trading value at some point in Gabe's life, so he stashed the goods on the pinto. Gabe led the horse to the picket line where the army horses were tethered and tied the Indian pony's head. Now the scout finally had a horse to ride back to the Mormons.

The rain had quit for now, but the sky hung low with overcast clouds. The smell of new, fresh rain was everywhere. As the morning moved along, Gabe wandered back and forth through the cook fires of the troops, having a conversation where it was afforded. The troop was made up mostly of young volunteers anxious to see the West. There were some veterans of the Civil War sprinkled in the mix and several Spanish Americans involved. They had not seen much action to date, and all of them were looking forward to a skirmish with the hostiles. The troop had seen enough carnage to convince them that their mission was warranted. Lieutenant Bryant was a West Point graduate, and his service to date was raw and inexperienced. He would need to muster up if the troop came under serious attack.

The army had placed several Pawnee scouts in this troop and one interpreter. He was a French Canadian named Louis Douix. The troops called him Dewey. His experience was essential to this patrol. He was an experienced woodsman and trapper of the days of old. He knew this country like the Indian, and his advice was the law out here. Gabe had been around men like him earlier in his life, and the scout had learned to listen when the old scouts like Dewey spoke. Those old wise men of the prairie as they were called, could save your hair on the worst of days, and safely guide you through the storm. Dewey had been sent out earlier in the morning with the scouting parties, and Gabe was anxious to talk to him upon his return.

Sometimes things don't end up the way you would expect in life, and this day was turning into a real winner. Gabe had just finished his sixth cup of coffee when a familiar sight strolled into the valley. It was Old Smoke being led by a group of the scouting party Pawnees. The horse seemed in fine spirits and had all his usual apparel still attached in order. Hell, even the Henry was in the scabbard. Old Smoke was prancing along like he was in a parade. Little did the jughead horse know that he almost cost his owner his hair. After all the tender loving care Gabe had provided over the years the big horse looked like he enjoyed being without the scout.

The Pawnee scouts brought their horses to bear on the picket line and tied them in with the other horses. Gabe strolled on over to the grey horse and put his hand up to his nose. Smoke pushed up against the pressure and made his usual nod that he recognized the smell. Gabe was examining him all over when Dewey came up to him. Dewey introduced himself and said how he admired Gabe's actions in the early morning battle. He told Gabe of the war party and showed the scout his thoughts on the position of the hostiles in regards to the troops and the Mormons.

The Pawnees had brought word of the wagon train and Dewey had deduced that Gabe had been a scout for the train. He had cut Gabe's trail several days back when Davey and he had found the boy on the prairie. Dewey figured sooner or later the two men would meet up. The wise old scout Dewey was everything Gabe had supposed. He was seasoned and tough as boot leather. He had the scars and weathering to prove it. He spoke perfect English and could read sign with the best Indian on the plains. His skills would get the lieutenant another bar on his sleeve someday if he heeded Dewey's advice. As the two men stood there conversing, another group of scouts rode in and dismounted. One of the Pawnees came over to Dewey and made a sign for a sit-down talk. The men invited Gabe to come along, and they proceeded to get the lieutenant involved.

The group of scouts all sat down around one of the small fires the Pawnees were cooking coffee from. As is the custom, a pipe was filled with tobacco and all parties partook of the smoke. The talk began with the news that the Pawnees had found tracks on the trail. They had found where the main raiding party had moved northeast toward the South Loup River drainage. This would put them in a crossing path with the Mormons if they stayed on their course. The Pawnees figured that some advanced scouting parties from the marauding Indians had already made contact with the Mormons and were in spy contact with them. They were setting up to assault the train when the moment presented itself. The raiding Indians would probably not risk an all out attack on the train because of its size. They were, no doubt, looking for livestock and any other thing they might run off with. As the group of Indian fighters sat there, it was obvious to all of them that there was great danger in the vicinity of the Mormon wagon train. Gabe would have to get to them as fast as possible and be very careful to skirt the hostiles in the process. That task would certainly be a risky one.

Finally, a plan was made for the army troop to continue on its course toward the Mormons. Gabe could move much faster going alone than the troop could, so he started immediately. The immediate goal was to alert the Mormons if possible and have them hold up and make camp. While the hostiles were preparing for a raid, the army would split into two squads and try to come up behind the Indians and pin the hostiles between themselves and the wagon train. Word was sent back to the main column to drop all supplies and make haste to a point determined. Then the Pawnees would bring them up to a point for an attack on the main hostile camp. Gabe just loved it when a plan would come together. But this plan had more holes in it than mouse cheese. This would be a fine plan if the hostiles were to stay put and wait to be attacked like the army proposed. The hostile Indians would have scouts out in all locations looking for just such a sign. The lieutenant was set on the plan, and Dewey could only advise. His advice was to wait for the main column before moving from this position and never split up the troops. This would make them easy picking should the Indians turn and fight. Logic would not run the lieutenant. He was determined to get some glory here, and this was his opportunity. The order was given and the camp was ordered to break.

Gabe walked over to the grey horse and started fixing his saddle when he heard a motion behind him. The scout turned around, and there were four Pawnee scouts with their weapons in hand staring at him. Gabe made the sign that he was in a hurry, and the Pawnee's signed back that he was not leaving there with the buffalo horse. Gabe pulled around and started to prepare his saddle bags when he heard the hammer on a rifle pulled to lock. The scout turned again and found himself staring down the barrel of an army issue carbine. One of the Pawnee scouts was pointing it directly at Gabe's head. Gabe was in the process of figuring a way out of this when Dewey calmly walked up and asked what Gabe's intentions were. Gabe told him, and Dewey said the scout was free to take the Indian pinto, but the Pawnee brave that had the rifle pointed at Gabe's head had found the buffalo horse abandoned on the prairie and had claimed him. Gabe noticed a slight smile on Dewey's face as he told him of the Pawnee's position on the matter.

One way or another, Old Smoke was trying his best to get him killed, Gabe thought to himself. Gabe was about to challenge the brave for the horse rights when Dewey came to the rescue. He suggested a trade. Dewey put it to the Pawnee brave, and with some reluctance the Indian asked what could be worth the value of the great buffalo horse. Dewey asked Gabe with a grin and said the scout needed to make an impression, or the grey horse would be lost. Gabe thought quickly and asked the brave to lower the rifle so Gabe might think. As Gabe turned to cuss the grey horse for putting him in that position, a brilliant idea came to him. Gabe walked over to the pinto, who was loaded up with all sorts of war spoils.

Gabe calmly led him to the circle and presented him to the Pawnee holding the rifle. At first Gabe thought he had failed, but when the Indian brave walked around the horse and saw the scalps hanging on the mane of the horse, he let out a loud yell three times, "Yee awh, yee awh, yee awh!" The other Pawnees joined in in unison. Gabe knew that the Pawnee were graven enemies of the Sioux and Cheyenne. They had been enemies for hundreds of years. They had raided the Pawnee and stolen women, children, and livestock for ages. They had killed many Pawnee in battle, and almost everyone in the Pawnee tribe had lost a loved one to the Sioux and Cheyenne at one time or another. Those scalps were big medicine among the Pawnee and a valued prize. Gabe also reached in the medicine bag on the pinto's saddle and pulled out the medicine pipe and presented it to the brave.

The Indian quickly handed it back and made the sign that the pipe was not for trade. It was bad medicine to the Pawnee to own or smoke from the enemy's pipe. He made the sign that the Indian pinto and all the booty would suffice for trade. The deal was done. Dewey never took the grin off his face the whole time. He had this deal done in his mind before Gabriel Tanner, mighty scout of the plains, even conceived it. Dewey was enjoying this too much. As Gabe turned to finish up getting the grey ready for the hard ride, Dewey put his hand on Gabe's shoulder and said, "Scout, there was someone out there watching out for you today, and I hope some of that magic rubs off on the rest of us. We are going to need all the help we can muster in the next few days. Keeping the lieutenant alive is starting to be a real chore."

At those words, Gabe bid him good luck as he stepped into the stirrups. Gabe was about to turn and leave when Dewey made another remark that got Gabe thinking. Dewey mentioned that one of the Pawnee scouts had run into a lone Indian on the plains. He was a Ponca Indian, and they were friendly with the Pawnee nation. He was searching for his granddaughter that had been abducted in a raid by this same group of hostiles the army was engaging.

Gabe thought this must be the Indian whom he had seen previously on the prairie and had made the track in his camp several days ago. Gabe thought he had seen a captive Indian girl in the night camp of the hostiles when he and Davey found the boy Will on the prairie about a week before. As Gabe started the grey horse out of the troop camp, he thanked Dewey for the information and told the lieutenant as he passed by him he would be well advised to heed Dewey's words.

CHAPTER 7 - MULES IN THE MIST

Haley Johnson came from the old country when she was just thirteen. Her parents had migrated from England when the Mormon missionaries had converted them back in 1861. They came by ship through the main harbor port at Ellis Island. Her father had applied for citizenship and was granted his request. He was a college professor by trade, and her mother was a school teacher. They had both applied their teaching skills in upper New York State before the Civil War. Haley was an only child, and she was raised with all the book fanfare a set of scholars could bestow on one child. At the age of seventeen, she taught grade school at the local town, while trying to maintain a low profile with all the surrounding soldiers stationed nearby. She was courted by many and had received the reputation of being a prune in disguise. Her parents guarded her virtues and kept her life in a scholarly condition. Everything she knew about life was contained in the books that she read continually day and night.

Her father was finally called into service late in the war. He was put in an intelligence unit because of his education and age. This left her and her mother to run the household alone and fending for themselves. Money was tight because of the war, and teaching brought in little income. They were pressed into various jobs of labor, and Haley got her first taste of physical hardships. She seemed to weather this challenge well. At the tail end of the war, her father was released from service, and the family decided it was best to follow the Mormon prophet's council and move out to the Utah territories. The majority of Mormons were already living there, and her father was asked to go out and help start up a university for the Saints. They had been living a low profile with their religious beliefs since they had arrived in America. And this new move would allow them to have the freedoms they wanted in expressing their views.

A plan was set in motion. Haley's parents would take the next wagon train west, and Haley would follow in the late summer, when she graduated from school. She would stay with some Mormon friends until that time. If the continental train were finished by the time she got out of school, she would take that passage to Utah. Otherwise, she would embark on the first Mormon wagon train heading west. As it turned out, the train was not finished due to Indian troubles, and the Mormon company lead by bishop Stone was her only option. She paid her passage fees to the church and was allowed to travel with the widow Sister Mays. They were outfitted with a wagon, and a set of elders were in charge of the teams and livestock care as provided by the Bishop. In turn for the services of the livestock care and harnessing the teams each day, they would cook for the elders assigned to them.

Everything was taken into consideration by the bishop and the elders in charge. The church had made this excursion to Utah many times. It was made as comfortable as possible with the limited funds available. Life on the trail was a fascinating adventure for Haley. There were so many sights to see. The drudgery of the trail work was swallowed up in the vast prairie skies. The wagons moved at a snail's pace along the winding wheel furrows that had been cut into the buffalo grass by thousands of previous migrants. When the wagons caught sight of the first buffalo herd, the order was given to halt so that the elders might procure some meat. The herds were so numerous that several days would pass before the buffalo would disappear on the horizon. The first time Haley tried buffalo meat, it was given to her by one of the elders. Sister Mays and Haley put on a camp pot and boiled the meat down to a tender morsel. She preferred it to beef. The two women learned how to dry the meat over a small fire as shown to them by Davey and Tim.

As the trip went along, Haley seemed to adjust to wagon life, and she never complained. She took to the task of the prairie like she had been born into it all her life. It would amaze some of the other sisters as she fell into the work with a song on her lips and a smile for everyone around. She made the dull camp come to life as all of the other women would see her work and laugh at some of the most tiring of chores. She was a breath of fresh air amid the dust and mud that were heaved upon the Saints as the wagons slowly crawled west. If someone were in need of assistance with their children, they could depend on Haley to help out. She helped nurse the sick ones and taught the smaller children how to read as time allowed along the trail. She was a valued commodity to the company and someone everyone was glad to have along.

As the trail came and went Haley and Sister Mays asked the elders to teach them how to fire the weapons. Davey took a special interest in this endeavor because Haley was teaching him some further education as they traveled. One day the wagons were encamped along the South Loup River, Davey rode up to the wagon and asked Haley and Sister Mays if they would join him on a shooting expedition. The two women were very excited. Davey had saddled two mules and placed the sisters on them. He led them out of camp several miles along the stream and came to a place that offered a steep cut bank on the other side of the stream. They all dismounted, and the targets were set. Several bottles were lined up, and the rifle was loaded. Handing the gun to Sister Mays, she pulled the rifle to her shoulder and squeezed the trigger. The gun roared up and nearly threw her on the ground. They all laughed as the next round was chambered for Haley. The weight of the barrel was nearly more than she could manage.

As the sight came across one of the bottles, she pulled back on the trigger and the gun rocked in the air. The bottle smashed into pieces, and the group burst into cheers. This was only the third time she had fired a rifle, but the impression would last her a lifetime. Both women were rubbing their shoulders and reluctant to shoot anymore, so Davey called it quits. As the party was mounting up, Davey noticed a lone Indian sitting out on the nearest hillside about a mile away. He was sitting on his horse, watching them intently. Davey pointed him out to the women and told them to stay close to his horse and keep up the pace back to the wagons. As they moved along, Davey kept his eye on the lone rider. He never moved.

When they were out of sight of the Indian, Davey picked up the pace to a trot. He pushed this speed all the way to the wagons. When he arrived there, he took the women to their wagon and made quick speed to Otis and the bishop. Some of the elders had assembled as the news rippled throughout the camp. Since Gabe was still on a scouting trip, it was decided that Davey and Tim, being the most experienced at this sort of thing, would ride out a small way and check for Indian sign. Haley had gathered with the elders to see if she might be of some assistance. She told Davey that she would put some food together for the brothers and pack it in a sack. The brothers started putting their gear together for the scouts.

As the two brothers mounted their horses and started off, Haley said a small prayer in her heart. She would pray every time Gabe would go out as well. She was sure that her prayers were keeping the men safe on their dangerous missions. Since cholera had attacked the Mormons, the overall mood among the saints was a sober one. The news of the lone Indian was not welcome throughout the camp. The elders armed themselves, and the women gathered the children into the wagon areas. The stock was rounded up, and the guard was put out around the camp. The Mormons settled into this defensive posture and waited for some news. Haley had been given a pistol from the wagon where the Mormons stored their guns and ammunition. She had fired it several times and had become somewhat knowledgeable about its functions. She put the pistol belt around her waist and made sure the gun was loaded.

As she was in the process of doing this, young Will came up to her for conversation. Haley had been teaching him along with others in the company to further their reading and arithmetic skills. He had grown quite fond of Haley as she reminded him of his young mother, who had perished at the hands of the hostiles. She had taken a liking to Will as well. He was like the little brother she never had. The two were often seen together reading and writing in their journals to pass the time away. They would go out with others and gather berries and wood when daylight afforded the venture. This day was another one of those days except for the lone Indian sighting.

Young Will had brought his journal, and the two of them sat beneath the wagon and penned their notations as the light rain fell on the camp.

Davey and Tim rode out to the west. They worked along the creek bed toward the last sighting of the Indian. As they came to the place where they had been target practicing, Davey showed Tim where the Indian had sat his horse. The two Choctaws decided to ride to that spot and pick up the sign. As Davey and Will neared the hill where the Indian had been, the rain started to increase. From the view of the hill, they could only see about one hundred yards through the dense fog that was coming off the water course below. They slowly walked their horses to the area where the Indian had been. Davey dismounted and surveyed the track.

The Indian appeared to be alone. He had ridden off to the south and didn't seem to be in any hurry. He must be fairly close since he seemed interested in the Mormon camp, Davey thought to himself. These were the thoughts of the young Choctaws as they followed the trail carefully. Both brothers had their rifles across their saddle horns in a defensive position. Both rifles were on half-cock, and the two young Indians had their hands in position to raise and fire if needed. Slowly they inched along the trail. They had gone about two miles when a sound made the boys freeze in their tracks. It was the call of the wren. The problem with this call is that there were not any wrens around. The two brothers dismounted and moved through the timbered forest on foot. As they were rounding a small amount of knocked down windblown birch trees, they came face to face with the Indian. He was sitting on his horse, staring at them from about thirty feet. He could have easily killed one or both of the boys, but he didn't have his rifle raised at them. Davey was in front on the trail and the closest to the Indian. The Indian wasn't dressed for war. His face and body were not painted. The boys were not sure what tribe he belonged to. Davey slowly raised his left hand and made the sign of peace. All this time he kept his right hand on his Winchester. The Indian made sign back that he wanted no trouble. He came in peace as well. He made the sign of smoke and talk.

The rain was constant and the timbered area where they were offered no relief. The lone Indian turned his horse around and made the sign to follow. The boys were hesitant, but the fact that he turned his back to them showed he did not fear them. Was he setting them up for an ambush? What was his mission and purpose out here in the rain? These and other questions were in the minds of the two brothers as they followed the Indian's horse. The boys kept their hands ready for anything that might pose a threat as they walked through the pouring rain. The Indian led them to a dense stand of timber and stepped down from his horse. He pulled a buffalo robe from behind his saddle and pitched it over several fallen timbers. He started to gather some sticks for a fire as the boys dismounted. The two brothers stood motionless as the Indian made a small makeshift fire and sat down beneath the robe and signed to sit with him in peace.

The Choctaws tied their horses and sat down under the cover opposite the Indian. They each kept their rifles at the ready as they sat cross-legged near the small fire. The Indian pulled a pipe from a sheath and filled it with kinnikinnick[2]. The boys were used to the smoke as the Indian took a long draw and passed the pipe to Tim. He puffed and blew, then handed it to Davey to finish the ceremony. The Indian introduced himself as a lesser chief of the Ponca tribe.

The Choctaws were familiar with the small nation of the Ponca. They had been decimated by smallpox back in the early 1800's and had been a small nation since that time. The Indian told them his tribe was less than seventy warriors at that time. The Ponca chief was on a mission to rescue his granddaughter. She had been taken in a raid by Sioux and Cheyenne warriors down in the Indian nations of Oklahoma about two moons ago. He was following the raiding party when he ran into the white man's wagons. There was something about the old Indian that Davey couldn't figure out. He asked the old Indian where the father of the captured Indian girl was. The Indian told them that he had fallen in battle with the Sioux and Cheyenne during the raid. It was then his responsibility to search out the daughter of the dead warrior and return her to her people.

---

[2] This ingredient was a staple smoke out on the plains when tobacco could not be had. It was made mainly from dried Bearberry leaves.

Davey asked if the fallen one was his son, and the Indian stared long into the fire and then nodded his head. Davey had known of a great chief among the Ponca named White Eagle. He asked if this Indian knew of this great chief. He nodded his head again. Davey asked him if he would be that chief. The Indian said that he was no longer the great chief. He was called Mahan by his people, and until he returned the Ponca maiden to her family, he would be known as Mahan a lesser chief. Davey knew this Indian sitting across from them had big medicine in his past. He was known far and wide across the plains as a warrior of great magnitude.

His exploits were known to the white man as well. He had brought peace to the white man and fellow Indians alike. But the Ponca had been besieged by the warlike Sioux and Cheyenne since their numbers declined over the past decade. This Indian had made serious war on his enemies when his people were accosted. The word *Mahan* meant great one in the universal sign language which the plains Indians shared. Just being in the presence of this Indian gave the boys a sense of wonder.

As the two brothers shared the fire and smoke with Mahan, he told them that he had seen the great white buffalo horse of the plains and was able to touch him and see that he is real. The boys asked if he had seen the scout named Gabe lately. Mahan told them of his encounters with him. He told them that he was on his way back to the wagons after meeting with the blue coats. He told them he had taken scalps in battle, and he fought this battle without the help of the buffalo horse. As the news reached the ears of the Choctaws, they were pleased to hear Gabe was alright and on his way toward them. Then the words from the great Indian got very sober. He told the two boys that they had been watched by war party Scouts of the Sioux for the last three days.

They appeared to be ready to make a raid on the wagons and that the hostile Indians were waiting for the right opportunity.

Mahan had been watching the hostiles from a distance of concealment, waiting for his chance to regain his granddaughter. He told the two boys that the Indians were made up of about seventy warriors. The main group was camped southwest from the wagons about a single day's ride. A small group of seven warriors watched, the wagon camp as they spoke.

Davey asked Mahan if he thought the Indians would attack the wagons in force. Mahan said it was likely; they were looking for an easy war and big gains. They would probably stampede the stock with a few warriors and try to draw the whites out from their defensive positions. This would make it much easier to raid the main group and keep them occupied while the small raiding party made off with the animals. This sounded like a well thought out plan, and Davey asked the great warrior if he had thought it up. He said that if he were making this war, this would be his war plan if he wanted success.

Mahan said there was a mighty warrior in the Cheyenne group called Black Tongue. He was a ruthless warrior and very cunning in his war ways. He had killed many Crow and Pawnees in battle, and his own people feared him. Mahan said that to get back his granddaughter he would have to meet this warrior Black Tongue in battle someday. Mahan told the two boys of his dream in which the great white buffalo horse would save his life in battle with the Cheyenne warrior. He didn't know how this would be possible because he didn't own the horse. It was his vision and to an Indian this was big medicine.

One thing the brothers knew was that Gabe would not part with Old Smoke unless he were dead. So the dream would be put on hold for now. The Young Choctaws needed to get back to the wagons and relay the words that they had learned from Mahan to the Mormons. The Choctaws told Mahan that they would let the white men in the wagon camp know that he came in peace. He was welcome there anytime, and he had permission to ride into the camp unmolested. These words were welcomed by Mahan, and the parley was ended with a sign of friendship. The two brothers mounted their ponies and made fast tracks for the wagon train.

As Haley and Will wrote in their journals, the rain was starting to ease up. Their camp was a muddy water soaked mess. The prairie grass had been eaten away by the stock animals that were in the center of the wagons. The constant rain of the past two days had penetrated the exposed topsoil and made a mud mash. Walking from wagon to wagon, the Mormons were slogging through six inches of slick mud. These conditions made the camp almost unbearable for the women and children.

The elders were on guard in shifts. Some watched the stock while others cared for the needs of the women and children. They would take the women out in groups to fetch water and wood for cooking. Sitting in the wagons and living in these conditions would produce sickness if the wagons were not soon moved. Everyone was on nerves end, and the only thing that could help with the misery was the hymns that were being sung from wagon to wagon. Prayers were offered for everything needed. Thanks was given for life and the opportunity to go west. The bishop made the rounds through the wagons and comforted the Saints as they waited for the unknown.

With the recent cholera and misery that had been brought to the Mormons, the bishop had been trying his best to offer something in the form of comfort. Now with the threat of hostiles and being stuck here in this quick mire was almost more than the Saints could endure. The heavy rains made it impossible for the teams to pull the wagons through the thick mud. This left the Mormons in a position of stalemate. The bishop decided that he would assign teams to go out and procure wood for the day. A group of six women with two armed elders to guard them would be the order of the day. Haley and Will were asked if they would help with the wood chores. They cheerfully accepted the offer so they might get out from under the wagons and get a breath of fresh air. The area they were assigned was just north of the camp about a quarter of a mile along the stream course. It had a variety of downed hardwoods that made for hot fires and plenty of cooking coals.

As Haley and Will went out with the elders, the rain was nearly gone. A heavy mist hung in the air, and the prairie seemed real quiet. Even the birds were still folded up on the limbs, trying to keep dry. There were a few deer moving about, but not much of anything else was stirring. One of the elders, named Brother Sikes, decided he might take a chance at one of the deer that was walking along the opposite side of the stream. He left the wood party and waded over to the other side and continued up the far bank and into the forest beyond. Haley and Will were busy piling up dead wood on a makeshift skid. This skid was harnessed to a mule for easy hauling. The skid made it so the Saints could gather a lot more wood than just carrying it with their arms. The skid was made of smooth timbers that had been cut and milled on the bottom of the skid to make it slide like a sleigh.

The wood was piled upon the skid and tied down for the trip back to the wagons. After nearly an hour of gathering wood, everyone was in the process of securing this task when a call was made to Brother Sikes. The wood party was ready to go back to the wagons. He did not respond when called. Everyone in the party started to call out his name as they searched the far bank with their eyes. Elder Paul was the other man in charge of safety. He motioned for the party to start back with the wood skid while he found Brother Sikes.

As Haley and Will watched, Elder Paul went to the spot near the stream that Brother Sikes had waded, and he followed that trail. As he reached the opposite side, he called out to Brother Sikes in a loud voice. Nothing could be heard on the plains but the soft swishing of the stream water as it meandered along its path. Elder Paul walked up the far bank and stood motionless staring out into the forest in front of him. He turned back to the wood crew and shrugged his shoulders as if to say he couldn't see anything.

Everyone in the wood detail was watching his movements as they started back for camp. The rest of the detail consisted of Haley and Will and three other sisters. One of the sisters had the lead rope on the mule, and she was pulling him along toward the wagons, which were within sight of the party. The wood party could see Brother Paul standing back there on the bank calling out to the other elder when he flinched backward and turned toward the group with an arrow sticking out from his upper torso. He fell back into the stream face down and then tried to get up on his knees. It all happened so fast that everyone was in shock. Sister Jones had a hold of the mule when she let out a scream that shook the valley floor. The mule spooked and jumped sideways. When he did this, the skid tightened up against his harness making the mule run from the pressure. He lit out across the prairie with the skid and wood flying in all directions. He continued past the wagons and out of sight.

Haley and Will were stunned. Their first instinct was to run toward the wagons. As they started that way, a loud scream was heard across the prairie. It was a man screaming in misery. It was coming from the wooded area where Brother Sikes had disappeared. All of the sudden a mass of yells and screams came from the wooded area. They were blood-curdling sounds in a hideous manner. As Haley looked back over her shoulder, the scene before her nearly made her heart stop. At least twenty mounted Indians were charging down on them from across the creek. They were coming fast, and there was no time to make it to the wagons before they were overrun. As she ran, Haley pulled the pistol from the holster and tried with all her might to pull the hammer back without stopping her run. She was in the back of the group almost twenty feet behind Will.

The other women were running towards the wagons as fast as they could. As she cocked the gun, her grip was so tight that the gun went off in her hand. The ball passed harmlessly in front of her on the buffalo grass. She looked up to see some of the elders running towards the group with their rifles in hand. As she witnessed this site, another group of Indians came at the wagons from the south end of the camp. They ran right through the wagons, yelling and screaming at the top of their lungs. They were waving buffalo robes and all kinds of leather skins to stampede the stock. This tactic by the Indians made the elders stop running toward the women. They immediately stopped and knelt for better gun mounting positions. The sounds of gunfire could be heard throughout the camp, and black powder smoke could be seen in the air. As Haley was running her lungs were burning. She felt like her strength was beginning to fade.

She finally pulled the hammer back one more time and turned just in time to see a mounted Indian closing in on her with a war club raised high above his head. She half-heartedly slowed and turned to face the threat. As she did the warrior rode past her with his stride. Her actions had confused the brave and he could not slow his horse down to counteract her movements. He rode past her and selected the next victim in front of him. Haley couldn't fire at him for fear of possibly hitting one of the others in the wood detail. As his horse lunged forward, he met with Sister Jones. The force of his running horse hit her in the back as she ran. This sent her sprawling out onto the prairie grass. As she tried to get up, the Indian wheeled his horse around and came at her before she could rise up. He hit her with his war club on the side of her head. As she fell to the earth, her head was a bloody mess. Death was instantaneous she never moved again.

Now the Indian had his sights on Will. The young boy had broken off from the group and was running back toward Haley for protection. This brought the Indian in line with Haley and the pistol. She raised the barrel and held on the running horse as the threat bore down on them. Will ran to her side and had just grabbed onto her shirt when she pulled the trigger on the gun. The Indian was so close that as the bullet passed through his lower neck, his momentum flung him off the horse and onto Haley and Will. The weight of the Indian knocked the pair to the ground with force. As they tried to gather themselves and get on their feet, another Indian came swooping down on the two of them from about fifty feet. There wasn't enough time to cock the hammer on the gun, so Haley pushed Will toward the wagons and told him to run. She stood there to face the enemy. She was trying to pull the hammer back when the Indian grabbed her by the hair and pulled her up on the side of his horse. This made her drop the pistol underneath the moving horse. She fought valiantly to free herself as the Indian turned his horse and ran for the timber. Twice the Indian lost his grip, and she plunged to the earth, only to have him grab her again and secure her to the horse's neck. As the Indian reached the stream side, he threw Haley from the horse and jumped down on top of her.

With all her strength, she was no match for the strong Indian. His face was painted crimson red, and he had the look of a wild animal as he wrestled her on the ground. He finally pulled leather thongs from his waistband as he sat on her chest. Then he proceeded to bind her hands. She fought continually through this maneuver until the Indian had had enough. He belted her upside the head with his knife handle, and that was the last Haley would remember.

As Will ran toward the wagons, a large herd of horses and mules came thundering out from the camp and right toward him. They were being chased by many Indians who were yelling and screaming as they ran from the Mormon camp. He had no choice but to fall to the ground and take cover in the fetal position. As the herd ran over the top of him, he was knocked several times on the back and buttocks by the frightened animals.

When the herd had passed, he rose from his hiding place and ran to the nearest wagon. As he reached the wagon, he was pulled under it by Otis. The elders were firing their guns and shouting about as the Indians made for the far timber to the north of the camp. Will had a terrible feeling in his stomach as he lay there under the wagon. He rose up and asked Otis where Haley was. Had she made it to the safety of the wagons? His question was answered with a resounding, "No, she never made it, son."

He lifted from his place under the wagon and started to crawl out from the safety to go after her. Otis grabbed the boy by the pant leg and pulled him back to safety. Otis told him that was the surest way to get killed. The Indians might not be finished yet. They would just stay under cover for a while and see what happens. Will started to cry. He felt like he had lost his best friend. Haley meant everything to him. The Indians had killed his parents and friends, and now they had killed or captured Haley. It was very difficult for him, not knowing of her condition. Otis told him that he had seen her being carried off by an Indian over near the creek. But he couldn't shoot the Indian without hitting Haley, so he had to watch as she disappeared from sight. They would go look for her as soon as the raid was over.

Davey and Tim heard the gunfire as they were about two miles out from the wagon camp. They could only presume to know the cause, but they were sure that the hostiles were raiding the Mormons. They slowed their march and decided it would not be wise to go charging into the camp with all the gunfire. It would be best to approach slowly and make sure they didn't run headlong into the marauding Indians. As they came within sight of the wagons, they could see a large plume of smoke within the camp. It didn't appear that any of the wagons were on fire, so they assumed it to be from the outdated black powder muskets that the Mormons had purchased before the trip. They could see men running around the camp, and horses and mules standing outside the wagon circles grazing on the prairie grass. When they got within rifle shot of the camp, they halted and decided to wait out the situation. Eventually, the two brothers were recognized, and the sign was given for them to come on in.

As they came into the camp, they were greeted by the bishop and Otis. Several elders had been taking inventory on the camp, and the mood was an angry one. As the two brothers dismounted, the elders were busy providing the bishop and Otis with the details of the raid. One-fourth of the stock had been run off. Five people were wounded slightly, and two elders and Sister Jones were dead. It appeared that Haley Johnson had been taken captive. The whereabouts of brothers Sikes and Paul were unknown. Upon hearing this information, the Bishop requested the Choctaws to go out and find the missing people if possible or, at least, pick up the trail of the hostiles and report back to him. In the meantime, he would gather together a party of the elders to try to retrieve the lost stock and Haley Johnson. Otis was given command of the wagons and was told to make preparations to break camp and move west to the next camping spot as shown on their maps. He was instructed to make a secure camp in case the Indians decided to raid again and then wait there until the bishop arrived with the party of elders.

The two Choctaws informed the bishop and Otis of their meeting with Mahan. They told everyone in the camp that he came in peace. Most of the elders were not in the mood to hear anything about Indians coming in peace, so the subject was dropped. The brothers rode out to the last known sighting of Haley Johnson. As they dismounted to examine the sign, Will Conner rode up on a mule and said he was going with them to find Haley Johnson. Davey grabbed the reins of the mule and pulled him aside. He told Will that this was grown men's business. The odds of being killed were very good with all the hostiles in the area. Davey motioned for him to go back to the camp at once. But Will would not submit to the words he was being told. He had grabbed a pistol from one of the wagon boxes, and he was bound and determined to find his friend. He kicked the mule in the ribs and pulled away from Davey's grasp. The mule broke into a trot and headed for the water stream.

Tim mounted his horse and ran after the young boy. As the mule reached the stream bed, the animal flinched sideways and unloaded the young boy flat on the ground. The mule ran off back to the wagons. As Will was getting to his feet, Tim rode to his side. He grabbed the young man and held him firmly by his suspenders. Davey rode up as the trio witnessed the scene before them. The mule had spooked from the human form in the stream. The pool that surrounded the body was full of crimson red blood. It was Elder Paul. The arrow was protruding from his upper chest, and he had been scalped. He lay face up in the water. It was a terrible sight for a young man of Will's age to witness. Davey took the suspenders from Tim's hand and pulled the young boy onto the back of his horse. Without a word, he turned and rode swiftly back to the wagons. He rode up to Otis and told him what had happened. Otis put Will in the wagon box and took the pistol from his belt. He told him that he would need his sharp eyes on the trail ahead. He promised Will that the brothers would find Haley and return her to the wagons safely. This would have to suffice for now; the company needed to get moving.

The Choctaws read the battle sign as they moved across the stream-bed. It was obvious that Haley had put up quite a fight. They found the dead Indian she had shot in the neck and identified him as a Sioux warrior. They suspected that his Indian brothers would come for his body at some point in time, so they left him where he had fallen. They followed the trail into the timber about one hundred yards when they discovered the remains of Elder Sikes. He had been scalped alive and then killed. His body showed the effects of torture. He had two arrows shot into his dead body as a warning to anyone wanting to follow the trail. The brothers marked the spot for the bishop's party that would be following them and proceeded along the trail. The hostiles had kept the stock mostly in the thick timber to avoid being caught out on the open plain by anyone following.

The forested area offered a place of protection should a fight begin. The two brothers followed this trail for nearly five miles before the trail turned northwest and out onto a more open hilly plain. It appeared that the Indians were taking their plunder toward the upper nations of the Sioux and Cheyenne towards the Dakota Territory and possibly the northern Wyoming territories. As the Choctaws moved along, they encountered horses and mules that had gotten away in the hurried departure of the raiding party. They would leave these for the Mormon party that would be following them. The break in the weather was not going to hold very long as the clouds were low and thick. As they ascended out onto the surrounding hills, the low hanging clouds formed and eerie fog that permeated the valleys. They would have to go slow so they wouldn't run into the raiding party and get killed. There were thirty-five riders in the group the Young Choctaws were following. Mahan said he had counted over seventy warriors. This meant they had a predetermined rendezvous somewhere ahead. If they reunited in force, this would make the task of collecting Haley Johnson almost impossible.

The two brothers were looking the trail over for any sign of the women when they heard riders coming on the run toward them. Through the dense fog, they could see about twenty Indians headed straight for them in a menacing way. The two turned their horses and ran them back toward the forested water course. If they could reach that before they were overtaken, then they might have a chance. The two pressed their horses for the nearest set of hardwood trees that dotted along the ancient river path. The wet prairie floor made the horses work extra hard to maintain their footing as they ran as hard as their riders could push them. When the riders reached the timber, they shot down into it like fleeing deer. They wound down into the maze back along the route they had previously taken. They were hoping to run into the bishop's party for relief.

The tangled limbs and branches tore at their buckskins and leggings as they dodged left and right through the thick forest. They could hear the whoops and yells of the charging Indians that were closing on them as they ran from the danger. As they reached the bottom of an ancient river channel, they turned east toward the wagon train. The pace was much faster along the creek bed for the two Choctaws, and their horses' footing was easier. They started to out gain the war party following them. Coming down the creek area at full speed, they were surprised to see a lone Indian sitting his horse just up on the opposite bank. It was Mahan. He made the sign for the two to come his way. The brothers pushed their horses up the steep bank of the stream and ran their horses hard to the spot where the Indian was standing. He made the sign to follow, and the Choctaws never missed a stride. They followed Mahan out of the stream area and into a tangled path of creek willows. He halted inside this stand of scrub and told the two young men to be prepared for another run if necessary.

The charging Indians hit the timbered area with a dead on assault. They were confident in their numbers and could smell blood in the air. They were yelling commands and talking excitedly as they slowed down and started to track the two brothers' horse trail. They were like a set of hounds on a lion track. As one Indian would see the sign, he would yip and yell out to the others. They were busy in this fashion when the first rifle exploded from the surrounding trees. The front Indian pitched off from his horse with a ball shot through his center chest. All at once the forest floor erupted in a roar of gunfire. The bishop's party had arrived on the scene just in time to get into a position of attack. They had witnessed the whole affair and were secretly stationed in the timber for maximum effect. The rain of balls cut through the leaves and branches all around the frightened Indians as they tried to pull back and recover from the fire. Several warriors fell from their horses in the onslaught.

As the Mormons were reloading their muskets, the Indians gained their composure and pulled back out of range of the Mormon muskets. The Indians still had a numerical advantage and immediately split into two groups and started to flank the concealed Mormons on two sides. The main force of four braves returned the fire from the front while the other two parties pushed into position for the kill. It appeared to Davey and Tim as they watched from the willows that the whole affair might end up in a massacre. The Mormons were not Indian tactical fighters they were green when it came to fighting. They had made a surprise volley of fire into the unaware attacking Indians, but now the battle would turn into cunning and position. Most of the Indians were firing repeating rifles while the Mormons were equipped with outdated Civil War muskets. The rate of fire was three to one from the Indians. The Mormons were starting to fall back from their positions of cover. As they did this, the Indians would rain fire into their positions. There appeared to be about eight Mormons total. Not nearly enough to stand off this assault from the Indians. Davey and Tim decided it was time to join the fight. They both had repeating Winchesters that Otis had given them before the trip had started. This would make a difference in the fight if they could get in a position to use the fire power.

Mahan motioned for the two brothers to follow him on foot. The two brothers could see he had a plan in mind and followed him through the thick willows. Mahan and the two brothers were sneaking into a position behind one of the flanking parties of Indians. If they could pull this off it might make the Indians nervous and want to quit the battle.

The trio moved along the willow path unnoticed to a point where the Indians' backs were exposed at about one hundred yards. This was short work for the Winchesters. The brothers took a position of concealment, and watching Mahan for the signal, the three fired down into the unsuspecting hostiles. The first barrage of shots hit two warriors in the back. They were dead before they reached the ground. Another brave was hit in the arm, and a third was shot through the upper shoulder. The Indians crawled out from under the deadly fire and reached the safety of their horses. The battle was silent. The forest dead quiet.

Nothing moved, but the leaves as the wind would rustle through them. The Mormons were reloaded and ready for the next charge. Mahan and the Choctaws were reloaded and ready for the next assault. Nothing happened. Suddenly the forest was full of bird sounds back and forth. The Indians were going to regroup or quit. The sound of horses running away brought the parties out of their hiding places. The Choctaws and Mahan called out to the bishop's party and identified themselves. The three men gathered their horses and rode over to the Mormons. The bishop was glad to see the trio. The Mormon party had lost one soul. Brother Winslow had fought valiantly but died as a result of a bullet shot to the head. He was being loaded on one of the mules as the party was preparing to return to the wagons. The roaming stock that could be captured would be taken back by the party as they hung their heads in sorrow and started back. Four of the elders had taken wounds in the Indian battle, and the overall mood was one of defeat.

Mahan told the brothers that he had unfinished business and that he would continue on his way. He stayed long enough to remove the scalps of the fallen warriors. This was the Indian way, and it made a statement for those who came to remove the dead that the slain Indians were killed by powerful medicine. Indians were superstitious about these matters, and it made a difference should they encounter Mahan in the future.

Mahan didn't start this warpath, but he would see it through to the end. His whole focus was on returning his granddaughter to her people at all costs. He found two of the Indian ponies and presented them to the Mormons along with the rifles that had fallen in battle. He did this before their departure. The bishop told Mahan that he was welcome to come among the Mormons anytime and that he would be honored by them for his deeds in battle. He thanked the white chief of the wagons and shook his hand. The great chief Mahan informed the two Choctaw brothers that he would bring back the white woman captive if the Great Spirit would bless his medicine. He would bring her to the white man's fort at Laramie Creek if he could. Mahan mounted his mustang and made the sign of friendship as he rode away.

The rain had left the forest floor very wet. The leaves were soaked with water, and a thick mist hung over the wooded land. As Gabe and Old Smoke worked along the river chain back to the wagon train, the pair was soaked. Gabe was traveling very cautiously with all the hostiles in the area. Man and horse were united again after the lightning incident out on the plains. The morning incident had placed the big grey alone on the prairie and the scout on foot. Luckily Old Smoke had been found by the scouting Pawnees. The bargain to trade the Pawnees back for the big horse was a costly one. Gabe was in the process of working the grey over verbally when the horse's ears went forward on the animal. Gabe pulled up on the reins and drew the Henry rifle from its scabbard. He pulled the hammer to half cock and nudged the grey horse forward. Through the mist, he could make out a pair of mules ears. Then another pair came into view as the scene before him unfolded. There, in the fallen hardwoods, stood two mules. One was intently foraging on the forest floor vegetation, and the other one was bound down tight to the fallen timber by its harness apparel. The big mule had wound itself around the fallen timbers to the point that the mule could barely stand. The other mule was keeping company as mules usually prefer companionship. The tangled mule was attached to a wood buck that Gabe recognized from the Mormon camp.

"How did this wreck happen?" Gabe asked the mules as he rode onto the scene. Talking slowly and reassuring the mules, he pulled his bowie knife and cut the leather straps from off the trapped mule and freed him from his peril. The big mule stood up straight and walked several feet and put his head down to eat. He wanted to get his share of the browse. Gabe looked around the scene and found nothing of concern. It looked like the mules had spooked and ran away from a wood party. He would tie the mules head to tail and pull them along with him back to the wagons.

As he mounted the grey horse, he reminded the mules of how fortunate they were that he had come along when he did. He told them they were wolf meat for sure. Or worse, they could have been taken by Indians who usually roasted the mules over a slow fire for food. He reminded the big grey horse that he had faced the same threat when he decided to venture out on his own alone. The scout smiled to himself as he worked the trio of animals along the forest game trails and east toward the Mormon wagons.

Cautiously the scout moved along the edge of the stream. He knew that there were hostiles in the area, and another run in with those painted fellows might prove unhealthy. He kept his eye on the plains to the south of him and occasionally looked back over his trail. He knew he must be close to the Mormons because the mules would not run very far with the wood buck in tow.

As he was settled into the ride, he noticed the ears on the grey intently forward and on alert. He passed his eyes over the mules, and the same signal was coming from the lot. He paused on the trail and decided to wait out the noise just in case it might be Indians. Along the edge of the prairie to the east of him, he could make out the first figures as they came in view. It was the Mormons all right, and he was relieved to see them. He kicked the grey into motion with his left leg, and the party started off at the trot toward the wagons.

As he came within proximity of the wagons, he noticed Otis and the young boy, Will, in the front wagon with Tim riding his horse along the side. Otis recognized Gabe and gave out a holler. The scout rode up, and the party halted. Gabe noticed that something was wrong almost immediately. The train was less burdened with stock animals, and everyone was armed and ready. Otis climbed down from the wagon and proceeded to tell Gabe of the battle. As the two men were in conversation, the bishop and several of the elders rode up on some of the mules and dismounted. They looked like they had seen the devil and lived to tell about it.

The story was hard to Gabe's ears, and he felt like he should have been there. As the words were hard to swallow, the final part of the story hit Gabe with a shock as he learned of the mishap with Haley Johnson. He was numb all over, and a funny feeling was stored up in his stomach. He had never experienced such a feeling in his life. He couldn't figure out why he felt the way he did. But it was a terrible knot that was twisting in his guts. His mind was racing with all kinds of thoughts. He wanted nothing more than to climb back on the grey and ride off to be by himself. The scout stood there and heard the rest of the grim story of the bishop and others as they piped in with comments.

The Mormons had buried their dead and were moving toward the next camping spot shown on their maps. In their minds, nothing could be done about the stock or Haley Johnson. They had resolved to turn the matter over to the military at their first opportunity. Gabe couldn't believe what he was hearing from these immigrants. The angry scout was on the verge of laying into them for being cowards when Otis grabbed his arm and pulled him back from the group. He talked sense to him in his stern calculating way. Gabe was not himself, and he couldn't figure out why he felt so burdened with all this. The bishop and his men stood back and were frightened of the angry scout. They had never been around Gabe when his hair was raised for war. Gabe spit on the ground at their feet and cursed the lot of them as he walked to the water barrel on the side of the wagon. Otis was at his side, trying to reason with him. Otis knew Gabe was on the verge of something he might regret later. It was times like this in his life when the only thing the scout knew how to do was fight. He knew it would be the only medicine for this empty feeling in his stomach. It was not the right way, but it was the only thing that would make him feel better.

As Gabe drank from the water cup, he sized up the situation. Otis had his eye on him in case he decided to take out his frustrations on the bishop and his men. Gabe asked Otis where Davey was, and he told him that he had ridden out about an hour before the scout showed up. He was staking out the next campsite and was expected back anytime. Gabe told Tim to get on his track and bring him back, that Gabe had a plan and it involved the Choctaws.

Tim swung up on his horse and rode away on the gallop. Gabe kept his distance from the Mormon men as Otis and Will gave him some food to eat. The bishop and the elders just stood there on the prairie and looked down at the ground like they were ashamed. They didn't know what to do. As Gabe sat leaned up against the wagon wheel eating vitals that were given him, he noticed the bishop finally got the nerve to approach. He stood over Gabe and apologized for the way he handled the rescue of Haley Johnson.

After a long while, Gabe finally looked up from under the brim of his hat and told him that he was not to blame. If it was anyone's fault, it might as well be Gabe's. If he had been there, it probably wouldn't have happened that way. Gabe finally reassured the bishop that he was not holding him responsible. The damn Indians were the culprit here, and Gabe was going to get a plan together and find the girl if possible. Bishop Stone asked Gabe if he thought it was possible that she might have survived. The scout told him that she would be big medicine to the warrior that had captured her. With her yellow hair and blue eyes, she would be the prize of the prairie. Gabe told him he felt like she would either be made an Indian wife or she would be traded for a lot of goods. This would keep her alive while Gabe had time to find the trail and take up the search. Gabe told the bishop that he knew he was a God-fearing man and his people needed him to see them through to Salt Lake. Gabe would take up the trail and find Haley Johnson. Since the Choctaws had not found her body on the trail, they followed after the raid, meaning, there was a very good chance that she was a captive. Gabe reassured him that the scout was prepared to ride to the ends of the earth for the girl if needs be. He would return her to the Mormons if she were alive.

As Gabe sat there resting up and waiting for the Choctaws, he had Will grain the grey horse and gather his mules together. They had survived the raid and would be a needed commodity on this venture. The two men packed them with all the provisions they could bare. Gabe would be going light and fast on this trip. The mules were in good shape from feeding on the lush prairie grasses and lack of hard work. They would probably lose a hundred pounds or so on this trek. The scouts made sure to pack enough oats for several days on the animals, just in case they ran into some rough country with little forage.

About the time that they finished packing the mules, the Choctaws rode into the wagons. The elders had gathered around, and the plan was laid out. Gabe informed the bishop of the presence of the cavalry. He was relieved that they were within a day's ride of the column. Gabe told Tim where he might find the Pawnee scouts and that he should take a message to the soldiers and bring them to the wagons, that they might escort the Mormons through to Fort Laramie.

The wagon train was to continue to the next camping spot and wait there until contacted by the soldiers. Gabe told the bishop about the other Indians that the Pawnees had encountered. Gabe supposed the hostiles had split into several groups to assault the Mormons and the soldiers. In their conversation, it was evident to all parties that there was a large force of Indians out on the prairie looking for a war on the whites. All of the elders were instructed to stay on guard and go loaded. Gabe would be leaving the party and strike out on his own to retrieve Haley Johnson. Otis and the Choctaws would see the party through to Salt Lake as planned. If possible, Gabe would meet up somewhere on the trail or in Salt Lake, depending on his circumstances. The scout would leave a word of his whereabouts if possible. Tim struck out for the cavalry on the fastest horse the Mormons owned.

The plan was set, and the bishop came to Gabe, shook his hand, and wished him success. He apologized again for the circumstances that Gabe had been placed in and asked if there was anything else he could do.

Gabe turned and looked him square in the face and said, “You can work up one of those prayers you Mormons are saying all the time, and see if your God will help me bring back Haley Johnson safely to her family.”

He smiled candidly and said, “We will pray for both of your lives and safety.”

Gabe nodded and stepped into the stirrup as Otis handed him the lead rope for the mules. He wished him luck and told Gabe he expected to see him again sometime. Gabe told him to take care of the Conner boy Will, and that he would see them in Salt Lake, God willing.

Gabe was turning to leave when Davey rode up beside him and said he would be going along on this trip. He was his own man and could go his way in life. He had discussed this with Otis, and he had given his consent. Gabe couldn't say no to this; Haley Johnson had been a good friend to Davey from the start of the trip. His keen senses and Indian ways would be of great importance for this venture. Gabe told him that he could not guarantee his safety, that the two might get scalped in this charade, but that he was welcome to come if he had the nerve. He said he was loaded and ready for the trail. With determined minds and a motive, the two scouts moved their horses out away from the wagons, turned once in the saddles, and waved a good-bye to the Mormons.

CHAPTER 8 - CAPTIVE HEARTS

The dream was very uncomfortable, and this was a strange place. Why did she feel tired? Why couldn't she move her arms? She felt like she was falling and being bound all at the same time. Her muscles ached, and she was thirsty. A small light opened in the dark place where she was being kept. It started small and then amplified into a glowing bright haze. As she came to consciousness, Haley's head was on fire. She realized that she was tied at the waist and had her wrists bound to the neck of a horse running in full motion. At each step the horse took, she would reel with pain. Her back and shoulder muscles ached from the constant pounding the horse she was riding produced as he trotted in unison with the other horses surrounding him. She could barely see through her swollen and bloody eyes.

The events of the morning raid were coming back to her as she desperately tried to maintain her balance on the running horse. At each step the horse took, she would nearly pass out from the pain in her head. She could barely see other riders around her. But she could not make out their identities. All she wanted was to be rid of this intense pain in her head and neck. Now and again the horses would come to a halt, move off in a slow walk, and finally, start galloping again. This pattern was repeated several times after Haley regained her consciousness. She could feel the rain through her cotton shirt. It would run down her back and along her ribs, soaking everything she had on. It was cold on her bare skin, and she shivered uncontrollably each time the horses broke into a run. As she came to her senses, she tried to free her hands from the leather thongs that bound her around the horse's neck. It was useless; the wet leather had shrunk, and it made the thongs cut into her skin as she fought to free herself. Her situation was hopeless, and she wondered if she might go into shock from all the pain. Is this her plight in life? To be captured by savages and tortured to death on this miserable horse? If only she could free her hands and sit up, she might be able to make it through this ordeal.

As she was pulling and bobbing up and down on the horse's neck, trying to get free, she was caught by the back of her hair, and the horse was pulled to a stop. Someone had her by the hair from behind, and she was being cut loose from the horse's neck. As her hands came free, she was pulled from the horse's back and landed on her back on the ground face up. She was staring up into the eyes of a half dozen painted savages looking down at her from their horses. The sight was horrifying. They were painted in all sorts of hideous manner. As she lay there, she wanted to die before they tortured her to death. She had heard all of the stories that were circulated back east about the evil ways that Indians tortured their captives. And she supposed that this would be her fate.

One Indian slid off his horse, and grabbing her by the hair, pulled her up to her feet. He put his face up against hers as he inspected her closely. He smelled like a dead animal, and he had the look of death in his eyes. He pulled her close to his body with one hand on her hair, and with his other hand, he pulled out his knife from its sheath. He started to pull the knife to her throat when another Indian caught the hand of the warrior and yelled out something in their native tongue. The Indian loosened his grip on Haley's hair and stood back from her. She had been spared for the moment, but why?

She trembled as she stood there facing her captors. There appeared to be about twenty mounted Indians. Their horses were painted in all manner of colors. She recognized several bloody parcels of hair that were attached to the horses' manes. These proved to be white scalps taken in the raid. They were heavily armed with rifles and pistols. Some had bows, and others had warlike clubs tied on their wrists. The whole war party looked like the devil and his demons running loose on the plains. She stood there, staring at her captors, waiting for the next move.

Her clothes were soaking wet from the rain and sweat of the horse she was riding. This made her shiver uncontrollably as she tried to maintain herself in front of the Indians. All of her senses were returning to her mind and body as she felt a wave of pain from head to toe. She tried to wipe the dried blood from her face with the sleeve of her shirt. As she did this, she noticed that she was still bleeding from her head wound. The war club had struck her along the hairline on the right side of her head. She could feel the wound as she pressed against it with her wrist. From the amount of blood she could see on her shirt cuff, it didn't seem to be life-threatening. Standing there alone and frightened she realized that if the Indians were going to kill her, then they would have done so by now. She found some comfort in this thought.

The wet clothes she had on and the cold misty air was making her very uncomfortable. She needed to relieve herself in the worst way. A defiant thought found her mind, and she mustered up her courage and walked swiftly away from the Indians and over to the other side of a small herd of grazing horses that had been captured from the Mormons. As she walked out, she waited for some sign of resistance from her captors, but nothing came of it. Haley concealed herself as best she could from the prying eyes of the Indians. She unlatched her belt and pulled her britches to her knees and quickly emptied her bladder. As fast as she could she belted up, and once again stood looking at the Indians. One of them motioned for her to come back where she had originally been. This was a great victory for her, and she knew that for the moment she was safe from harm or rape.

Several of the Indians were intently watching their back trail for signs of movement. From time to time, they would converse in their native tongue as they would point to the area they had just come from. There seemed to be a pecking order among the Indians and a large framed Indian with a very impressive yellow horse was doing most of the talking. He made several gestures toward Haley pointing with his war club, and the others seemed to be in unison with his commands.

As the war party was gathered there on the plains, one of the Indians slid off his horse in the direction of the large Indian and pulling some dried meat from a hair skinned bag on his horse, gave a piece to Haley. She immediately put the jerky to her teeth and pulled at it with vigor. Haley was famished, and the dried meat tasted so good. The meat went down quickly as she wiped the dried grease from her mouth. A large soft-skinned bladder was handed to her, and she was instructed in sign to drink. Pulling the stop, she pressed the orifice to her lips and poured the water down her throat, spilling some on the front of her cotton shirt. Three times she pulled from the makeshift canteen and finally replenished her need for water. She handed the bladder back to the young Indian and said, "Thank you."

The horses that surrounded the group grazed intently on the scarce prairie grass that afforded them some pickings. They didn't stray far from the Indians, for they were trained to stand nearby as their riders were afoot. It seemed to Haley like the Indians were waiting for others to arrive. That or they had some other plan to waylay an unsuspecting foe that might be following the group. She put her hand to her forehead to block the light sky and perceived to see some riders off in the distance. The Indians were already watching the approaching horses.

There were about twenty horses in total, and they were all being ridden by horsemen. As the group came within earshot, the leader in the front raised his war club and let out a loud yell. The Indians around Haley answered back with all sorts of yips and yells in deathly array. She had never heard such a terrifying display in her life. It frightened her to the bone, and she reminded herself that her situation was perilous. The advancing group rode in among the standing Indians. One lone brave with a headdress of feathers adorned on his head quickly slid off his horse and walked swiftly up to Haley and grabbed her by the arm. He held her for inspection and turned her around as if to size her up. She protested with all her might, but it was useless against the strength of the Indian. His face was painted similar to the others with yellow and vermillion red across his forehead. He appeared to be the leader of this new group. He let go of her arm and walked up to the other Indian that rode the yellow horse and began a heated discussion concerning Haley. She could tell that she was the author of attention because the two Indians would point their clubs toward her as they argued back and forth. Finally the Indian with the headdress walked back to his horse and pulled himself up on the horse and rode swiftly away toward the far distant hills. About six other Indians joined him as they quickly put their horses into running speed.

As Haley looked over the new group of Indians, she stopped and stared at a small Indian on a painted horse that seemed to be bound at the waist and hands. The small Indian appeared to be some kind of captive like Haley. The Indian would look at Haley now and again, and several times their eyes would meet. Haley could only wonder why she was bound and what her story might be. As she stood there staring at the small captive, an Indian grabbed Haley by the shirt and signed for her to mount the horse she had been riding. After pulling herself up on the horse, the Indian fashioned a set of leather throngs onto Haley's wrists and around her waist similar to the small Indian captive. Her horse was led by one of the Indians, and the whole group turned, mounted their horses, and pointed them toward the direction the previous Indians had ridden. Swiftly they broke into a trot and then at a full gallop as they herded the loose stock and all their mounts toward the distant hills.

Gabe and Davey were following the trail left by the hostiles at a good pace. The only thing that slowed down their travel was the mules they were pulling along. Gabe had a bad feeling inside him, and he couldn't figure out what it was. He felt like he had lost something of great value. This feeling was new and strange to him. He rode along with this overhanging cloud surrounding his head. His heart was sore and full all at the same time. He wished he could shake this feeling. He had been sick before but nothing compared to this despair he felt inside. In one moment, he would cuss the Mormons for not protecting Haley, and in the other he would cuss himself for not being there to see that this affair never happened. Gabe would catch himself in thought and suddenly realize that he was talking to himself. Several times he would look back over his shoulder at Davey, who followed behind him on the trail. Davey knew the reason behind Gabe's weird behavior; he had seen it since Gabe had recovered from the grip. He was not the same man as before. Something had disturbed his soul during the sickness, and it would take a time to heal fully. The two riders rode along in silence with their keen senses tuned into the surrounding setting.

Here and there Gabe and Davey would run into a mule or horse that had gotten away from the Indians in their hasty retreat. The only thing they could do was leave them in the hopes that someone might come by and capture them. They couldn't afford to stop and gather them up. They were on a mission, and Gabe would see to it that nothing interfered with their goal. He was anxious to overtake the Indians and set the whole thing in motion. His days of Indian fighting had taught him a lot about Indian ways and habits. He knew that the Indians were headed for the broken country along the Wyoming territories. They would find safety there in numbers and concealment. Most raiding parties made for the north country with their booty, so they were left undisturbed to vanquish in their spoils. Gabe assured himself that this would not be the case as long as he was alive. He would hunt to the ends of the earth to recover Haley and return her to civilization. She deserved a civilized life. She was educated and brought happiness to others around her. She didn't deserve to be hung out to dry by a group of hostiles bent on misery and slavery. He would get the girl and right the score for Will and the others who had lost their loved ones in this raid.

As the two riders followed the track, they were aware of a lone rider parallel to them at about four miles out from their position on the prairie. Gabe suspected that the Indians had left a scout on the back trail to warn the main group if the army or a large group of the Mormons were coming up the trail. It was about two hours before sundown, and the two riders decided to continue along until dark, then they would gather up the lone scout and find out what he was up to. The trail led out on the prairie north from the watershed toward the broken country, as Gabe had suspected. The riders came to an area out on the plains that made them dismount and investigate the sign. A large group of horses had milled around for an hour or so about three hours before them coming to this junction. As Davey and Gabe inspected the sign, they were reading the tracks for clues. Suddenly Davey motioned to Gabe, and he walked over to the Choctaw. There in the dirt was the unmistaken boot print of a small person. It was Haley's boot track. She would be the only one in this group to wear handmade boots.

The rest of the tracks were all made by moccasins. She had stood in this spot for some time and had barely moved from this point. She seemed to be surrounded by Indians and horses. Davey estimated that they were following two groups that consisted of thirty-five warriors and about sixty head of loose stock animals. Gabe intently worked the tracks, looking for some sign of trauma, but he found nothing. As he stared at the little boot print, his heart was held captive for the moment. He could only visualize Haley's condition at the hands of the hostiles. He found himself flustered, and the palms of his hands were sweating. He had never been like this in his life. He needed to regain his composure, or he would not be any good on this war trail. Gabe walked over to one of the mules and pulled a water bag from the sawbucks. He pulled the cork and poured the water over his face. He drank one big gulp and then spit in the dirt in front of his feet. Gabe cursed the fate that had been brought upon Haley Johnson. His angered spewed out from beneath his shirt collar, and he reddened at the thought that was formulating in his mind.

He handed the water bag to Davey and said, "This is going to be a hard trail from here on out."

We're outnumbered at least thirty-five to two. They are headed for the upper Sioux nations along the Wyoming territories. If they get into that country, we will never see the girl again. I figure we need to ride hard until we can catch site of the party, then we can make a plan."

Davey agreed with Gabe's comments and said that the tracks he was looking at were of two different groups of Indians. He suspected Cheyenne and Sioux. If the Cheyenne were holding Haley captive, they might split off from the main group of Sioux and head over to the Yellowstone River country. This would give them a better chance of rescue.

The two riders mounted their ponies and started off in the direction of the track trail. They would ride quickly but with their guard up. There was still a lone rider out on the prairie they had to navigate before they could close the gap between them and the war party. Along about sundown, the two decided to leave the trail and make for the direction of the lone rider to see what his intentions might be. Gabe instructed Davey to flank him as he secured the mules in a small arroyo out of sight. He would ride straight at the lone rider and try to either flush him or make him fight. If he ran, they would know he was a lookout. If he stood to fight Gabe alone, then he might have others nearby hidden from sight for an ambush. The plan was made, and the sun was almost below the horizon. Gabe pulled the Henry from the scabbard and instructed Davey to lay out about a half mile off of his position.

At any sign of trouble, he was instructed to maneuver into a position at the rear of the trouble and make his war from there. Gabe told him to watch his back trail and hang onto his hair. They would meet back at the mules sometime during the night or at daybreak. Gabe rode out from the Arroyo first so the lone rider would not see two riders. He had instructed Davey to wait until it was nearly dark before he made his move from the mule's position. The air was filled with the coolness of the rain that had fallen in the previous day. The earth was soft, and the noise from Smoke's hooves was fairly quiet as Gabe nudged the big horse along. He had seen the lone rider several miles out to his left just as the sunset, and that was the direction he pointed the horse.

As Gabe approached the last known sighting of the lone rider, the light was still bright enough that he could fire his rifle if needed. He checked the lever and started to inspect the ground for some sign. As he did this, he heard a horse coming quickly from behind his position. He swung around and leveled his rifle, preparing for the worst when he caught sight of two riders headed straight for him. He quickly dismounted and knelt to get a bead on the front horse when he realized that the front rider was Davey waving his arm in the air. He had stopped just out of gun range and was trying to signal Gabe.

Gabe pulled up on the rifle and stood up. He waved back at Davey and made the sign to come in. As the two riders approached Gabe, he recognized the horse of the second rider as the lone Indian he had seen previously out on his scouting trip. What could this be about? And why was Davey riding with this Indian? Gabe kept his rifle handy as the two approached him. He never took his finger off the trigger the whole time they rode up. This could be a trick of some kind. He looked over his shoulder to see if there were more Indians around, but he couldn't see anything. Davey would not call out, for he knew that others might be about, so he rode straight into Gabe's position.

As he got close, he signed that everything was okay. Gabe relaxed his grip on the Henry and stood staring at the Indian behind Davey. He made the peace sign, and the Indian did likewise. Davey dismounted and informed Gabe that this Indian was the great chief Mahan. He told him of his previous encounter and suggested they make camp back at the Arroyo and smoke the pipe. Gabe agreed, and the three rode back over to the tethered mules and started to make a small camp. It was agreed that no fires were necessary and that the camp would stay cold. There was just enough light that Gabe could make out the Indian Mahan in the dark as the three of them sat down to talk. Mahan had put the sneak on Gabe and Davey that day, and his medicine was big. Gabe sat there amazed, staring at Mahan. He knew the Indian could have taken both he and Davey out of this life if he had wanted to. Gabe had heard of a great Indian Chief down in the nations from one of the civilized tribes, but he had thought it was folklore tales. Now this Indian was introduced to Gabe by Davey, and he was the genuine article sitting right in front of the scout.

The pipe was flamed, and the smoke was passed back and forth until all had partaken. Davey and Mahan could speak each other's language, so the ceremony went along smoothly. Mahan told his story to Gabe as Davey interpreted for him, and he mentioned that this war trail they were following was his war trail as well. He would follow until his granddaughter was freed from the war chief Black Tongue. He would have his revenge on Black Tongue for killing his son before he could return to his people, or he would die in the act. As Gabe watched the Indian in the shadows conversing with his hands and sign, he couldn't help but notice how the great Indian held himself with prowess. This wasn't a normal Plains Indian sitting here in front of Gabe and Davey.

The stories that Gabe had heard on the prairie about this great chief were nothing short of superhuman. His enemies feared his name, and he was known far and wide among tribes as an Indian you didn't molest. Even before the Ponca Indians became a friendly tribe with the whites, he raided all along the western Missouri River valley, creating fear and death among the settlers that dared to wrong his people. He led his people with pride and power. Even the other Plains tribes were in awe of his greatness and seldom molested his tribe for fear of retribution. As his story was unfolded to Gabe, the scout realized that this Indian was the moccasin track he had seen in his camp next to Smoke days earlier. He asked the great chief why he didn't take his horse a few days ago when he had a chance to. Mahan replied that the horse had special medicine in his dreams and that he would not steal the great horse because that would cheapen his vision. He told Gabe that he had seen the great horse nearly a year before this in one of his dreams. When he came upon the horse in Gabe's camp that day, his heart was warm for the horse and not full of war. He didn't want war with the scout or the Mormons. He only wanted his granddaughter returned to her people and the scalp of the war chief Black Tongue. His heart was on the ground and held captive by his enemy. In his dream, he would avenge the death of his son and release his son's spirit so that he may go live in the lodge with the Great Spirit.

Gabe asked Mahan why he had come into their camp. Mahan told him that the great buffalo horse was seen in his dream and that he did not know how this would come to be. He decided to trail the big grey horse and see if his dream would come to pass. Gabe told him that he thought they shared the same war trail and that together they would be stronger than one. He welcomed Mahan to ride the trail with them and that they would see this to the end. Mahan made the sign of friendship and told Gabe that he would welcome his white brother to join him in this mission. The two of them shook hands, and a mutual admiration was formed on both parties. They discussed the trail ahead of them and ways in which they might be successful. Davey fixed a small cold meal of jerky and hardtack as the three of them relaxed in each other's company. Along about midnight, the trio decided to press the trail again in hopes of closing the distance between them and the war party. They mounted their horses and moved out quietly into the night with Davey following the tracks. It was decided that Mahan would ride out about a mile on their flank in case of an attack from the war party. This would give them an edge if they were surprised.

There was a soft breeze in the air, and it made the night fairly chilly. It could get downright cold out on the plains in the late summer, and Gabe knew that Haley must be very cold and miserable this night. His thoughts went to her, and he wished he could comfort her in this hour of need. If only he had stayed closer to the wagons. This and many other thoughts were racing through his mind as the horses and mules moved along on the trail. Pulling these mules would slow the party down, but the supplies they were carrying were invaluable to the survival of the men. They would need every bit of food and water on this trip. They couldn't take the time to hunt or search for food and water; they needed to stay the course and keep pushing the trail in front of them.

At this rate, they would soon be upon the war party. The Indians were herding horses, and that was a slow process. Mahan had mentioned that he thought they would be in sight of the war party within a day at the rate they were traveling. This was welcome news to Gabe because he had a score to settle. His mind was filled with anticipation. He had been in situations like this many times in his service as a scout with the Pawnee Battalion. Chasing Indians on the plains had been his livelihood for the past six years. He had grown accustomed to the rigors associated with the war trail. Long hours in the saddle and little food and comfort were the order of the day. Only this time he had personal business to conduct, and he was keen to the task.

Sometime along sundown, the war party slowed their pace and walked the horse herd along. Haley could see that the Indians were searching ahead for a suitable campsite for the night. Finally, the Indians stopped and dismounted their horses near a small bluff that offered some protection and a small vantage point for a lookout. A signal was given by the Indian with the feathered headdress on, and the Indians split into groups preparing a camp. Some rode out of sight behind the group while others tended to the horse herd. Several Indians started to gather up small wood for cooking fires, and the whole scene became a working order. Haley and the small Indian captive were pulled from their horses and sat down on the ground next to some rocks that protruded from the bluff. Haley's hands were sore and tingly, her wrists bloody and raw from the leather straps that bound her.

As she sat there looking at the camp being made, she wondered if she would ever see civilization again. She had been praying since the time she reached consciousness for some escape, but she knew that was impossible for the time being. She was saying a prayer in her mind when she spoke to herself out loud and said, “Please, God, ease my burden in this awful state. Help me escape from my captors.” The words seemed to come out softly as tears fell on her cheeks.

She was caught off guard when, suddenly, the small Indian sitting next to her spoke in perfect English and said, “Do you pray to the Great White Spirit that lives in the clouds?” Haley just stared in disbelief at the small Indian sitting there. She couldn’t believe what she was hearing. Haley looked at the small Indian without replying and studied her features.

The Indian appeared to be a small girl. She was filthy dirty from head to toe and had seen much abuse at the hands of her captors. She looked like she might be fourteen or fifteen years old. And she was quite beautiful in her worn state. Haley asked her where she learned English, and the young Indian girl told her that she was taught by the Black Robes along the big river when she was living there with her people. She introduced herself as Pitani, the daughter of Crow and Little Swan of the Ponca Indian nation. As the two young women were meeting one another, one of the Indians came up to them and stared down at them for a moment. He pulled out a five-foot-long strap with a loop at each end and placed one loop around Haley’s neck and the other end he placed around Pitani’s neck. This would keep the pair from running away. It appeared that they would be bound together for a while. He handed them jerky and a gourd of water. The two captives wasted no time in devouring the jerky, and each drank their fill from the gourd.

The camp was made, and the cooking fires were lit. It appeared to Haley that the Indians didn’t have any fear of being followed. This made her heart sad, for she realized that her life and a few Mormon horses and mules were not worth risking any lives for. She knew the Mormons were not Indian fighters, and the loss of some stock would not bring the

Mormons out from the safety of their wagons. She was all alone in this, and the thought of no one coming for her brought tears to her eyes once more. Pitani noticed Haley's sadness and moved closer to her to comfort her and gain the necessary body heat that she knew the two of them would need before morning. She cuddled her arms around the white woman and seemed to be more confident in her mind than Haley.

Pitani asked Haley why she cried, and Haley confessed her hopelessness to the young girl. Pitani could only offer words of comfort, for she was in as perilous a situation as Haley. In fact, Pitani had felt like she might be killed at any moment since her capture. The Indians had argued the fact in front of her several times. She told Haley that she understood the language of their captors. She had learned it from a Cheyenne woman captive in her village many moons ago. She comforted Haley with the thought that she would not be killed because she was big medicine to the Cheyenne with her yellow hair and blue eyes. She would either be traded for a large sum or made into a wife for one of the braves. This would be her plight in life from this point forward. Pitani, on the other hand, was an enemy to the Cheyenne. She would either be killed or made into a slave at some time in the future. If she was lucky, she might be made into an Indian wife and be able to live among her captors as a souvenir war trophy. Any way the girls looked at their situations, it seemed an awful way to go on living. They would need more than courage to face the future.

As the night settled in the young women huddled close together with their arms around one another. The prairie breeze was chilling to the bone. The Indians had made fires and were comfortably sitting around them and conversing. The girls could only stare at the flames of the fires and pretend to feel the warmth they provided. They had placed the young women about twenty feet from the main camp area. At least they had the shelter of the rock they were pressed against. Without that, they might freeze to death before morning. The Indians seemed to be discussing their plans for the next few days. Pitani would catch certain words she could hear and relay them to Haley. The two women would whisper in each other's ear so that their captors couldn't know they understood them.

The main leader of this group was an Indian named Black Tongue. He was mean and warlike. He wanted to kill all enemies in his path and ravage the women. The only thing that prevented him from doing so was an Indian named Yellow Hand. He was revered by his people and was a well-respected war chief. He was a big chief among the Sioux, and he had influence with the other warriors on this raid. They all listened to him, and he kept the order of things somewhat civil in the camp. If he was not along on this war trail, Pitani was certain she would have been raped and killed by now. Yellow Hand wanted to trade Haley for a big bounty, and Black Tongue wanted her for his wife. Black Tongue felt like she was his captive since he was the one that had captured the yellow-haired white woman. He had also killed the Ponca warrior, Crow, in hand-to-hand battle and captured his daughter. So he felt like the small Indian girl was his as well. The two Indian leaders would duel this out in heated words as the night passed away. The other Indians grunted and nodded their approval for one comment or another.

This kept the girls entertained most of the night and allowed their cold, miserable condition to be bearable. Along about early light, the camp was broke, and the girls were put on their horses and bound again at the waist and pulled out along the trail in front of them by their captors. The Indians rode along silently and stealthily. They seemed to be made of the elements.

CHAPTER 9 - THE DEVILS IN THE DETAILS

The weather had been rainy and wet for the last several days, but this day it would break into the sunshine and welcome warmth to the captive women. As they rode along, Haley could feel the first rays of the sun as it pulled its way through the partly cloudy skies. Another day and she was still alive. Her hopes of rescue had faded with her thoughts, and she was left with each new day and what it would bring.

The Indians were strung out single file, riding along a long winding prairie ridge. Haley could see buffalo in the distance scattered about on the plains. She wondered if they might have fresh meat at some time shortly. Her stomach growled with pain as she thought of the tasty morsels of meat that a buffalo provided. The women had not had anything to eat since early last night when they were given a small amount of jerky and water. Haley was growing weaker by the day, and she knew she wouldn't last very long at this rate of pace. She looked back at Pitani on the horse behind her and tried her best to smile. Pitani would smile back, and it was the two girl's way of reassuring themselves of their situation.

Haley's legs were starting to cramp up. She was not used to riding on a daily basis. The insides of her knees were sore and raw from the horse's coarse hair. Pitani, however, was comfortable in this fashion, for she had been raised on horseback from a small child. This was a nomadic Indian's lifestyle and one that Haley was not accustomed to. Haley's mood was a solemn one with hope fading fast. She had been raised to teach and help others in need, and God had brought her to this plight. Why would he do such a thing? She had never prayed so much in her entire life. Had God forsaken her in her time of need?

Several Indians were riding up very quickly from the rear of the group and rode to the front of the column. The band halted its march as Yellow Hand and Black Tongue heard the report. There was some confusion in the group, and the two leaders started debating the issue. It became heated this time, and the two men's voices could be heard across the plains. Suddenly Yellow Hand reached out and grabbed the arm of Black Tongue and pulled him from his horse onto the ground. In one swift movement, Yellow Hand slid off his horse and landed on top of Black Tongue while he was trying to get up off the ground. The war chief Yellow Hand grabbed the other Indian by the hair, and pulling his arm around the warrior's neck, held him face down on the prairie floor. Black Tongue was powerless to do anything. He finally quit trying to resist and subdued himself to his situation. Yellow Hand released the brave and stood up over him. He was shouting out commands the whole time in his native tongue.

The other Indians stood by motionless as the scene unfolded in front of all to see. Black Tongue rose to his feet and spit out dirt he had taken in the mouth. His face was ferocious and defiant in nature. He stood there as a proud man who had not been thoroughly defeated by his foe. He stared at Yellow Hand with vicious eyes. He was a warrior from head to toe, and his every move in life was one of cunning and pride. This was an insult to his manhood, especially in front of his peers. The two war chiefs stood face to face with clenched fists and stern looks. Finally, Yellow Hand turned his back to Black Tongue, a sign of further insult to the proud warrior. Yellow Hand waved his arm at the onlookers and mounted his horse with instructions for the band to make haste.

The Indians quickly kicked their ponies into high speed as the main group rode out leaving Black Tongue standing there alone. As Haley rode past, she kept her head down and stared at her horse's neck. She could feel the eyes of the proud warrior looking at her. She had been advised by Pitani not to look the warriors in the face as it was a sign of disrespect. As her horse moved away from the scene, she glanced back to see the defeated warrior mount his horse and ride out to the west of their line of sight.

Yellow Hand had made it known to the rest of warriors that he would lead this war trail, and none other would interfere. Yellow Hand had been told by the rear riders that they were being followed by three men with pack mules. The men had been observed reading the trail sign, and it was possible that they were following the war party. Black Tongue had wanted to turn around and make war on these three men since they were few in numbers. Yellow Hand didn't like this maneuver because the party had seen the sign of the bluecoats some days earlier and stopping for a small war with the three strangers might mean great danger from the horse soldiers. This decision had been challenged as cowardice in the eyes of Black Tongue and resulted in the dispute between the two chiefs. Yellow Hand knew this country very well, and he knew that when the war party reached the broken country that they would be safe from all enemies. That was the order he gave to his warriors. Make quickly for the broken ground and then they could rest and hunt for meat.

Gabe was watching the trail they were following for any signs that Haley might leave. This occupied his mind for the moment and kept him from swelling up inside with his frustration. About mid-morning, Davey rode back along the trail to where Gabe was following and made the sign for trouble. At this same time, the riders could see Mahan riding towards them. He rode up to them and motioned with a sign that they were being watched by two Indians about a mile to their front. Finally the chase was on, Gabe thought to himself. The sign of these two warriors would mean that the war party would soon know the whereabouts of Gabe and his companions. Mahan estimated that the main party would probably maintain their continued march toward the broken country and that several others would try to make war with the three men following. Just how many would come for them was not sure, but he suspected, at least two warriors for each of them. He surmised that Indians liked superior numbers when it came to war.

It was agreed between the three of them that their original plan was the best one, with Mahan riding out on the flank of Gabe and Davey. Davey would cautiously survey the trail ahead and look for signs of an ambush. It would be rather difficult to surprise the three of them out on the open plains. If the three of them stayed out of the valleys and rode mostly on the prairie ridges, it would be difficult for someone to make an ambush. Mahan was the ace in the hole if such an event took place. He would stay in the arroyos and valleys to one side and keep his presence unknown to all. He would meet up with Gabe and Davey after dark if all were safe.

The three riders turned their horses and made best of the plan laid. They would be traveling at a much slower pace than before. Gabe looked forward to this new adventure, and his former thoughts left him. As he rode along, he checked his firearms and made ready for anything that might come his way. The big grey horse he was riding could sense its rider's movements, and his nose and ears were full alerts for smell and sound. He had been taught at a young age to key on his rider's movements. The clicking noise of guns and smell of burned powder made the veteran horse tense with anticipation. He knew all too well that those sounds usually ended up with running and shooting. And he would be right in the middle of it. The big horse felt like he was born for this sort of thing. He would do his best if called upon.

Gabe talked to his horse as the two followed the trail. This was customary when they were alone. Gabe felt like the horse understood his words, and he confided in him often. Out on the prairie scouting, they had become good friends through many battles over the years. Each had come to the aid of the other when the chips were down. This time would be no different. The sign in front of Gabe was clear and easy to read. Many mounted warriors and a bunch of loose stock being herded. He had not seen any sign of Mahan's granddaughter, but if the great Indian chief said she was with the war party, then he would not question his word. Gabe had seen the young Indian girl the night he put the sneak on the Cheyenne camp when he and Davey had found Will up the tree. She was alive at that time, and he could only hope she still was.

Gabe approached Davey and his horse. The Choctaw was bent down examining something on the trail when Gabe rode up. Davey gave the sign for Gabe to look at the tracks made in the earth's surface. Gabe proceeded to that spot, and upon examining the sign, he could see where two small prints were clearly seen upon the soil one of Haley's small boot tracks and the other a very small moccasin track presumed to be that of Mahan's granddaughter. It appeared from all sign that the pair had been tethered together throughout the night and that they were still alive and captive. This was good news to Gabe, and he needed this bit of refreshing sign.

From the other signs, Davey read that morning the trail was becoming obvious to the pair of seasoned scouts. A scuffle had taken place, and Gabe and Davey could only guess as to what had caused the dispute. The Indians were in disagreement, and at some point, a lone Indian had ridden off in the direction of Mahan on their flank. The rest of the party had resumed their march toward the broken country to the northwest. It was clear to Gabe that the hostiles were making a run for that portion of the territories that would afford them the upper hand in an escape. The only options for Gabe and his partners were to continue and hope that the Indians would stop their march long enough to rest their horses and hunt for meat. The pair of scouts mounted again and started off in the direction of the tracks.

Black Tongue was furious with the treatment he had received at the hands of the Sioux chief, Yellow Hand. He swore to himself that he would avenge the slander on his person and gain the upper hand with the other warriors. He would need to count coup on his enemies and regain his status as the war chief. As he pushed his war pony along the prairie ground with his war club in hand, he took his anger out on the horse with swift blows to the flanks each time the horse would wonder which direction to go. The horse wanted nothing but to return to its former herd and take up that trail with safety in numbers. Black Tongue knew this as he punished the horse for this weakness. The horse would whinny and blow out his nose in hopes of hearing one of the other herd horses in the distance. Each time the horse resisted the direction taken by its rider, the more Black Tongue would punish the horse with his club.

Finally, the horse gave up in vain and settled down to the task it was given. As the pair rode along the rim of a prairie hill top, the warrior pulled up hard on the mouth of the horse and turned the pony in a full circle with the rawhide bit in the horse's mouth. Quickly Black Tongue recognized the threat of a lone Indian rider out some distance on the plain. It must be one of the three riders that were following the war party. Black Tongue had not been seen, he was sure of it. He quickly turned his mount north and clubbed the horse with all his might across the rump. The horse broke into a swift gallop and then into a full out run. The pair put distance between themselves and the lone rider. Black Tongue knew that if he could reach the war party and warn them of the impending danger that he would be given a reprieve by his fellow warriors and regain his prowess among them. He pushed the big black war pony as fast as the animal would carry him across the open prairie.

The Indians were pushing the loose herd of stock animals along as quickly as possible when a rider was spotted in the rear, closing fast. Yellow Hand sent out two warriors to investigate and make war if necessary. The warriors turned their horses and made tracks toward the new threat. They had not gone very far when they realized that the rider coming at a swift pace was the war chief Black Tongue on his magnificent black war horse. The sight of the running horse with its warrior rider made the two braves envious of the scene that lay before them. They halted their advance, and within several minutes the proud Indian Black Tongue rode his horse in among them. He told them of the danger he had seen and the approximate distance from their position that he thought the lone rider was. The three immediately took off in a gallop back to the herding warriors and Yellow Hand. The party stopped long enough to hear the news and make a plan.

This time, the threat was too close for comfort, and war would be made upon the following riders. Yellow Hand barked out his orders to seven of his braves, and the whole lot of them sprang into action. Black Tongue was forgiven for all offenses toward Yellow Hand and reinstated as the war chief of the Cheyenne that was part of the raiding party. He was instructed to continue towards a place the Indians knew as Traders Creek in the broken hills. He would set up camp near the trading post that a white trapper named Frenchie operated for trade with the Indians. There the Indians would make a trade for the yellow-haired woman. She would bring many guns and white man's whiskey for her value to the white man. Black Tongue wanted to argue the commands he was given. He wanted to make war on the three following, but instead he thought he might gain some advantage on this new war trail that he would be in charge of.

He gathered up the Cheyenne that were with the war party, and in number they amounted to sixteen. He gave his commands, and the group moved out with the stock and the female captives. As Black Tongue rode along, he decided to himself that he would have the yellow-haired white woman for his own. He would take both captives for wives, and there would be no trade. They were his captives, and he had the rights to them by Indian laws. If he were forced to make war upon Yellow Hand, then he would do so in his own time. But the captives were his to do that which pleased him. For now, he would go along with Yellow Hand's plans, but someday soon he would take the scalp of the Sioux chief and place it on his war lance for all to see his power.

Yellow Hand would not be menaced in his country by those who followed his trail. He would make war upon the three who followed, and he made preparations for this action. His warriors were nearly three times the size in numbers of the enemy who followed so that the war trail would be an easy victory. They would quickly route and kill the followers and then make tracks swiftly back to the broken hills and catch up with Black Tongue and Cheyenne. These were the orders he instructed to his fellow warriors as the hostiles prepared for battle. They were mostly armed with bow and arrows. Some had taken rifles and pistols in previous raids. And a few were left with older muzzle-loading firearms of bygone days. Painting themselves and their horses with crimson and yellow paint, the warriors prepared for the war trail. Yellow Hand was a seasoned warrior and had ridden the war trail for many moons. Most of the warriors were young and inexperienced, but they thirsted for the scalps that would give them power among their fellow group.

There was a wild excitement among them as they painted themselves and chanted their war songs to the Great Spirit in the sky. As they made the war songs, they mounted their ponies and swiftly rode out to meet the following three. This would be a day that would be talked about among the tribes when the warriors returned to their families with the spoils of war. They would sing songs and dance around the fires well into the night with all the tribe as witnesses to their bravery and cunning. They would be revered with pride and rank among their fellow tribesmen for this war that they would make this day.

The first thing Gabe noticed was the tense motion in the movements of his trusted steed. The big grey horse had a nose full of something, and he was wound up like a top. Gabe had only seen him like this on one other occasion, down on the Arkansas River when he and Pawnee scouts were jumped by a group of Sioux warriors. That day the big horse had alerted him to the dangers, and it had proved to be lifesaving in its nature. This was the same way he acted back then and he was only a three-year-old at the time. He was a real seasoned horse now, and Gabe knew he was all business. Gabe pulled the Henry from the scabbard and placed his hand on the hammer. He made the sound of a prairie quail with his hand to his mouth that warned Davey to turn around and come back to him. The two scouts had rehearsed these sounds and signs since the Mormon train had left Omaha.

They were in unison with one another as Davey turned his mount around and headed back to Gabe. Davey noticed the big buffalo horse's tense posture and made the sign to Gabe that he acknowledged him. Gabe pointed to a small bluff with some protruding rocks, and the pair pulled the mules along to that high prairie point. The animals were all hobbled and tethered to each other, and the two scouts prepared a groundwork defensive maneuvers. What brushwood and rocks that the scouts found were forded up into a breastwork. The men worked feverishly to their position. Gabe knew they would be attacked, and he felt like they might have the upper hand with elevation and firepower. If they could hold off the hostiles long enough, then Mahan could make a surprise move from the rear of the war party, and they would have them in a crossfire. But of course, war plans usually don't end up the way you lay them out.

Plains Indians were the best guerrilla fighters in the territories. They were a very formidable foe on those mustang ponies and made for hard targets as they raced them across the plains. Gabe put his hand to the nose of Old Smoke and let him smell the sweat of his hand. This seemed to calm the big horse down as Gabe rubbed him along the neck and front shoulders. The scouts would keep their riding horses close by in case they needed to make fast tracks out of the fight. Davey sat down behind the breastwork and proceeded to place paint on his face that he had brought with him in his medicine bag. Gabe looked on and realized that no matter how civilized the young Choctaw was in living the white man's life, he would never be able to overcome his native Indian roots. Davey would prepare himself for war and possible death as he had been taught by his forefathers and their fathers before them. He started to whisper his death songs as the two scouts prepared for the inevitable.

The first Indian to show was a lead scout for the main war party. He cautiously looked around as he came in view of the makeshift breastworks. He halted his approach and sat on his horse, studying the situation before him. Slowly he rode off over the hill and was gone from sight. Gabe and Davey had seen the scout and cocked their rifles. Gabe told Davey that he thought they would come straight at them one time and see if they could route the two from their position of defense. If they succeeded, then they could make short work of the scouts out on the open prairie. He told Davey not to move from this position even if Gabe were killed. Their only hope for survival was their rifles and their hidden element, Mahan. If the Indians couldn't take them out in the first rush, then this small war would take on a sniping battle between the two enemies. The Indians were very good at maneuvering and sniping at an enemy, especially when they held superior numbers. They would try to surround and flank the position until they could pick off the two scouts from long range. But for now it would be an all-out assault on the breastworks to see if that plan would work. The scouts would have the first advantage on the charging warriors. They would need to take out as many as possible on the first pass. Gabe thought that if they could kill or wound several on the first charge, the Indians might not think this little war worth the effort and ride away. Usually, Indians on raids didn't like to lose too many warriors in matters that were meaningless. This was a threatening posture on behalf of the Indians, and if they were to succeed with some scalps and trophies, then that would make a great little war. Otherwise, it would not be worth the risks.

As the two scouts leveled their rifles toward the last seen Indian, they waited with fear and anticipation. Even though Gabe had fought many Indian battles in the past, each one brought a fear inside his guts that would nearly make him sick to his stomach. He noticed that he was sweating profusely on his face and forehead. He took one last look at their position and felt like it would do. Davey nudged his arm and pointed as the two men looked at their fate. The war party came over the horizon and stopped just out of range of the scout's rifles. They were surveying the scene and looking for an edge. Yellow Hand didn't like the breastworks. He had thought they might take these followers by surprise. Something in this plan made him uneasy. He had fought many battles and seen the power of the white man.

This party looked like white men from the wagons they had raided. He suspected they were an advanced scouting party trying to keep up with the slow moving

Indians herding the stolen horses. This they would do until reinforcements could arrive. Yellow Hand knew that the war party must make a quick war of these three men and get away fast. He gave instructions for the group to hit the breastworks from two sides at once. Three warriors were assigned the task of running off the horses and mules while the others would kill the white men scouts. Yellow Hand gave instructions that the large buffalo horse belonged to him and that he was claiming him as chief. The rest of the spoils would go to those individual braves that captured them. The plan was set in motion as the war party split up and rode apart.

Gabe instructed Davey to hold his fire until Gabe fired first. He could see the young Choctaw was shaking with fear. He put his hand on his arm and told him that Otis would be proud of the young Indian. The first group of warriors let out their war whoops and screams as they came charging up the valley floor. They were going to be the first group to reach the scouts' position. This was an old Indian tactic, and Gabe was well aware of it. He told Davey not to shoot until the second group of warriors charged; he would take on the first group alone. As he got the words out his mouth, Gabe took a fine bead on the lead rider and pulled the trigger firmly on his Henry rifle. The Indian fell off his horse, and the horses following behind him ran over his body as they galloped onward. Gabe pulled the lever down on the rifle and took dead aim again and fired at the next lead horse's head. The horse went down end over end in a most devastating fashion. The horse and rider were sprawled out on the prairie floor.

Other riders and horse veered off to the left and right of the downed horse. One warrior's horse could not keep from tripping over the downed horse and half-heartedly tried to jump over the scene of carnage. He came up short and piled into the ground nose first. His rider flew from the mount and tumbled several times out on the ground. He rose slowly, and as he did Gabe put a bullet through his chest. He fell dead where he was. Cocking the Henry Gabe pulled up on the next rider as the Indians fired their guns and bows at the makeshift defense. There were only three left in this first group, and they seemed to pull off to one side and ride clear of the men and their horses. Three more Indians came from the rear of the scouts waving blankets and yelling at the top of their lungs. They were trying to run off the horses and mules. The whole scene erupted in one violent hair-raising event.

Davey pulled around and fired across the mules' heads at the charging Indians. His first shot missed its mark. He barely had time to cock his Winchester when the three Indians were upon him. He fired quickly and hit the lead warrior in the hip, knocking from his horse. Gabe turned around just in time to jump out of the way of a war club intended for the back of his head. As the Indian brave galloped past Gabe, he pulled the Henry into his shoulder and fired at the back of the passing Indian. The warrior fell from his horse and tried to get to his feet. He turned and started to run at Gabe. The scout leveled the rifle one more time and put the Indian to the ground.

Meanwhile, the other Indians paired off and galloped back down the valley from where they came. Yellow Hand could not believe the marksmanship of the white men. He made signal for his warriors to dismount and move into positions around the enemy and start sniping at their position. He gave instructions not to shoot the big buffalo horse, but the others were of no concern. He wanted this war over quickly before his warriors grew tired of the killing. He had already lost too many to the deadly fire of the white man's rifle.

Mahan heard the report of the first shots. He knew immediately that the two scouts were under siege. He cautiously put his horse into a gallop toward the sound of the guns. He could hear more firing, and from the sounds of the shots he estimated it to be the rifles of his friends. These were well thought out gunshots, and he knew they were from Gabe's Henry rifle. Mahan admired the rifle and knew it was a deadly weapon in the hands of the White Pawnee scout. As he rode close to the scene, he circled from afar. He needed to locate the war party before he could construct a plan of attack. He left his horse on the back side of a small rolling hill and crawled to the top for a look. Before him was a scene of death and carnage. He could see several dead animals and warriors lying on the ground. He could barely make out the scouts lying behind their breastworks.

As he intently studied the view, he could not help but be amazed at the cunning of his friends. The white scout was definitely a seasoned Indian fighter, and Mahan could not have chosen a better defense himself. He marveled at the deadly marksmanship of the two scouts and realized that the enemy had been dealt a huge blow in the first fight. Lying there Mahan took notice of the wind and clouds in the distance. A storm was approaching from the west and would be upon the scouts by midday. This would make things real ugly for the war party. Indians don't like making war in bad weather. They feel like they did something to upset the storm maker and chose to abandon selfish ideas. The storm could make the difference between life and death for all concerned. Mahan worked back down the hill to where his horse was tethered and made himself ready for war.

Gabe and Davey had withstood the first assault without injury. The only fatality was one of the pack mules had taken and arrow in the neck. The mule was lying where it fell, and the others just stood by, waiting their turn. Gabe looked his big grey horse over and told him that everything would be okay. The big horse just stood there nibbling at the bridle straps from one of the mules standing next to him. Gabe reassured Old Smoke that there were several mules surrounding him and they would see that no harm would come to him. He made light of the fact that the big horse was the easiest target on the prairie and that if he should go down, the Indians would make good use of him as a grand meal later that night. Davey laughed out loud as he heard Gabe talk to the buffalo horse standing between them. He knew that the pair had made a bond that would last the lifetime of both parties. Gabe would give his life for the horse, and the reverse was true of Old Smoke.

Gabe handed Davey a water pouch and some jerky. They were in the clear while the Indians figured their next move. Gabe noticed a change in the wind, and looking out on the sky for the first time in a while, he could see the storm clouds gathering and the sight of distant lightning. This was going to be the day of all days when that storm hit them. They were exposed completely to all the elements where they were entrenched. He motioned with his arm, and Davey looked just in time to see a bright flash many miles away. Gabe could not decide which was worse, the Indians or the storm. He hoped one would erase the other if God would have anything to do with it. He found himself mumbling a short prayer as the two men hunkered down behind the homemade cover.

Yellow Hand noticed the changing wind as it hit him in the face. He did not like this new challenge. He had learned that the Great Storm Maker could avenge for all the wrongs committed by his people if he chose to do so. He had been out in storms of the past that had taken many lives as the angry Storm Maker brought the Indian to his knees. The war party would need to end this battle soon, or they would be at the mercy of the Great Storm Maker. He did not know if this storm was meant to punish his band of warriors or that of the white men. The storm was heading straight for them, and he knew that they might perish if they persisted in this small war. He instructed his warriors to crawl out on the prairie and take the battle to the white scouts. He would leave two warriors behind to watch the ponies, should the bluecoats show up on the battlefield. He would direct the gunfire from a point of vantage across from the valley floor, which gave him a position above and behind his warriors. The warriors dismounted, and six of them crawled into positions for firing. They were stealthy in their endeavors and closed the distance to within rifle shot before being discovered by the hunkering white men.

Gabe saw the smoke from the first rifle and heard the bullet whiz overhead. He told Davey to train his shot at the lowest point of the smoke and hold steady. The next shot hit the breastwork and harmlessly fell short of its mark. Immediately Davey fired for the smoke point, but his bullet was high above the mark and hit the earth, knocking up a dust cloud. Each scout held off firing just for the sake of it. They would only shoot when a target presented itself. A bullet hit the top of the breastwork and sent pieces of splintered wood spraying down on the two scouts. Gabe located the smoke and held a tight bead on the bottom line of rising smoke and touched off the Henry. Immediately a warrior moaned out loud but didn't show himself. This type of warfare went on for nearly an hour as the warriors closed in a little at a time on their enemy.

At some point, they would be within easy sight of the white scouts and could make a quick war on them. Gabe knew it would just be a matter of time before they came under direct fire from the warriors. He supposed that Mahan had run into trouble and was possibly taken out by the war party. It would be up to the two men to make the Indians pay dearly for this war in their last dying efforts. Gabe had resolved his death in his mind, and he would take several warriors to the great hunting grounds in the sky with him. As the bullets started to pierce the homemade shield, the two men came to grips with the situation. Davey looked at Gabe and told him that he was prepared to die. Gabe nodded the same back, and the two men continued their fire as targets became apparent.

Mahan had located the main party and moved to flank them. He had an idea that might change the outcome of the battle. He proceeded upwind of the hostiles, and this gave him the advantage he was looking for. He closed to within several hundred yards and quickly dismounted his horse. The war party had all their eyes focused on the breastwork and were not watching their backs. Mahan used his fire flints and started to light the prairie grasses on fire. He moved swiftly and in no time at all he had several fires in the direction of the wind. As the storm front was moving along the plains, it would create gusts of wind that would fan the fire in all directions faster than a horse could run. He methodically moved from one direction to the next, firing off the flints and igniting the flames towards the unsuspecting war party. Mahan knew that once Gabe saw the fire, he would know who was behind the spark. The war party would be in the fire's direct path, and they would have to move quickly from their naked defenses, making them easy targets for Gabe and Davey.

As the fires spread, Mahan decided to move over to the west flank of the Indians and set himself up for war. He found a nice bunch of rocks and set himself down in the middle of them and waited for his enemy to pass by. He would count coup this day and avenge for some of the misdeeds put upon his people in the raid by the war party that had killed his son. He took the token from his medicine bag that had belonged to his son and tied it to the stock on the rifle he held in his hands. Now it was just a matter of time until the war would come to the war party.

Gabe smelled the smoke several minutes before he saw it. Immediately he told Davey that Mahan had set the prairie on fire. He instructed the youth to wait out his shots until the warriors had to move from their positions to avoid the fire. The scouts made ready as they could see the ominous blackened sky, which made nearly a full circle around them. Gabe knew that they might perish in this fire, but at least they had a chance for escape as the smoke and fire would prevail upon all parties at once. If they could somehow escape in the confusion of the flames and smoke, then they could put some distance between then and the war party. Gabe doubted that the Indians would be up for much more fighting after this charade. He wondered where on the plains Mahan might have positioned himself from a tactical advantage. Gabe knew the war chief would be looking for scalps and payback for his people. The two scouts lay in waiting for the inevitable outcome with rifles at the ready.

Some parts of the fire were several hundred yards behind the hidden warriors when they noticed their dilemma. Yellow Hand smelled the smoke long before he saw the flames of the fires. He didn't know if the fire was intentional or from the distant lightning he had seen with the storm. He made a sign to the warriors in waiting that they must give up this battle and leave this part of the world. He suspected that the Great Storm Maker was unhappy with him making war on his white children.

As he signaled for the retreat of the warriors, the fire blew down on them in a terrible way. It spread almost without warning, and the six warriors that lay upon the ground sniping at the white scouts were consumed in smoke and flames. Yellow Hand rode his horse over to where the horses were being tended and motioned for the braves to mount and follow him with the remaining Indians. All of the Indians rode out among the flames and smoke at a rapid pace to the west. As they galloped through the smoke, they could only see a few yards in front of them. Some of the horses were wild with fright, and their eyes bulged out of their heads with fear. Some of the Indians could not control their mounts as they ran wild upon the prairie. The warriors held onto the necks of their horses and tried to stay mounted in the awful inferno.

Gabe saw the first warrior rise and quickly put a bullet into him. Davey did likewise, and the whole affair seemed to get out of control. There were Indians running through the smoke in all directions, and targets were scarce. One Indian brave ran right into the breastwork in his lost confusion. Gabe hit him in the mouth with the stock of his gun as he ran by. The two scouts stood up from their position for the kill. They would pick the warriors off one at a time as they revealed themselves in their fright. Within seconds, the fight was over, and all the warriors were either dead or running out on the plains, trying to avoid the flames.

Gabe knew this was their chance and told Davey to get mounted and follow him through hell. The pair of scouts mounted their horses in a minute as Gabe led a path with his big grey horse right through the smoke and fire. The big horse knew the danger and plodded fearlessly along as the rest followed. Old Smoke was no stranger to prairie fires. He had seen them before and each time his trusted companion had led him through to safety. Having a good steady horse under these conditions made it possible for the scouts to gain a position of safety.

As the pair of men cleared the fire area, they looked at one another and their outfit for damage. Gabe looked at Davey, and the two men started laughing from the faces they were seeing. Each of them had blackened faces and had the look of the devil and his hosts. The two men nearly fell out of their saddles, they were laughing so hard. Gabe was just happy to be alive, and he knew they had just dodged a bullet headed for their heads. Having their scalps made the two men laugh even if they were singed nearly off from the heat. They turned and rode out away from the flames upwind.

Mahan could see movement in the smoke. He raised his gun and pointed at that direction. One by one the war party filed by his position. He took aim at the first target he could see through the smoke and fired. The warrior fell from his horse as the others realized they were vulnerable and ran out in all directions under the cover of smoke. The rifle came up to Mahan's shoulder, and he pulled the trigger again. Once more a riderless pony came charging out of the brimstone. Now the prey knew his position. Fearing he might become the hunted, Mahan mounted swiftly and rode south away from the flames. As he looked back on the scene, the whole plains were a mass of smoke and fire. The plan had worked, and the war party had become the hunted. Now he must wait and let the fire play out and then go look for his friends. Hopefully, they had made it out of the Bad Spirit's path and were safe somewhere. He would search when he could.

For now he had counted coup on his enemies, and two of the war party had felt the wrath of his son's spirit. He held the token of the son in his right hand and squeezed hard on the chalice in the memory of his fallen son. This war trail would not be over until Pitani was returned to her people. Mahan figured that Pitani must be farther up the trail with the Cheyenne. He had not seen any Cheyenne warriors in this battle. He had hoped for a chance to kill the snake they call Black Tongue, but he had eluded Mahan for the moment. He would press the trail once again and find his granddaughter. Mahan had been on this trail with a riding party many moons before, with a raiding party trying to take back stolen horses from the Cheyenne. He knew they were headed for the broken hill country and to the safety of the big trees that cry when the Wind Maker is blowing his cold breath upon the land. There he would find Pitani and avenge his son's killer.

Mahan rode in a big circle back southeast and then turned back northwest to the scene of the battle. As he came upon the burned prairie, he noticed the bodies of the fallen Sioux warriors. Each in his death left exactly where they fell. Mahan knew that this was an insult to the Sioux by not being able to retrieve the bodies of the fallen warriors and place them in proper burial stands. The Sioux would not risk coming back along this trail for fear of more death from the Storm Maker. He dismounted his horse and walked through the charred battle scene. He was looking for signs of his friends when his horse lifted his head in anticipation of other animals and looked to the east. There were his friends riding down upon him and he was glad they had prevailed from the Bad Spirit that cleans off the land with fire.

Gabe and Davey rode into the burned valley and recognized Mahan from the color of his horse and put their rifles back into the scabbards. They had not been sure if it were more Sioux warriors looking for their dead, and both scouts were prepared for more war if that was the case. They were very glad to see Mahan because he had saved their lives, and they owed him a great debt. As the two scouts approached, Gabe put out his hand in friendship sign and Mahan did the same. The party dismounted and surveyed the battlefield. The war had gone well for the scouts, and the Sioux warriors that had fallen were now hunting a different range. With the loss of just one mule, the scouts had prevailed against great enemy numbers and were victorious. Gabe pulled a water pouch from one of the mules and passed it around as a celebration toast.

This ceremony was all new to Mahan, but he participated in the white man's pleasure. Mahan walked over to the closest body and scalped the dead brave. He held up the patch of hair in his hand and yelled out his war chant, repeating it twice. He would walk from warrior to warrior and repeat the scene until all were scalped and the dead left to their designs. Gabe and Davey stood by quietly until this part of the death dance was over. They would honor the Great War chief with their silence and respect.

Mahan returned with a fist full of bloody scalps. He took leather sinew out from his war bag and placed a hole in each scalp. Running the leather string through several at a time, he walked over to one of the mules and tied the bunch of scalps to the sawbuck and told Gabe that they were his trophies. Gabe acknowledged the gift while Mahan tied the other scalps to his horse's tail. Displaying them in this manner would insult and infuriate his enemies. This would play into the war chief's plans for the future. He turned and made an overture to the Great Spirit and then bowed his head in silence.

When the ceremony was done, the three scouts made a small fire and smoked the pipe. Gabe cooked some coffee as the rain started falling on the prairie. He passed around some jerky and hardtack to the others as the three sat and discussed the day's events. The clouds were covering the sunset. It would be dark soon and the trio needed some rest from all the stress of the battle. They would make a small shelter with a buffalo hide from one of the mule's packs to escape the pouring rain. When rested they would take up the trail sometime in the night.

The Great Storm Maker has frowned on his people this day, Yellow Hand thought. The Great One was upset and had taken out his fury on the fallen warriors. Dejected and angry, the Indians followed Yellow Hand in a solemn single file line toward the broken hills. They could not send their fallen friends to the Great Spirit's lodge as ceremony called for. They had lost many and gained nothing for their efforts. This war trail was bad medicine, and they wanted to get out of this country for good. It would be told in the lodges of the Sioux people from that day forward how three scouts had big medicine and could call on the Bad Spirit Maker as an ally against the Sioux warriors.

The war party rode silently and quickly as they put the miles behind them from the bad little war that took many Sioux lives. Yellow Hand had lost his prowess with the group. They thought his medicine weak and wanted to quit this war trail that they were on and return to their families. As soon as they caught up with the Cheyenne, this war trail would be finished for good. Yellow Hand had promised the braves scalps and trophies in this raid, and in the early parts of the raid, this had been the case. But when the Sioux made war on the three scouts, the war path had turned on them and no longer smiled on his people. He would leave this land and try to repair his status among the remaining warriors. If he could make a big trade for the yellow-haired white woman, then he might regain his position among his people. She would be worth many guns and kegs of white man's whiskey. He would make the trade and all would be good before the war party returned to their families. There could still be a victory in this trail. And the small Indian girl captive would make a nice slave wife on those cold nights when the Cold Maker would blow his breath on the land of the Sioux. Yellow Hand would claim the captive Ponca girl as his very own when the time was right. He was a greater chief than Black Tongue, and he led the war trail they were on. It was his right to take whatever he deemed necessary and leave the leftovers to the remaining braves. These were the thoughts that filled the war chief's mind as the Indians filed along the trail in the darkness and pouring rain.

CHAPTER 10 - THE LESSER OF TWO EVILS

Haley was so sore from the constant pounding of the horse she was riding that she could barely stand the pain any longer. She would look back from time to time and smile quietly at Pitani. The two girls had formed a bond for life, and they were in this together, even if it meant their deaths. Pitani knew that Haley was very uncomfortable and wished she could do something to relieve her pain. The Cheyenne were pushing the stock animals and the captives at a deadly pace. Several of the stolen horses had fallen down from exhaustion and were left behind by the war party. The group had been riding in the broken hill country since about mid-day. It had rained on and off and brought relief to the weary captives as they would try and refresh themselves while riding and catching the rain on their faces. Black Tongue was riding at the front of the war party, and his pace was swift. The giant black war horse that he rode was a tremendous mount. He was larger than the rest of the war ponies, and Black Tongue sat on him like a proud warrior with no fear in his heart. Haley could see the back of the war chief's shoulders as he rode in the front. He was a well-muscled Indian and seemed to be larger in stature than the other Cheyenne warriors. He would point out the war trail with his club and bark orders to the others as they filed along behind him. He never stopped for anything other than to occasionally look back on his trail. He continually kept watch for Yellow Hand and the Sioux warriors.

Sometimes as he glanced to the rear, his eyes would cast down upon Haley, and he would size her up and down with malice and content. Haley knew that if he could, he would kill her quickly and be done with the matter. Her only reason for being alive on this war trail was because Yellow Hand had other designs for her future. Throughout the day, Pitani would whisper things that she noticed and heard among the warriors, and kept Haley informed of what the group would discuss. Both captives knew that others were following and that the Sioux had split off to make war on them. The girls knew that there was bad blood between Yellow Hand and Black Tongue because of the women. Pitani had informed Haley that the Sioux chief Yellow Hand had intentions of trading her for guns and whiskey at Traders Creek Store. The two girls knew of the hate and deadly intentions of Black Tongue as well. Haley prayed continuously through the day and into the night.

Sometime in the night the war party stopped their advance and set up a small camp. Sentries were put out on guard, and the warriors sat down to smoke and eat some dried meat. The girls were given nothing but water, and their hands were bound tighter than before and they were staked to a large cedar tree. Throughout the night, the girls would hear the warriors' chant and dance to songs of war and victory. This went on well into the night until finally the two women fell asleep bound to the tree in a sitting position. Sometime during the night, Haley was awakened by the sound of running horses coming toward the camp. She tried to strain her eyes to see what or who it might be. As she stared into the night, she could make out the shapes of horses and riders converging on the camp in a rapid motion.

Pitani awoke, and the two girls watched as Yellow Hand and what was left of his Sioux warriors filed their horses into the camp at a walk. The other Indians stood around the fire staring in disbelief as the story of the small war on the three was relayed to the group. Pitani relayed the details as the girls overheard the conversations between the warriors. The girls finally knew more about their situation than before. The raiding party was being followed by three scouts that had taken out the lives of many brave Sioux warriors in a battle fought earlier on the plains. The Storm Maker had come to the aid of the three scouts and helped them defeat the Sioux and drive them from the battle like frightened children. The Storm Maker had made an angry fire that devoured the warriors just as they were getting ready to kill the three scouts and take their scalps in victory. The mood among the Indians was a solemn one, and the only warrior that spoke was Black Tongue. He called the Sioux weak in their hearts and minds and said that the Cheyenne should have been allowed on this war trail. He told the group that his medicine was much stronger than the Sioux and that he should lead the war trail from this point forward.

This was a direct challenge to Yellow Hand, and he immediately jumped from his horse and stared defiantly in the face of Black Tongue. He said that this was not the time to settle this matter, that they were being followed by the three scouts, and that they would bring the blue coats with them. If the Indians didn't get farther into the broken hills, then they were in jeopardy of losing the herd of animals and possibly their lives. Black Tongue backed away because he knew that Yellow Hand was right. There would be another time to challenge for the right to lead the trail.

The Indian camp was broken quickly, and the warriors made haste in getting the roaming herds of stolen stock animals on the trail and moving towards Traders Creek country. The captive women were thrust upon their horses and tied in the same manner as before. The entire time it took the Indians to break camp and get moving was a real surprise to Haley. Every movement the Indians made was done in a methodical approach. It was like they had done this hundreds of times before. The whole event took less than five minutes, and the entire group was in motion, moving quickly into the dark night. The news that someone followed was puzzling to Haley. Who would risk their lives for the sake of one white woman and an Indian captive girl? Surely the Mormons would not risk this kind of adventure for her or some stolen horses because they had their families to protect. She had no idea what to think about these circumstances, but she had hope in her heart and that would get her by for now. Someone was coming for her, and it had the Indians nervous.

The pace was fast and strenuous for the women on the bare backs of the Indian ponies they rode. Haley could hardly stand the pain that was once again rubbing her inner legs and thighs raw from the rough hair of her horse. Haley closed her eyes and asked God for the strength to live a little while longer. She made a pact right there in the darkness that if she were permitted to live and be free from her captors, she would raise up a righteous family in the eyes of God. She would follow God's counsel throughout the rest of her days and live his commandments as she had been taught by the Mormons. Haley put her head down on the horse's neck and tried to wipe her tears on her shoulder. She was bound so tightly to the horse that it took all her effort just to maintain her balance as the raiding party rode through the night air.

The rain had stopped, and the night sky looked clear and full of stars. Gabe wondered if Haley was looking at the same set of stars that abound the sky. He thought she must be ready to give up or just die from exhaustion with the force march that she had been regimented to by her captors. He could only hope that she could hold on long enough for him to reach her and try to free her from this awful situation she found herself in. The three scouts were well on the trail in the middle of the night and expected to come within sight of the war party within the next two days. They were obviously gaining on the raiding party because the Indians had felt threatened enough to stand and fight.

The scouts were moving faster than the Indians because of the stolen stock that the warriors were being forced to herd along as they traveled. It had been decided during their camp talk earlier in the night that the three scouts would pursue the war party until they were sighted and then a plan would be devised for the release of the women captives. Gabe had suggested trading for the women, but Mahan thought the Indians would rather kill the women instead of trading after the small war that had been fought and the lost lives they had encountered at the hands of the scouts. He told Gabe that the honor of the war party had been violated and that they would be in no mood for trading. He supposed that the only way for the women's release would be through force. This was fine by Gabe since he had an anger built up in him that would take some time to calm down. He wanted only one thing; the safe release of Haley Johnson. He would ride to the ends of the earth for that outcome.

How it had come to this he couldn't understand. He hardly knew the young woman, but just the thought of her made him feel good inside. He was not the same man he had been before the grip took him and she nursed him back from the other side. If nothing else he felt like he owed her his life, and that would keep him following the trail until it ended. Gabe pushed the big grey horse, his knees nudging the beast forward at a quick pace. He knew that the next few days would mean the end of this trail, and he was anxious to see it through.

Yellow Hand led the war party through the canyon bottom and out onto a big plateau to the west. This long ridge would lead the party westward to the valley of the Traders Creek. It would be there that they could be free of the women captives and make a trade. He suspected that the raiding party would be in sight of the trader's cabin around sunset later in the day. It would be a hard ride, but the Indians were used to the rigors of the trail life. He thought of the captives and how much whiskey the yellow-haired woman would bring. Many times before this time, Yellow Hand had ridden the war trail and made a trade with the bearded trader named Frenchie. The Indian felt like he had bested the short, stout man in every trade they had made. This time would be no different. The Indians had a lot of good Mormon horses and mules and packs full of clothing and plunder that they had taken from the dead as they raided the plains. This war trail had been kind to Indians with the exception of the small war on the three who follow. Yellow Hand would deal with the scouts on another day.

This day would be a day of good medicine for the war party. He looked back over his shoulder at the following horses and braves. His eyes looked at the captives and then glanced over at Black Tongue. The warrior had an evil grin on his face that made him look devilish in the early morning shadows. Yellow Hand knew that he would have to kill the Cheyenne warrior before the trade was made later in the day. Black Tongue would never agree to allow the yellow-haired woman to be given in trade. He would claim his rights to her as he had taken her in battle. This was the Indian way, and Yellow Hand would have to challenge this right in front of the other Indians. It would mean a fight to the death, and the victor would prevail over the captives. Black Tongue would be a difficult foe. The young Cheyenne chief was a master of war on his big black stallion. It would take all of Yellow Hands cunning to defeat the young warrior and claim the rights to lead again. Yellow Hand put the war club to the butt of his horse and quickened the pace. He wanted to press hard and reach Traders Creek by sundown.

Charles Deschard, as he was named from birth, went by the name Frenchie. He had come west in the year 1838 and trapped with the Hudson Bay fur trappers' company for nearly ten years. He had become a real mountain man and decided to make it his life's passion. He had fought Indians and lived with Indians. He had married into the Mandan tribe and raised a family. All things in his life were good until the pox took his entire family one winter while Frenchie was away trapping. After that he left the Mandan tribe and wandered farther west, finally settling down in a small canyon in the Wyoming territories. He found it to be good for water and grass for livestock. It had plenty of local cedar and pine wood, and protection from the cold Wyoming winds. He hunted buffalo for the hide value when the fur trade fell out, and he cut himself a homestead in the vast rugged wilderness with his bare hands. He managed a fair relationship with the local Indians in trading for the white man's goods, and he was a master of the old art of brewing distilled liquors. This had kept his hair on his head many times in the past when Indian raiding parties would descend upon his makeshift cabin and demand whiskey.

The Indians had allowed Frenchie to live in their prime hunting grounds as long as he provided them whiskey and trade. He had become a source of value for the Indians, and he would bring the white man's trade goods to their encampments and thrill the Indian women with the marvels of modern society. The warriors would benefit from this trade, and the Indian women would make teepee life very comfortable for them. He was a man for all seasons, and he could come and go with safety among the warring tribes of the Cheyenne and Sioux nations. Frenchie had become a loner and never took another Indian wife. He had been offered many in trade, but he refused them all. He would live out his days in a solitary state of mind.

As the morning sun came over the ridgeline up the canyon. Frenchie pulled on his leather shirt and laced up his moccasins. Today he had many chores to do and needed to get going. The hint of fall in the air made the inside of the small cabin very chilly. He fired the stove up and put on some coffee to boil. He had a wagon he needed to unload that had supplies he had traded for down at Fort Laramie. The supplies were purchased with eight hundred and eighty buffalo hides that Frenchie had hunted while out on the plains the past winter. He had made a good trade for the supplies of mash that he needed to keep his whiskey supply going. Frenchie had also purchased some fine Spencer rifles that would come in handy for negotiations with the local Indians. He knew about the law of the land forbidding any trade of guns and liquor to the Indian peoples, but he was so far removed from society that he felt like the law didn't pertain to him. He made his own law, survival of the fittest, and to be the most cunning man alive.

Frenchie was a cunning sort. He would double the value of trade to the duped Indians as they came clamoring out of the hills begging for his elixir. He was the man of the hour, and he knew it. Nothing could stand in his way of becoming a rich man at the hands of the childlike savages that surrounded his meager abode. Frenchie traded only for horses and gold. He would hide the gold in the ground until he had enough to leave the frontier and become a wealthy man in his native Quebec. The horses he traded for were usually sold to the bluecoats at the local forts that dotted the prairies.

Frenchie had a complete circle of commerce going for him, and his wealth was increasing at an alarming rate. As he sat and sipped his coffee, he looked out the window of his cabin and noticed that the horses in his corral were all on alert with their ears perked forward and looking up the canyon. Frenchie knew from past experience that this sign usually meant that Indians were on the prowl. He finished the last bit of coffee and pulled his rifle from its position above the door buck. He checked the lever of the Winchester and peered outside into the morning light.

Frenchie looked up the canyon trail from where he thought the sign might come from, and he could barely make out two Indians mounted on ponies looking over his cabin. They sat on their horses like so many before them and just surveyed the situation until they felt safe enough to proceed toward the white man's post. Frenchie walked out the cabin door and stood facing the two Indians. They were well out of rifle shot, a tactic usually deployed by warriors. If they had squaws and children with them they would usually have the women walk into the trading post as the warriors stayed out of harm's way and ready for trouble. Even though the local Indians frequented the post, they were always on guard and looking for signs of war. These two would wait until they were ready before proceeding forward to the cabin area. After several minutes of tense study, one of the Indians made the sign for peace and talk. Frenchie did likewise, and the two warriors slowly rode into the trader's camp.

As they came forward Frenchie could tell they were from a raiding party. They had their war implements with them, and they were all painted up like warriors do when they are on the warpath. This made Frenchie nervous, and he squeezed his hands tighter on his Winchester. Finally, the two Indians were within rifle shot, and this made the whole affair seem less threatening. They would not expose themselves to fire if they meant war on Frenchie. Frenchie smiled his usual fake smile and waved his arm in a friendly gesture as the warriors approached his cabin front. Frenchie could tell they were Cheyenne warriors from the markings on their apparel and the way they wore their hair.

They dismounted their horses and never took their eyes off of Frenchie. One of the braves rubbed his stomach and made the sign for hungry. Frenchie held out his hand and gave the sign that he would get them something to eat. He turned sideways and slowly walked back to the cabin door while keeping his eye on the two warriors the whole time. As he went inside and retrieved some dried meat and coffee, he never let the two warriors out of his sight. He had learned that it didn't matter how friendly the Indians acted, you could never bet your hair on their honesty.

When Frenchie walked back through the cabin door, the two warriors were seated on the ground like little children waiting to be fed. It almost made him laugh out loud at the thought of how great his position was over these childlike men. He handed the food to them, and they devoured it without looking up. The pact was made, and the two warriors were in Frenchie's living room parlor on the wilderness floor. There they sat like begging dogs, looking for a scrap of meat. Frenchie felt like he was the king of the frontier. He inquired of the two what it was they wanted. The Frenchman had a commanding gift for the various tongues that the indigenous peoples of the prairie spoke. He was fluent in Sioux, Cheyenne, Crow, and all manner of Missouri river tribes. He could make the sign with the best of them and was quite prolific in his manner. He sat down as custom would allow in front of the two warriors and made their native tongue come to life. He was told that they were with a war party that was coming to Traders Creek with many items to trade. They were sent ahead to have the long beard make ready for his Sioux and Cheyenne brothers that would arrive around sunset.

"The great chief Yellow Hand of the Sioux Lakota nation sends his wishes that the long beard of the Traders Creek will welcome his Indian neighbors with whiskey and trade," said one of the men.

The warriors mentioned that they had captives among the war party and that one of them was a white woman that would be offered for trade. This was stunning news to Frenchie; he had never made a trade for captive white women. He was not sure about this, but the time would come when he could decide what to do. Maybe there was a way for Frenchie to really take advantage of his Indian neighbors and make a good profit in the meantime. Frenchie concluded the meeting by smoking the pipe with the two warriors. This was done to show his agreement to their chief's wishes, and then he sent each of them off with a jug of whiskey. He knew that when the two braves got back to the war party with the gifts of whiskey the whole group of Indians would partake of the white man's firewater. By the time the war party reached his cabin they would be drunk and easy to take advantage of in trade. He watched from his cabin door as the two warriors rode back down the long canyon and out of sight. This was shaping up to be a grand day in the wilderness for Frenchie. He would prepare a place to one side of his cabin with buffalo robes spread across the ground. This would afford the interested parties a place to sit and haggle out the terms of the trade as the process would allow.

The weather was perfect and the sky cloudless. This would allow the trading to go well into the night if needed. Frenchie intended to scarf off all the possible booty that the Indians had stolen on their raid. He would not be satisfied until he had bested them all from their trophies of war. Time and time again he had taken advantage of the Indians as they would fill up with the liquor he made and then lose their valuable furs and horses in stupidity of it all. He knew the Indian was a sucker for the white man's whiskey, and he fully intended on its use for his gain.

Frenchie made a makeshift lean-to from the outside cabin wall and set everything in its place for his guests' arrival. He cut wood for the fires that would serve for cooking and comfort, and he placed all of his trade goods in bundles against the outside wall of the cabin. He would sit in front of all his prizes and let the Indians view the enormous amount of goods that were stacked along the cabin wall. He placed many jugs and several barrels of whiskey in plain sight. All this could be theirs if they made the right trades and allowed the Frenchman to milk them out of their goods. When the morning sun came up tomorrow, Frenchie would be the wealthiest man in the territories. He would take his gold and horses down to the fort at Laramie and sell the horses to the soldiers for a high price, and then he would take all of his gold and make his way back to his beloved

Quebec. He would be a king with all his wealth among his old friends. He might even settle down and take a white woman to wife. These were the Frenchman's thoughts as he prepared his camp for the rendezvous.

Yellow Hand could see the approaching riders for several miles along the plateau as they came in his direction. He knew it was the two Cheyenne braves that had been sent ahead to the long beard's trading post. As they came in front of the group of anxious warriors, the war party let out a series of yelps and howls that scared off some of the herding horses. Haley looked out to see what the commotion was as the pair of Cheyenne warriors rode into the horses being herded along. She could see the warriors holding up the jugs in their hands and shouting praises of victory while all the other Indians rode their horses in tightly around the two warriors and all took a swipe at the prize whiskey. The whole group came to halt and dismounted as they passed around the jugs. They drank and screamed at the top of their lungs. They would hunch their backs and make dances in the dirt. Their bodies were contorted in all manner of weird fashion as one after another partook of the firewater. Haley and Pitani sat their horses in view of the prairie party before them. They could only look on as the helpless warriors poured down the elixir and screamed louder.

The jugs were flung from one Indian to another until all had drunk their fill. Some of the Indians began to stagger around while others fell to the ground and lay sprawled out on the plateau rocks. It took less than an hour for the whole scene to calm down as the majority of the braves were in a drunken stupor. Finally, Yellow Hand gathered up what was left of the jugs and tied them to one of the pack animals that had been taken in the raid on the whites. He barked his orders and went around kicking the defenseless Indians as they lay passed out from the effects of the whiskey. After another hour of this method, Yellow Hand mounted his horse and told the group to either follow him quickly or give up their scalps to the three who follow. Some Indians crawled to their feet while others were helped on their horses and pushed along the trail. Finally, the war party was moving again in the direction of the Traders Creek canyon. Hungover and still within the effects of the liquor, the war party slowed its march down to a walking pace. All of the Indians were riding with heads down, some sick to their stomachs. The whole scene was shocking to the women as they filed along in the aftermath before them.

Yellow Hand felt sure that once the war party was in the canyon of Traders Creek that they would be safe from their enemies. He would leave several warriors to guard the entrance to the canyon, to warn the party if anyone was following the group. If the war party was being pursued, then he could mount an attack on the enemy from the sides of the canyon as the enemy marched along the canyon floor. This would be his war plan if the need should arrive. He led the party down into the canyon and made his choice from the sober Indians as to which ones he would leave behind to guard. The order was given, and three braves were selected from the hungover bunch of Indians. Two braves would guard the entrance and the third one would ride forward and alert the war party of any impending dangers as they traded with the long beard.

Yellow Hand instructed two more braves to ride forward and shout the coming of the war party to the long-bearded Frenchman at Traders Creek. Tell him to make ready for trade and to have all his whiskey and guns made available to the war party. The Indians would only stay one night, then they would move on to their lodges. The two braves galloped their horse forward in advance of the war party to deliver Yellow Hand's message. The women heard the instructions, and Pitani relayed the conversations of the warriors in whispered tones to Haley. Both women knew that something would intervene in their lives by tomorrow's sun up.

Haley silently prayed to God as the Indians pushed the captives and their stolen horses up through the canyon floor. The only time the Indians stopped was to let the stock animals drink from the fresh water that meandered down from the flowing stream at the bottom of the canyon. Haley thought to herself that this must be Traders Creek that the Indians had mentioned earlier. Her mind was filled with anticipation for what she might face at the end of the day. She had been taught by the Mormons in her conversion that she had a constant companion in the Holy Ghost. Now more than ever she would need this comforting gift from God if she was to survive this ordeal. She constantly prayed as the group rode in sight of the trader's cabin and corral area. The Indians dismounted and placed their riding horses in a line close by. This was done in case of danger. The stolen stock animals were herded into the corrals that Frenchie had provided for their safe keeping. Yellow Hand and Black Tongue were the first to greet the white man trader. He presented them with two new blankets and two jugs of whiskey. They shook hands, and he led them to the side of his cabin where he had prepared some buffalo and beans to eat.

The women were pulled from their horses and tied to the nearest corral post in a sitting position. They could see the trading area from where they were bound up. The Indians all filed into line and received their blankets and jugs of whiskey. As each one got his prize, he found himself a place on the buffalo robes and sat down to drink and eat the buffalo that had been prepared. Stories were told, and every now and then an Indian would get up and act out some form of heroism of his deeds in battle. This was done for several hours until the Indians were liquored up and they became drunk from the whiskey.

Finally, Frenchie stood and announced that the trading blanket was set. He placed a bright red blanket on the buffalo robes and spread it out for a place to make the trade. He motioned with sign language and spoke in the Sioux tongue that he had twenty new rifles that he had purchased from the soldier fort at Laramie. As he did so, he passed one of the new Spencers around for all the Indians to handle. He would trade the rifles and all the whiskey stacked against the cabin wall for all the horses and ten pouches of gold nuggets. Yellow Hand countered this offer with half of the horses and five pouches of gold nuggets. Frenchie asked the Sioux chief if he had the gold with him. Yellow Hand replied that he could have the gold there by sunrise the next morning. Frenchie spit out his tobacco plug and haggled for more horses and more gold. The trading had come to an impasse. The scene went quiet, and some of the Indians returned to their jugs as Frenchie put more wood on the fires. The sun was starting to set, and the long shadows were reaching out to cover the ground. Frenchie knew that this ploy by Yellow Hand was only the beginning of the trading.

The girls were thirsty and tired. Haley was so sore from the horse that she could hardly move her legs. As she tried to straighten out her legs, the pain nearly made her pass out. Finally, one of the braves tending to the horses came over to the women and put a water bladder up to their mouths so that they could drink. He did this until each woman had drunk enough. Haley noticed that he was the same Indian that had given her water and food earlier in the week. The Indian brave pulled some jerky from a pouch and put one large piece in each of the girl's mouths. This would be all they got, and they chewed and licked until the morsels were gone. Their hands were still bound, and they could not escape their captors.

Finally, the young Indian came back over to them just before dark and pulled them to their feet. He loosened their rawhide ties and led them over to the side of the corrals and motioned for them to relieve themselves if they needed to. Both women were in need and immediately squatted in the darkness and did their business. After they were through, the Indian gave them one more piece of meat and another drink of the bladder. Then he tied them tight again and sat them down secured to the nearest corral post. Haley and Pitani were amazed at the generosity of the young Indian. He didn't seem to be like the rest of the war party. He had taken pity on the girls, and they would remember his kindness. Pitani and Haley spoke to one another as the young Indian left them alone by the corral. Pitani could hear the men speaking and informed Haley of the sudden stop to the trading. Both women wondered how this whole scene might turn out.

The Indians were drunk and in a somber mood. Yellow Hand and Black Tongue had drunk very little whiskey. They knew the traders trick of getting them drunk and then stealing from them in trade while they were under the influence of the white man's whiskey. They stared at the fire and then at the Frenchman. Finally, Yellow Hand motioned for one of the braves and gave him a command. The Indian came toward the girls and reached down and cut Haley's hands loose. He pulled her to her feet and grabbed her by the hair and shoved her toward the cooking fires.

As they approached the firelight, Yellow Hand stood up and grasped Haley by the arm and offered her in trade along with six bags of gold for all the Frenchman's whiskey and twenty rifles with ammunition. Immediately Black Tongue sprang to his feet in protest as Yellow Hand hit him across the side of his head with the butt of his knife. It happened so swiftly that the Cheyenne war chief never saw it coming. He fell forward on the trading blanket and lay there motionless. Yellow Hand told some of the other Cheyenne warriors to take him away before he killed Black Tongue and scalped him where he laid. They did as they were told, and several of them dragged him off into the darkness of the night. Yellow Hand resumed his stance and regained his grasp on Haley's arm as he stared at the French trader sitting before him. Frenchie knew he might not get out of this night alive if he were to best the chief standing before him. He could only guess what might be the trouble between the young Cheyenne war chief and Yellow Hand. But the Sioux chief had made it clear that he wanted the last say in this trade.

The liquor had made the war chief angry and dangerous. Frenchie knew his only out was to accept the war chief's offer and make the trade. He stood and made the sign that the trade was a done deal. He reached out and shook the hand of the Sioux chief, and the proceedings were finished for the night. The Indians would finish their drinking now that the trading was over. Yellow Hand handed Haley over to Frenchie; the trader took her by the arm and pulled her over to the front of his cabin. He told her to go inside and wash herself up and make herself comfortable then he would be in to talk with her after he got the Indians settled down for the night. She was surprised that the French trader could speak good English as well as Sioux and French, living clear out here in this wilderness. He seemed to be somewhat educated in a rough manner.

Finally, Haley could relax a little bit, yet she trembled as she entered the musty cabin interior. There was a wash tin setting on a small table in the center of the room. She walked over to it and put her hands in the cool water and put her hands to her face. She was still in shock from the ordeal she had encountered the last few days. But she figured that God had delivered her out of harm's way and into the custody of the French trader. Haley peered out the open cabin door and could see Pitani still tied to the corral post. She felt helpless to do anything. Maybe she could talk with the French trader and he could interfere on her behalf. Something must be done. Haley could not live with herself if Pitani was not freed as well.

Frenchie walked out to the Indians and took his trade blanket and folded it up. This signaled that all trading was final and there would be no more tonight. Yellow Hand signaled to one of the braves, who immediately mounted a horse and rode off into the night. The warrior would ride out to a predetermined point and retrieve the trade gold as promised. The Sacred Black Hills were a source of gold for the Indians and were a place fiercely protected. Frenchie had heard of the gold and knew that this would be the source of his wealth come morning. The Sioux would have a stash of gold not far from his trader's post, which they had used in the past to gain whiskey and guns. Frenchie sat near the Sioux chief and poured him another cup full of whiskey from the jug at his side. Now that the trading was over, Yellow Hand had cause to relax and enjoy his new-found wealth. The war party would return to their lodges with plenty of whiskey to last the long winter and new rifles with which to kill their enemies.

The war chief put the whiskey cup to his mouth and drank heavily from the tin. He had won back the support of his warriors and put the skunk Black Tongue in his place. He still might find the Cheyenne war chief and kill him before the night was over. As the whiskey took its affect, Yellow Hand fell on his side, passed out from the alcohol. Frenchie looked at the war chief and shook his head. These Indians were nothing more than beggars and thieves of the prairie. Real men would never allow themselves to be taken in trade by the effects of whiskey. Frenchie would still get the best of this war chief. He had served only his best whiskey, but the kegs the Indians were receiving were tainted with all sorts of watered down concoctions. If he never saw any of the murdering savages again it would not hurt his feelings one bit.

Frenchie would be out of this territory and on his way to the fort as soon as the Indians cleared his camp. He would hire several local tame Indians to help drive the animals and the whole lot could be under way within a few days. Right now, Frenchie had other things on his mind, and he needed to tend to the yellow-haired white woman.

Frenchie entered the open door to the cabin and looked at Haley Johnson in the dark cabin light. He went over and lit a small kerosene lantern and set it on the small table. As he looked up and into the face of Haley, she seemed scared of his presence. Obviously she must have been put through a very difficult ordeal with the war party. Frenchie asked her name, and she told him. As soon as the words were out of her mouth, she asked the Frenchman to intervene on behalf of the other stolen captive, Pitani. The Frenchman laughed out loud at the preposterous suggestion. He told Haley that the Indian girl would be one of the braves' slave squaws and that if he even mentioned her to the Indians they would kill and scalp both he and Haley. He informed Haley that Pitani was from an enemy tribe to the Sioux and Cheyenne, and that it was a miracle that she had survived this long. Ponca Indians had been graven enemies of the Cheyenne for hundreds of years. That she had been the daughter of a Ponca chief was a great victory for the warrior that took her in the raid. Frenchie would not say anything to assist the young Ponca maiden. He valued his hair and advised Haley to do likewise.

As the lights of the small cabin glowed, Frenchie could see that his trade for the yellow-haired woman was a good trade. She had features that he had not seen in a woman in a long time.

Frenchie moved closer to inspect Haley, and she noticed his interest and moved away. The Frenchman reached out and grabbed her by the arm and pulled her close to him. Haley tried to resist, but she was no match for the trader's strength. Frenchie ran his hand through her hair as Haley tried in vain to pull away from him. He mumbled under his breath and then stepped back and hit her full in the face, knocking her down on the floor of the cabin.

Stunned and helpless Haley tried to crawl out the cabin door only to be grabbed by the hair and pulled back inside on the dirt floor.

The Frenchman pulled her to her feet and said he had traded in good faith to the Indians and now she belonged to him. She was his woman, and he would make her his slave wife. He slapped her again as she sprawled back across the cabin, hitting the table and knocking its contents across the cabin floor. Haley could feel the swelling in her mouth and the blood trickle down her chin. As she tried to regain her footing, the stout Frenchman grabbed her wrist and pulled out a leather thong. He tied her hands tightly and grabbed the collar of her shirt, pulling her along behind him outside and around to the back of the cabin. He bound her to a pole next to a woodpile and tied her feet as well. He spoke to her in his drunken tone and said this would hold her until morning. He warned her that if she tried to escape, he would give her back to the Indians as a gift. Haley was still stunned from the punches she had received. All she could see was the Frenchman standing and barking at her in his native French language. She passed out from the shock and slumped to one side as she was bound at the waist.

Pitani had witnessed the assault on Haley and sat helpless to do anything. She had heard the Indians talking about the French trader and knew he was a bad man. The French trader had returned to his cabin, and the lights were put out. No doubt he had succumbed to the effects of the whiskey like his partners in evil. As Pitani sat there in the night air she hoped Haley was still alive. She cried to herself and asked the Great Spirit to have mercy on the two women. While she was in the act of praying to her god, she heard someone approaching very quietly. It could only be an Indian. White men could not move that silently across the earth. She stared out into the darkness, trying to get some visual of the approaching person. Suddenly she was bound across the mouth with a piece of leather and pulled up from her sitting position. She was grasped and picked up off her feet and carried out into the darkness by some unknown person.

Pitani was carried out several hundred feet from the corrals and placed upon a horse. She was bound in the usual manner and led away by several braves in the darkness. She could not make out their identities, but she suspected they might be Cheyenne warriors, about seven of them. The warriors mounted their horses and walked them quietly away from the trader's cabin. The group silently left the area and worked their horses up a trail that led out of the canyon floor. Pitani had no idea what this new turn of events would lead to. Her horse followed along with several horses in front of her and some behind. She finally heard one of the brave's whispers and he was talking Cheyenne.

Black Tongue immediately whispered for the Cheyenne brave behind him to shut up. He firmly whispered a warning that he would kill anyone that raised the alarm to the Sioux. Finally, Pitani knew her fate as the horsemen ascended the canyon rim and rode out into the broken hills to the west. Black Tongue had made his move, and he would not be denied the rights of battle. He would make the Ponca maiden his slave wife, or he would kill her if she defied him. He rode along in the darkness, proud and full of himself for outsmarting the foolish Yellow Hand. By the time the Sioux realized the Cheyenne were gone, it would be too late.

The Cheyenne would be in their home country before midday, and then their brothers would seal the fate of anyone who followed the small war party. Black Tongue was angry with himself for not cutting the throat of Yellow Hand while the war chief lay passed out from the white man's whiskey. He could have accomplished this deed easily after he rose from his beating at the hands of the Sioux chief. He was engaged in this act when the French trader came around from the back of his cabin, singing a song in his drunken state. Black Tongue had crawled to within several feet of Yellow Hand when he was surprised by the trader. He lay on the buffalo robes like he was one of the drunken Indians until the trader had passed by him. Then he felt it not safe to engage the Sioux chief at that moment because the long beard was standing at the side of his cabin, pissing on the ground while he sang a foolish song in the night air. Yellow Hand's medicine had saved his life on that night, but now Black Tongue would be rid of the Sioux dictator and his orders. He would lead this small war party and return to his people with the captive Ponca woman as his trophy of war.

CHAPTER 11 - WHITE KING'S KNIGHT TAKES BLACK QUEEN'S KNIGHT

The entrance to the canyon could be seen easily from a position of protruding rocks that jutted out from the prairie floor nearly a mile away. The three scouts, Gabe, Davey, and Mahan, were nestled up in the rock crevices, spying on the entrance to the canyon in front of them. With his spy glass, Gabe could easily see the three Indians that had been placed in the canyon entrance as guards. He passed the glass around for all to view the scene. Mahan had a plan. He would find a way to encircle the three warriors, and when Gabe and Davey rode up to the canyon entrance he would be behind the trio and have a tactical advantage.

Gabe thought the plan out and agreed that this might be their only chance since their approach would definitely be seen by the three Indian braves in the opening. Mahan would go on foot since the steep canyon wall would not support a horse. He left Gabe and Davey sitting in the rock crevice and quietly and secretly crept around the three unsuspecting warriors. Mahan climbed through the rocks at the edge of the broken country and gained access to the canyon after a grueling ordeal. The canyon was very steep, and it took all of his strength to pull himself up the sharp jagged canyon to a point of ambush. He would give the signal to Gabe with his mirror when he was in position behind the three Indians guarding the entrance. After several hours sitting out in the early morning sun, Davey nudged Gabe and pointed to the flashing signal that Mahan was making with his mirror. The two scouts immediately mounted their horses and quickly rode toward the mouth of the canyon. Just as Gabe had figured, as soon as the pair were spotted, one of the Indian guards mounted his horse and sped away back up the canyon and out of sight. The other two warriors prepared themselves for an ambush.

As the lone Indian warrior filed past Mahan on his horse through the canyon, the great war chief knocked an arrow and with great skill let the arrow fly from his bow. The arrow was true to its mark and hit the young warrior just under the ribs on his right side. He rode for several yards from the point of impact and then bled out and fell from his horse down into the canyon water stream. Mahan quickly converged on the other two warriors that were preparing to ambush Gabe and Davey. Mahan came in from behind the unsuspecting warriors, and with a war club in one hand and a knife in the other, he quickly dispatched both braves with a blow to the head and a knife in the side of the neck to the other remaining warrior.

The whole death scene took less than five seconds, and two warriors were sent to the Great Lodge in the sky. As Gabe and Davey filed their horses and mules into the canyon entrance, the death scene before them became apparent. Gabe realized for the first time how great of a warrior Mahan really was. Mahan had just finished scalping his victims when Gabe and Davey rode up. He quickly mounted his horse in one motion and swiftly rode out of sight and up the canyon floor. Gabe knew that they were close to the war party and that Mahan would want to reach his granddaughter before the war party could kill her. If they suspected the scouts were in the canyon, they might kill her on the spot and make a run for it.

Gabe kicked Old smoke in the ribs and pushed him faster up the canyon floor. The big buffalo horse took the cue from its master and broke into a medium gallop. This rate of pace would be all the mules could do to keep up. Gabe knew at some point he would have to cut the mules loose because they were too slow. He wanted to get farther up the canyon before he did this in case they needed the extra ammunition that the mules carried. Gabe knew that there were at least twenty-five warriors in this group and they would have superior numbers over the scouts if they chose to turn and fight again.

Mahan had told Gabe and Davey of Traders Creek and that many Indian tribes would go there to trade with the long beard for whiskey and guns. The popularity of the trading post was quite well known among all the Plains Indians. Mahan had been to the post on two occasions and knew the layout of the canyon and its side trails. He had given the layout to Gabe and Davey the night before so that all of them would be in unison for an attack if warranted. Gabe figured that the scouts should arrive at the trader's cabin area around mid-morning. He suspected as did Mahan that the Indians would be there trading the horse herd for guns and whiskey.

Gabe could only hope that the women were still all right. The scouts had found the area where the Indians had made a prairie party with the whiskey they had received. There was not any evidence to suggest that the women had been harmed, and that was good news to the scouts. Gabe knew that there would be killing and death under the morning sky. His only hope was that Haley would be safe and that he could reach her in time. He figured that the Indians would probably not kill her since she was very valuable in trade. He suspected they might try to trade her at the post, or they would take her to their lodges and make her some warrior's squaw. Either way he would follow the trail until he reached her and brought her safely out of the Indian nations.

The Indians would have to kill him to make him stop the trail. As Gabe and Davey rode up the canyon floor, they came in sight of Mahan sitting his horse and staring ahead up the canyon. They rode up to him, and he pointed out a scene before them. Eight riders were scaling the side canyon trail and nearing the summit. Gabe produced the glass and handed it to Mahan. The war chief took one look and handed the glass back to Gabe. He spoke, "The Indian snake named Black Tongue has my granddaughter, and I must kill him this day and free her from his terror. It was shown to me in my vision. I will avenge my son on this day with the blood of the Cheyenne Dog Soldier. I will place his scalp on my war club for all to see and he will never make war on my people again."

Gabe looked at Mahan in silence and felt a bit of sadness for the sorrow in the old chief's heart. He could not begin to feel the sadness of losing one's only son to a cutthroat like Black Tongue. If the circumstances were any different, Gabe would follow the Cheyenne warrior and kill just for the sake of prairie law. Black Tongue had killed and raped many white and Indian people on the plains, and his reputation was among the most hated in the territories. The army had a standing bounty of one thousand dollars out for his scalp, but he had escaped all efforts to bring him to justice.

Gabe stepped out of the saddle and handed the reins of the big grey horse to Mahan. "You'll never catch them unless you ride Old Smoke. He can outlast any Indian pony on the plains.' It's the only way you can reach the war party before they get into the Cheyenne nations near the Devil's Tower country."

Mahan knew that what Gabe spoke was true. He slid off of his mustang and handed the reins in similar jester over to Gabe. The three scouts knew that they must split up and go separate ways from this point. There were two women captives and two war trails. Gabe shook the hand of Mahan and wished him good luck. This was strange behavior to the war chief; he wasn't sure about this thing called luck.

Gabe pulled the Henry from the scabbard on the grey horse and brushed the neck of the horse as he whispered in his ear, "Take good care of my friend Mahan and bring your ornery carcass back to me. I'm not through with you just yet. We've got a lot more trails to go down you and me so run fast and stay the course."

A small welling in Gabe's eyes went unnoticed by the scouts, but a wrenching feeling deep down inside made Gabe turn his face from sight, and he busied himself with the mules. Mahan mounted the big buffalo horse and said something in his native tongue to Gabe and Davey. He quickly rode out across the canyon floor and started up the trail to the summit. Gabe cocked the Henry and told Davey to make ready for war. The pair of scouts took what extra ammunition was on the mules and dropped their packs. The mules were hobbled and cut loose. They would stay near the captured Indian pony that Davey had tied to a nearby tree. The scouts mounted their war ponies and made a swift departure up the canyon creek bed.

Frenchie looked out the open cabin door and realized that some of the Indians were gone. He walked out the side of his cabin where several Indians sat trying to work out the effects of the whiskey. Yellow Hand was shouting orders, and the whole camp was trying their best to move around. The Cheyenne had snuck out in the darkness, taking the Ponca maiden with them, and the guards from the mouth of the canyon had not been heard from since yesterday evening. This was alarming news to Yellow Hand, and he smelled trouble. He knew the Indians were in no condition for a small war, and their only choice was to flee the area and get to the Black Hills for safety. It would be a hard full day's ride to reach the Black Forest, but once they were within the sacred area, there were many warriors who could take up the war trail and help them kill the three who follow.

A lone brave approached Yellow Hand and handed the gold pouches over to him that he had recovered in the night. Yellow Hand gave them to the long beard and said that their dealings were done here and that they would be leaving quickly. The Frenchman watched from his cabin door as the whole camp was broken and mounted in less than five minutes. The hungover Indians were a sorry lot as they rode off in single file following their leader. The Indians were soon out of sight over the summit of the canyon rim, and the trader's post took on a quiet sound.

Frenchie had unfinished business with his newly acquired slave woman. He would mold her in time, and she would do the necessary chores and make his life comfortable. If she refused, then he would cut her throat and be done with the problem. Either way, it didn't really matter much to Frenchie. He had been a loner for many years, and he enjoyed his own company. The only thought in his mind right now was the gold bags sitting on the porch floor. He would retrieve all of the gold and then make his way over to the fort at Laramie and sell the stolen horses. Thoughts of grandeur and fame filled the Frenchman's mind as he started his morning chores. Now and again his mind went back to the yellow-haired woman and her stunning beauty. He would have her before this day was through, he had decided.

Gabe took the trail leading up the creek to the trader's post. He had instructed Davey to take a side trail that led up out of the canyon to the rim, just in case the hostiles should make their escape with Haley in their procession. This way they would have the war party in a crossfire, should it be necessary to fight. Slowly Gabe slid off the mustang and prepared himself for battle. He put the colt pistol in his belt band and pulled his bowie knife up to his front pants pocket. This would make it easier to pull if he ran out of ammunition and needed to fight hand to hand. Fully loaded and ready for a war, he started sneaking along the edge shadows of the canyon. The morning sun had not fully hit the canyon floor, and there were still lingering shadows cast among the rocks and juniper trees that dotted the landscape. From one rock position to another, Gabe made his way among the creek boulders until he came in sight of the trader's cabin. He could see the Indians were not there.

He inspected every inch of the place for Haley with his glass but couldn't see her anywhere. His heart sank at the thoughts that she might still be with the war party and headed for the Sacred Black Hills. Gabe knew that if they got inside that fortress of canyons and timber, it would take him a long time to locate Haley. Gabe could see Davey from his cover position, and he signed for the young scout to climb to the rim and look for sign. Davey immediately moved from his position and started the long climb to the top plateau. Gabe decided to sit in cover for a while longer, watching and listening for a sign. He could see the corral full of stolen horses and mules, and several small fires were smoldering as evidence of the war party the night before. They must have just barely left, he thought to himself as he surveyed the trader's cabin.

Frenchie had just finished his morning chores when he decided it was time for the yellow-haired woman. He would take her some food and water and see if this might improve her mood. He entered the cabin front door and prepared some eggs and coffee. He went out the back door leaving it opened for the cabin to air out some from its musty smell. He would need the cabin smelling better if he were to bed the young woman. After all, Frenchie had been a lady's man down along the Missouri River trading posts back in his younger days. He had sparked the river whores all up and down the mighty river, and his reputation with the women was one of bragging rights to his fellow trappers. Today he would slick himself up just a bit and try to influence the young maiden tied up out back. He hoped he could loosen her bonds and that Haley might accept her plight.

Frenchie only wanted some loving companionship now and again as the mood arose. After all, it could be a lot worse for her; she could be some Indian buck's squaw. Frenchie had convinced himself that he was doing the young maiden a service. The Frenchman took the food out to the woman and poured water on her head from a bucket to wake her from unconsciousness. As he did this Haley moaned with discomfort and opened her eyes. She could hardly see the man standing in front of her. The trapper knelt down and spooned a mouthful of eggs in front of her lips. She begrudgingly ate out of sheer starvation.

"Now that wasn't so bad," the Frenchman said as he heaped the spoonful's down as fast as the woman could swallow.

Finally, he put the warm coffee to her lips and poured down the brew. Haley coughed and swallowed as the coffee was too strong and full of grit. She spat out a mouthful, and the discharge hit the trapper in the front of his shirt. The bearded trapper burst out laughing and nearly fell over. He stood and threw the rest of the brew down on the front of Haley's shirt as he walked away. It was time to show her some manners. Frenchie walked back into the cabin and finished his morning breakfast. He sat at the table, staring out the back door. All the while he ate, watching Haley tied to the lean-to post.

Finally, he stood and grabbed one of the jugs of whiskey and poured some of the contents in a tin cup and swallowed the liquor down. He did this several times, and finally he filled the tin to the brim. He walked out the back door, and reaching down he grabbed Haley by the chin and pried open her mouth and poured down the contents of the tin cup. Haley gagged and choked while thrashing her head back and forth from side to side. Finally, the Frenchman stood up and grabbed her by the hair. He pulled out his knife and held it to the side of her jaw. "You'll either like me, or I'll cut your throat and leave you to the wolves," he said. The blade was searing a small sliced wound in her cheekbone. Haley tried to resist, but it was all in vain. The Frenchman let loose of her hair and walked quickly back into the cabin.

Haley knew she would be killed if she didn't cooperate with the trapper, but she had decided she would rather die than submit herself to the terrible man. As she sat there in the morning sun, she made her resolutions with God and His Son. She asked that she be taken quickly and not left to suffer anymore. Haley's eyes were closed when the shadow of the trapper fell over her. She didn't want to open her eyes, but the thought of not seeing her death coming was more than she could bear. She opened her eyes and there stood the Frenchman with a leather shirt on and he was naked from the waist down. He was undoing her ties and cutting away at the leather thongs with a huge bowie knife. The second Haley was free from the leather bonds she sprang away on her knees, screaming as loud as she could, trying to crawl away from her tormentor.

The trapper grabbed her by the hair, and using his knife hand, he slugged her in the side of the stomach as she tried to crawl away. He pulled her back to her feet by the hair and threw her down on the woodpile that lay next to the cabin. The sheer force of the blow and the weight of her body hitting the wood knocked the breath out of the young woman. Before she could regain her senses the trapper was upon her with all his body weight. He raised up just long enough to grab her shirt and tear it from her body. Then he started to unbutton her pants as she violently fought with all her might. She bit the trapper on the side of his hand as he put it to her mouth to force his mouth upon hers. He pulled back his hand and looked at the blood starting to flow from the wound. The Frenchman pulled up the knife and was in the motion of stabbing Haley when he was struck in the head from behind with a rifle butt.

Haley could not see what was happening because the Frenchman fell forward on top of her with all his dead weight. She pushed violently back and forth, trying to free herself from under her attacker when a strange voice called her name and she felt the weight of the unconscious man lifted from her. It was Gabe. He took the Frenchman by the leather shirt and pitched him head first into the woodpile. The unconscious madman hit the wood with full force. He lay still, and Haley hoped he was dead. Gabe pulled her to her feet and tried to cover her nakedness with the remains of her shirt. He walked through the back door of the cabin and returned with a pail of water and a blanket. Haley kept staring at the scout while he tended to her wounds as she sat on an old log stump just outside the cabin back door, still in shock from the horror of her predicament.

Gabe nursed the swollen lips of Haley and put a soft wet cloth in her mouth to suck on. He wiped away the blood from her chin and made a poncho out of the blanket for her to cover herself. He took what was left of her shirt and cut strips and wrapped them around her sore and bruised ribs. This was the best he could do under the circumstances. There were many wild Indians in the vicinity, and Gabe and Haley needed to beware.

Haley rose to her feet and tried to straighten up, but the pain was too much. She almost lost her balance, but Gabe grabbed her and held her upright. The pair was just turning to go into the cabin when the Frenchman rose from the wood pile and grabbed an axe sticking out from a stump. He had the advantage on Gabe and swung the axe, aiming it at the center of Gabe's backbone. Instantly Haley and Gabe were sprayed upon with brain matter and blood as the front forehead of the Frenchman exploded into bits and pieces. Then they heard the report of the rifle from behind the trapper as the short fat man fell forward, landing face down at the couple's feet. Gabe had tried to turn during the assault and was in the motion of pulling the colt pistol in his belt when the shot went off. He would never have beaten the Frenchman to the draw, because he had his hands full in supporting Haley.

The whole incident happened in a split second, and as Gabe turned around with his pistol in hand he could see three Pawnee scouts and Dewey standing about seventy-five yards out and behind the cabin. A huge smile parted Dewey's lips as he yelled out, "Thought you might need some help there wagon scout."

Gabe grinned from ear to ear and told Haley that everything would be all right, and that this man and his Indian scouts were with the army and his good friends. Upon hearing the news, Haley lost consciousness and slumped to her knees. Gabe wrestled her in his arms and carried her into the cabin and laid her on the bunk in the corner. He put a damp rag on her forehead and covered her with a small blanket that he found in a cupboard. He went to the door and motioned for the scouts to come in and have some coffee. The scouts sat at the front of the cabin and rehearsed the events of the past week.

After some time, Davey rode his horse into the area and tied it up at the corrals. Gabe kept checking on the beautiful woman that lay unconscious on the cabin bunk. He was worried about her and thought maybe she needed medical attention that he couldn't provide. Davey went to her side and said that he had some medicine in his bag that would help the young woman recover. He proceeded to make a tea, and eventually Haley came to her senses and drank some.

Scout Dewey told Gabe that they were scouting north to the broken hills after hearing from Tim about the war party raid on the Mormon wagons. The Pawnees had cut the trail of the great grey buffalo horse and read the sign of the small war in the flames. Dewey decided to try to reach Gabe in time to help fight the war party if needed. The lieutenant and the rest of the company were two days back on the trail and headed their way. He had orders to capture the renegade trapper known as Frenchie and hold him over until the army could get there. Then he would be hanged on the premises and the trading post burned to the ground. This was frontier justice muted out in a way by the army to deal with bad men selling guns and whiskey to the Indians.

Davey came out of the cabin and closed the front door. He said that Haley was feeling better. She would need some time to get cleaned up and regain her strength. He had made her some soup and gave her Indian herbs to help heal her wounds. Davey told the scouts that after he topped out on the rim, he could see the Sioux in single file crossing the big plateau and making their way into the tall timber on the other side of the ridge. This would put them into the sacred Black Hills, and their medicine would be strong there. Upon hearing this news, the Pawnees advised against pursuing the war party any further. They knew of the strong medicine that the Sioux would have in their home country. Dewey would wait for the lieutenant and the company to arrive for more orders.

Now that the frontier justice was meted out against Frenchie, their job was complete. They would set a torch to this place and hang the Frenchman by his heels to show all that passed this way that there were penalties for selling whiskey and guns to the natives. Gabe told Dewey that he still had another mission to finish. He needed to return the Mormon girl to her people.

During the conversation, the Pawnees asked about the great scout Mahan. They had known of him before this trail and had cut his track several times in the last few days. He was revered by the Indians far and wide across the plains as a great warrior and someone not to be trifled with. The Pawnees had read the sign on the trail and knew that Mahan had ridden the grey buffalo horse after the Cheyenne war chief Black Tongue. The army scouts had no jurisdiction in the Wyoming territories and could not follow the trail and punish Black Tongue. Mahan would be left alone to his small war trail, and only the Great Spirit could ride with him. Gabe thought about Mahan and had made up his mind that he and Davey would take the trail of the war chief and see if they could be of assistance in returning his granddaughter. Gabe told Davey that he should make ready and they would ride down the canyon and pick up the trail. Gabe asked Dewey if he would watch out for the girl Haley until they returned in a few days. He agreed and the scouts prepared their horses and mules for the war trail.

Upon hearing the men talking on the cabin porch, Haley made preparations to leave. She would not stay behind with the army scouts, and she would not leave Gabe's side. She emerged from the cabin wearing a cotton shirt that she had found in Frenchie's supplies, and she had combed and fashioned her hair up and had placed a western hat on her head. As she came into the morning sunlight, Gabe nearly choked on his spit. She was more beautiful than he had ever imagined. After all Haley had gone through at the hands of her captors, she radiated beauty in a special way.

All of the men were speechless where they stood. Her presence made the morning light something special, and each and every man there around the corrals knew she was the most beautiful woman they had ever seen. Haley informed Gabe that she would accompany him and that he would not be able to get rid of her no matter what he did. She would follow if it meant doing it alone. The scouts couldn't believe the words she was telling them. They thought she would want rest and recovery time to heal and mend her wounds. Gabe informed her that the trail they were following was no place for a woman and they might have to fight in order to survive. Haley would not hear any of the things Gabe was saying. She had made up her mind and that was that. Pitani was her friend and if she needed help then Haley would do what she could to aid her.

Finally, Davey intervened on Haley's behalf and sided with her. He told Gabe that it might not be too bad of an idea because it would give him more time to apply some herbs and help Haley's wounds heal faster. That was bullshit to Gabe's ears. He was frustrated with the matter, but he didn't know what to do about it.

Dewey relayed the conversation to the Pawnee scouts and they all broke out laughing.

Now Gabe was the center of the joke, and he was mad about it. He put his head down and pulled on the rope packs, busying himself with the task of packing the mules. He mumbled to himself and groaned out loud when one of the mules stepped on his foot as he was not paying attention to it. The scouts and Haley burst into laughter again, and the whole scene was more embarrassing to Gabe. His face was beat red, and he could feel the heat on his neck from the morning sun. He needed a drink of water, so he left and walked to the creek with a canteen. He swore to himself that Haley would be his demise someday. He dipped the canteens in the creek and watched as they bubbled to the brim with the cool, sweet Wyoming spring water. Gabe walked back to the corralled horses and noticed one of them already saddled and ready to go. This must have been the one that Frenchie had intended on riding that day. It looked like a good stout bay gelding just the right size for Haley. He motioned for her to try out the stirrups. He helped her mount the horse and adjusted the length for her and told Davey they should get going.

Two of the Pawnee scouts decided they would take up the trail as far as the medicine rock but they would go no farther. Dewey said he would wait for the lieutenant and then see what action he might take. So Gabe, Davey, Haley, and two Pawnees set out on the trail of Black Tongue and Mahan.

It was midday, and the sun was high and warm in the sky. Mahan was following the trail made by the Cheyenne and Pitani. He could plainly see the track her horse made with the small amount of weight on his back. He could also see the powerful deep impressions that Black Tongue's stallion made. Black Tongue must have stolen the horse in the raid because no Plains Indian would ever find himself in the possession of such a fine animal without thievery involved.

The Plains Indians were the masters of horse thievery. They could sneak into a remuda and steal every horse in the pen in full sight of the horses' guardians and still make a good escape. He was cunning and knew all the angles when it came to acquiring horse flesh that didn't belong to him. The Indian prized the horse over all of his possessions and would keep his best pony tethered and ready at his beckoning side. This big dark stallion was a well-bred horse of English descent. He was much too fine for an Indian outlaw such as Black Tongue to own.

Mahan knew he must close the gap between the war party and himself. He would need to get in front of the group and then make his war. As he rode the trail, he thought back to the time he was made a chief among the Ponca and received the war bundle. It was an honor given from one holder to another after the recipient had proven himself worthy in battle. It would take some warchiefs an entire lifetime to earn such an honor, but Mahan had earned his in his first war on the Cheyenne. He had counted coup and killed five of his enemy on that first raid. He also captured seventy-five of the enemy's horses and brought home the scalps of his fallen foe.

The women of the tribe had performed the scalp dance after his return, and he was celebrated among his people to no end. He was given the war bundle in a ceremony that lasted many days, and he was made a chief of his people at the young age of twenty snows. Now the years had come and gone, and he had led his people to hundreds of raids and small wars against the Sioux and Cheyenne. He had grown old and tired of the war trail and had settled down to raise some horses and farming corn when Black Tongue had made his war on Mahan's family. Now Mahan must take up the war trail and avenge the death of his son. He quickened his pace as he felt he would see the war party by sunset.

Black Tongue looked back over his shoulder to check the back trail. Nothing could be seen, and the trail looked deserted. He thought this would be a fine time to rest the horses and gather some meat. He barked out his orders, and two Cheyenne braves rode away from the main war party and hunted some meat. The Indians dismounted and sat where they had stopped, each one of them holding the reins of their ponies in silence as they waited. Black Tongue pulled Pitani from her horse and sat her on the ground. As he did so, he noticed the blue dot tattoo in the middle of her forehead. She was pierced in each ear with bone loops and wore her hair pulled back on her skull. This was the first time he had taken notice of her. He realized that she was a chief's daughter. He knew that the Ponca tattooed their daughters when they received rank among the people such as being made a chief.

The tattooed person was not to be molested or touched by other members of the tribe. They were special women that were guarded and chosen to be made wives for other selected outstanding men in the tribe. They would be virgins until that time when they were chosen to be married. If they agreed, and their parents agreed then a huge ceremony lasting many days would fulfill the marriage rights.

This young Ponca maiden sitting before Black Tongue had not been inducted into marriage yet. She would have the marriage tattoos on her arms signifying her acceptance of the choice to lose her virginity. Black Tongue realized for the first time that she was big medicine and would be a great trophy among his people. He might even make a big trade for the rights to her virginity among his fellow warriors. Black Tongue thought to himself that the Ponca warrior named White Eagle that had ridden after the war party on the day of the raid must have been her father. The Ponca war chief had ridden into the band of Cheyenne that day with fury and madness to make war upon the Cheyenne war party. The Ponca war chief could hardly control his anger, and his disregard for his safety had led Black Tongue to place an arrow into the Ponca's breast.

Black Tongue had scalped the war chief and taken his daughter in the war. This would be the story told by the people for years to come. Black Tongue's medicine was strong, and he felt invincible. He looked the Ponca girl over one more time as the two Cheyenne braves that had gone for meat returned with a deer slung across one of the horses necks. A small fire was made and some meat put on sticks and cooked.

Mahan could smell the smoke and meat for several miles before he could actually see the line of smoke rising through the tall timber. He would finally have his day with the war party, and he knew by sunset that this war trail would come to an end. He quickly dismounted and made himself ready for war. He took off his buckskin leggings and shirt. This left him naked down to his breechcloth and arm rings. He took out the sacred war bundle and carefully laid it upon the ground. He sang the war song and chanted the phrases he had been taught as a young man many snows before. He painted his body with the usual black and red war paint of the Ponca Indian and placed the small dried hawk necklace around his neck. He took out his war weapons and inspected each one as he chanted the war songs over and over.

Mahan had worn his hair on this war trail in the customary comb style. His head was shaven except a center scalp lock that was combed and stiffened straight up on his head to appear as a rooster. His forehead and face were painted with red and black stripes as taught by his people, and he wore only moccasins on his feet. Mahan hung his bow and quiver from a strap he placed around Old Smoke's neck. He would use his pistol and rifle, and the bow would be used only in a backup. His war club was wrapped around his wrist and his knife on his side.

He sang to the buffalo horse as he painted the horse for war. He placed red stripes around the grey horse's legs with black handprints on his rump. He tied feathers and scalps of the dead Cheyenne warriors to the tail and mane of the horse and decorated him for war in the Ponca fashion. The only way you would know Old Smoke wasn't a member of a Ponca war party was the white man's saddle that belonged to Gabe. Finally, Mahan removed the saddle and placed it next to the war bundle making the horse a full member of the tribe. The usual Ponca custom at this juncture was to smoke a war pipe, but this would be too dangerous being this close to the enemy. Mahan said his prayers to the Great Spirit and ended the ceremony.
Horse and rider moved through the timbered forest at a walk. Mahan circled the unsuspecting Cheyenne and came to an open grass meadow secluded by the surrounding timber.

The meadow was about one hundred yards long and about seventy yards across. This would allow for enough room for the big buffalo horse to maneuver if necessary. The plan for Mahan was to remain concealed until the Cheyenne were within sight and then reveal himself and challenge the leader Black Tongue to a war. Mahan would display the Cheyenne scalps for all to see, bringing the warriors to anger.

By challenging the leader, Mahan thought he might kill Black Tongue and the other warriors would quit the war trail. If this didn't succeed, then Mahan would fight them all to the death for his granddaughter.

Old Smoke moved through the tall trees, picking his way back and forth. He knew something was in the air, for he could smell the other horses and the Indians that rode them. He had recognized this smell from many outings in which he and Gabe had encountered wild Indians and their hard ridden ponies.[3] As Mahan and Old Smoke circled the camp, Mahan reached down and put his hand to the animal's nose. He didn't want Old Smoke to call out to the other horses close by. This was just as he had seen in his vision thought Mahan. The Great Spirit was guiding this war trail for him.

Gabe and the Pawnees found the trail that Yellow Hand had taken out of the canyon from the trader cabin. The war chief had escaped this day, but his fate was sealed.[4] The Pawnees found the trail that Mahan had taken, and the pace

---

[3] The Indian horse is abused constantly from the pressure applied by the warrior rider. The mustang horses sweat all the time while on the move and the smell is easy to distinguish between another horse's keen sense of smell. The Indian horse is fed whatever he can browse through while the white man's horses are given oats and hay whenever available. Both animals produce a different smell that the Indian and horse alike can distinguish from.

[4] It would only be another snow, and the Sioux warrior would meet his maker at the hands of the great scout William F. Cody. The defiant war chief would challenge the scout Buffalo Bill to a dual on the prairie grass a year later only to be shown the trail to the Great Spirit's lodge in the sky. Buffalo Bill would be famous for this deed and play the part in real life at his famous Wild West Show. Gabe would see the show in his retirement years and marvel at the way the west was portrayed.

was set at a fast gallop. Gabe knew that the war chief Mahan would be no match for the Cheyenne dog soldiers by himself.

The Cheyenne dog soldiers were a society of killers. They were taken at a young age and taught the art of warfare and terror. They were an elite group of warriors that rode at the head of their nation's pride. They were a menacing force for the army, and the white man and the plains ran blood red from their depredations and raids. They had no equal when it came to guerrilla warfare and cunning. All the Indian nations of the plains held them in revere. They had become a graven enemy of the Pawnee and Ponca nations and other civilized reservation tribes. The dog soldiers made numerous murder raids on the peaceful Indians of the plains. The army would be called out after each raid to try to destroy the ghost-like war parties as they raided and murdered all along the Oregon Trail. It was in this capacity that Gabe had found himself scouting and guiding for the army in his younger days.

Now he was on the trail of one of the most bloodthirsty warriors he had ever trailed. Black Tongue was a proud Cheyenne dog soldier and war chief. He did not know fear and his warlike skills were the best his tribe could produce. He would lead the war trail with blood and carnage. Everything that came in his path had been destroyed and looted. He had managed to steal thousands of horses from ranchers, farmers, and unsuspecting travelers as they ventured into the land he called his home. He knew every trail and water hole in the prairie. He would herd his large stolen horse herds into the Cheyenne nations of Wyoming and then relish in his spoils as his tribe saluted his accomplishments. The War Maker had smiled on his Indian son, and Black Tongue was the greatest of the dog soldiers.

Black Tongue stood up and threw the meat stick from his hands. He made the sign for the war party to get mounted. Pitani was put on her horse, and warriors moved out through the timbered forest at a trot. Black Tongue was sure that the war party had not been followed. He had purposefully stopped and allowed the war party to eat just to prove his point. When nothing showed on the back trail, he knew he had nothing to fear. He slowed the big black stallion to a walk and laughed to himself at how stupid Yellow Hand had been for allowing Black Tongue to escape with the Ponca maiden and four of the Spencer rifles. The rifles would bring needed defense to his people from the encroaching armies that had built forts in the Indians' hunting grounds. Each rifle had been stolen from the trader's cabin with two boxes of bullets. Black Tongue knew that the rifles could shoot a buffalo with one shot from a long distance. They could kill as far as the Indian could see on a clear day.

The rifle Black Tongue held in his hand would bring many scalps and trophies to his lodge. The war chief was engaged in his thoughts when the black stallion raised his head and snorted from a smell in the air. Immediately the war chief halted the war party and surveyed the meadow before them. His eyes searched for the smell his horse had detected, but he found nothing. Maybe the horse smelled a bear, which frequented these wooded areas. Or maybe the smell was that of a game animal. Black Tongue nudged the stallion forward ever so cautiously with his hand on the carbine rifle he had in his grasp. He had barely come to the meadow's edge when he decided to circle the meadow and stay in the timber.

As he proceeded to do this, his eye caught the glimpse of the grey buffalo horse standing opposite him in the timber on the far side of the meadow. A warrior could faintly be seen astride the horse, and he appeared to be Indian. Black Tongue halted the warriors and pointed out his find to the others. The whole group sat on their horses, studying the scene before them, not sure what to do next. Black Tongue could not figure out how the big grey buffalo horse came to this Indian.

The last time Black Tongue saw this Indian he was with the three scouts that followed the war party. Was this Indian another Cheyenne or an enemy? Black Tongue made the usual hand signal to the other Indian, inquiring about his nature. Mahan made the sign of challenge and emerged from the timber into the clear view of all the Cheyenne. He turned the big grey horse around for all to see the scalps worn on him and called out a challenge in the native Ponca tongue. He repeated the challenge in Cheyenne and signed for the snake called Black Tongue to come out and meet him. Pitani instantly recognized her grandfather and gasped at the sight of him. Black Tongue turned around on his horse and stared at the Indian captive. He signed to her if she knew the warrior and she nodded back. How could her father come back from the Great Spirit's lodge and be here this day? Black Tongue thought to himself. What special medicine was this? He turned and held up his hand and signed that he would kill the Ponca warrior if he didn't give them the trail. He also signed that he would kill the Indian captive if they were not left alone.

Mahan stood his ground and called out in Cheyenne that Black Tongue was a coward and a snake. He hid behind captive women and was afraid to meet him in battle. He told the other warriors to go back to the lodges of their people and tell of the coward Black Tongue and how he crawled away from the Ponca warrior's challenge. Black Tongue turned around in his makeshift Indian saddle and looked at the warriors with him. He knew he could not get out of this latest challenge and be able to return to his people without meeting the Ponca in war. He gave instructions for the warriors to kill the Ponca maiden if he should not return and then kill the Ponca warrior, or Black Tongue's spirit would ride with them all their lives and make them miserable. The warriors nodded their agreement, and the war party split up.

The two war chiefs walked their horses to the edge of the clearing and stood ready for battle at fifty yards apart.

Black Tongue studied the Ponca war chief on the big buffalo horse. He had many questions in his mind that needed answers. He signed to the Ponca if he was the same war chief he had killed and scalped last moon. Mahan signed that he was the dead war chief's father there to avenge the death of the son. Black Tongue inquired how it was that the Ponca stole the great buffalo horse from the white man scout. Mahan signed that he was allowed to ride the horse because it was in his vision to do so. Black Tongue yelled out in Cheyenne that the Ponca warrior would meet his son this day at the Great Spirit's lodge in the sky. He screamed out his threats that he would also eat the heart of the Ponca chief and rape his granddaughter.

Mahan spun Old Smoke around in a circle and told Black Tongue that his scalp would be hanging on the tail of the buffalo horse before the sun set. Mahan raised his arm in a challenge and gave the right of weapons choice to the Cheyenne. Black Tongue was full of pride and arrogance. He was certain he could kill the Ponca with his war lance and shield in hand-to-hand combat. He motioned for the shield and club as Mahan threw down his revolver and rifle.

The two enemies stood facing one another with one big white buffalo horse staring down the black stallion of the Cheyenne Nation. Both men gripped their war clubs and nudged their horses into a trot. Black Tongue took his war club and hammered it across the rump of the black stallion, making the horse wince from the impact. This sent the steed into a full run straight at its intended target. Without cue, Old Smoke broke into a thundering gallop as Mahan reached down and laid his hand on the neck of the great animal and spoke out his medicine chant. The horse and rider were in full unison and were closing the distance between the warriors within seconds.

Black Tongue's eyes and face were full of anger and hate as the two men approached each other on the run. The two war horses hit head on in the clearing, and the sound of muscle and bone could be heard throughout the meadow. Right at impact Black Tongue swung his war club and hit at the head of Mahan. The Ponca warrior parried the blow with his buffalo hide shield as the two horses collided. Both horses lost their footing, and both Indians were thrown to the ground. Immediately Black Tongue was on his feet, but the Ponca Chief was quicker and had his war club coming down on Black Tongue with all his might. Just barely in time, the Cheyenne warrior raised his buffalo shield to absorb the blow. The force of the blow knocked Black Tongue to the ground, and he let go of the shield in order to break his fall.

As he rose to get up another blow, Mahan hit the Cheyenne warrior in the left shoulder, breaking bones as the sound of the club hit its mark. With one arm useless and only his war club in his right hand, Black Tongue swung with a low blow to the knee of Mahan knocking the old chief to the ground. With the swiftness of a young warrior, Black Tongue dropped his war club, and while pulling his knife he jumped on Mahan. Mahan didn't have time to thwart the knife, as it found his side. He rolled away from the blade and sprung to his feet faster than Black Tongue could get to his. Mahan swung his club once more down on the backbone of Black Tongue as the Cheyenne tried to regain his footing. The blow knocked the warrior back to the ground, and as he tried to rise Mahan threw down his shield and club and pulled his knife for the kill. Mahan could barely stand on his swelling knee but managed to grab the Cheyenne warrior by the back of his hair, and in one swift motion, while yelling his war song, Mahan put the blade of his knife to the side of Black Tongue's throat and pulled the knife across his throat with one swift and powerful swath.

Mahan made one more slice with his knife and removed the scalp lock, which he held in his hand for all to see. He tried to stand upright, but the pain from his knee made this impossible, so he knelt there with the scalp in his hand in the air, yelling his war chant. The other Cheyenne warriors were amazed at the swiftness of the old warrior. They looked at one another for someone to take charge of the situation and tell them what to do. Black Tongue was the chief of this war trail, and his death had not been expected. There was confusion in the ranks, and the young warriors argued amongst themselves as to what to do.

Meanwhile, Mahan crawled to where he had dropped his rifle and recovered both guns. The indecision of the war party would give Mahan time to prepare for the next assault. He swiftly crawled over to Old Smoke and pulled himself in a standing position. He inspected the buffalo horse, and he seemed to be in good condition despite of the menacing blow he had taken from the impact of the two war horses.

The black stallion was standing but had his hind leg lifted slightly off the ground, signaling that he was hurt. Mahan was looking over the back of Old Smoke, keeping the horse between himself and the war party on the other side of the meadow just inside the timber. He couldn't see Pitani, and he dared not fire a shot in that direction for fear of hitting her. His hand went to his side, and as he inspected the knife wound, he realized that it was serious and would need some attention quickly. He pulled his medicine bag from around the neck of Smoke and pulled out his wound moss and pressed it to the cut. Mahan winced with pain as the dirty moss mixed with his blood and entered the flesh. He knew he must end this war soon or he might die from blood loss. The Ponca warrior bound himself with a four-inch-wide strip of tanned buffalo hide and tied it around his belly as tight as he could allow. This would have to do for now.

Red Hawk had not been in favor of this war trail from the beginning. When the captive women were taken, he had shown mercy and gave them water and food. He felt like the medicine of Black Tongue was weak and would get all the Cheyenne killed if they persisted down this trail. He wanted to take the stolen animals in the beginning and return to his people. He knew that taking captives would bring trouble. Other people would come looking to rescue the women, and he knew that it would mean a war trail in the end. His medicine was not as strong as Black Tongue, so he had gone along with the war chief's orders. Now that Black Tongue was dead, Red Hawk would not take orders from the remaining warriors. He said that he was quitting the war trail and returning to his lodge alive. He advised the others to do the same and to release the Ponca maiden. Red Hawk turned his war pony around in the timber and rode off in the direction of his people. There were five remaining warriors, and they were all dog soldiers.

The group elected Conch to lead the rest of their war trail. He was older than all the others and seemed to have the most knowledge when it came to making decisions. Conch instructed the warriors to surround the Ponca warrior in the meadow and use their rifles to kill him and remove the spirit of Black Tongue from haunting them all their living days. He would take the captive girl and kill her as Black Tongue had instructed before his death. Pitani, understanding the language of the Cheyenne, knew her time on this earth would be short if she didn't act quickly.

With all her might, she kicked out to the side of her horse, hitting Conch in the waist with her foot. Her hands were still tied around the neck of her horse, but she had loosened her bonds during the ride up from the trader's cabin in the night. She kicked the small mustang into a trot and headed out into the meadow towards her grandfather.

Conch regained his balance on his horse and pulled up his reins and hit the side of his horse with his Spencer rifle. The blow made the animal jump into a running gallop. Conch was gaining on Pitani, and as he came along the side of her horse, he pulled his knife and made a lunge at her back. Conch was in the motion of swinging the knife blade again toward the woman when a bullet caught him just below the sternum, knocking him back off the running horse and to the ground. The bullet had passed completely through the dead warrior, and he was dead before his body quit rolling in the meadow grass. Pitani heard the report of the rifle and knew it was Mahan that had killed the Cheyenne Conch. She rode her horse over to the edge of the timber toward Mahan as he jumped up and tried to stop the frightened animal. He caught the horse by its cheek leather and swung the horse around to a stop. He quickly cut the leather thongs binding Pitani and pulled her down and behind a fallen log.

A bullet passed overhead and took the bark off the nearest tree to the side of Mahan's head. He quickly pulled the buffalo horse around to his side and mounted the tall horse with all his might. He threw the pistol down to Pitani and told her to kill her enemies if he should not return. He kicked the big grey horse in the flanks, and Old Smoke burst through the timber and galloped toward the puzzled Cheyenne warriors. Seeing the white buffalo horse charging at them and the Ponca warrior screaming a death song made the group turn and scatter in the timber. All but one ran for the back trail of Red Hawk. Lone Bull pulled up his new Spencer rifle and fired one last shot at the charging Ponca war chief.

Lone Bull swung his war pony around and beat a fast track through the timber and towards the other fleeing warriors. He never looked back on the meadow and the threatening Ponca warrior. Had Lone Bull looked back that day, his medicine might have turned in his favor, and he would probably have ridden into the lodges of his people as the next Great War Chief of the Cheyenne Nation.

CHAPTER 12 - REWARDS FROM HEAVEN

Mahan saw the smoke from the rifle and felt the bullet hit the big grey horse in the neck. Old Smoke lost all of his strength and went head down and back end over two times in the open meadow. The impact threw Mahan forward nearly twelve feet and he rolled several times coming to a stop face down and unconscious. Old Smoke lay on his side and tried to raise his head, but he gave up the fight and just lay his head back down on the cool meadow grass. He had served his masters well. He could leave this life with honor and respect among his fellow comrades. Smoke closed his eyes as the Great Spirit ascended on his fallen body.

A magnificent white stallion came prancing through the mist with its tail and mane flowing like angel's hair. The more Old Smoke looked, the more he thought he recognized the beautiful horse. As the stallion came nearer through the mist, Smoke realized that it was his father El Caballo Magnifico in all his glory. Smoke had only seen his father once down in Old Mexico. He and his mother had been sold to a ranch in Texas, and that was the last time the two of them had seen one another. His father approached and looked Smoke over. He said that he was glad to see his son and that the two of them had many good times ahead together. He said that their spirits were free in the Heavens to roam where they pleased. The Great Father in heaven loved all the spirits of the earthly animals, and they had performed a mission for him on earth. Now that they were free from pain and suffering on earth they could live with him forever in this mansion in the sky. Smoke stood and compared his stature with that of his father. The two horses marveled at one another and stood in awe of each other's prowess. Both animals had been outstanding steeds in their earthly missions. They had served mankind with compassion and endurance to the end. And together father and son walked through the beautiful canyons of heaven as they conversed and reacquainted themselves with one another.

Gabe, Davey, and Haley were riding up the timbered trail, following the Pawnee scouts in front. One of the Pawnees motioned for the group to stop. Another Pawnee scout rode out and disappeared in the thick timber. Gabe signed for Davey to stay with Haley no matter what the circumstances, and if there was any danger to take her back down the trail to Dewey and the army. Gabe signed that he would send one of the Pawnees back to get Davey and Haley when things were safe. He prodded the mustang horse in the belly and moved off in the direction of the Pawnee scout. Gabe pulled the Henry out just in case it was needed and checked the lever as he rode through the forest. He could see the two Pawnees in front of him, sitting on their horses and looking at something.

Gabe rode up to the two scouts and they pointed to the meadow before them. Gabe's heart sunk as he witnessed the scene before him. Pitani sat cross legged out in the open near Mahan's body and was chanting and singing her song of death. Gabe looked the area over and realized that the battle for Pitani was over. He rode slowly into the open meadow and toward his fallen horse. The big grey horse lay on his side and looked finished. Near him sat Pitani, and her grandfather. Mahan was barely alive, and Pitani was holding his head in her lap as she sat in the meadow grass. Gabe signed for one of the Pawnees to go fetch Davey and Haley as he slid from the mustang's back. He walked over to Mahan and gazed down at him. Mahan was clinging to life. The meadow grass that encircled the Indians was stained from the amount of blood the old warrior had lost. Gabe knew the old chief had traveled his last war trail.

As Davey and Haley rode into the scene, Gabe instructed the Pawnee scouts to make sure all hostiles in the area were gone. They mounted their ponies and swiftly rode away. Davey pulled his medicine bag from one of the pack mules and knelt down at Mahan's side. He touched Pitani on the shoulder to reassure her that he would try and help the dying warrior. Davey looked at the wound in Mahan's side and prepared a moss compress. He cut loose the makeshift bandage that Mahan had applied and viewed the knife cut in the Indian's side. Davey looked up at Gabe and said in Choctaw that it was finished. He covered up the wound and stood slowly and backed away. Gabe knelt down and put his hand on the hand of Mahan and told him that his granddaughter would be returned to her people. He gave his promise to the dying chief that this would be done on his life's word.

Mahan spoke slowly and said, "*Kweyachi atay ahei.* I go to the place of my father. My journey through this life is finished. I will ride the trail with my grandfathers before the sun sets." He told Gabe of the great battle the grey horse fought. He told Gabe that he would care for the great buffalo horse in the Great Spirit's hunting grounds until Gabe reached that place and could be reunited with his horse. Gabe cordially, thanked Mahan and looked up to see Old Smoke lying there in the afternoon sun.

As Gabe stared at his horse's form out on the meadow flats, Pitani suddenly screamed out and started wailing. Gabe looked back to see Mahan had taken his last breath. The mighty warrior chief had finished the war trail. Gabe stood and took his hat off in reverence and gratitude for the old chief's help in recovering the captive women. He and Davey owed their life to the proud warrior, and they would finish Mahan's vision of returning Pitani to her people.

The Pawnee scouts returned with news of the Cheyenne war party. The once proud Cheyenne warriors had made a fast retreat to the safety of the Great Spirit rock country. There they would be protected from their enemies by their people. The war trail was finished, and now it was time to bury the dead. Gabe instructed the Pawnees to make a platform scaffold in the nearby lodge pole pines. First Gabe went to the big black Cheyenne war horse. The poor animal could hardly stand. His back leg was broken, and he would surely perish if left alone to die. Gabe took out his pistol and put the horse down with a shot to the ear. Then Gabe walked over to the dead body of Black Tongue and scalped the dead warrior. Mahan would take that scalp to the Great Spirit's lodge with him that day. When the Pawnees were finished, the body of Mahan was wrapped in buckskin straps and bound tightly with sinew.

Gabe and the scouts placed Mahan's body on the platform supported by the log poles. Mahan had told Gabe that if he should die on the war trail, he wanted to be buried in the way of the old ones. Since the introduction of Christianity to the Missouri Indian tribes, most of the nations buried their dead in the ground as taught in the Bible. But the old Indians were placed out in the open, up in the air on scaffolds, and left for the Great Spirit to take their bodies to his lodge in the sky. This was the dying wish of Gabe's friend, and he would see the task through.

Gabe tied all the Cheyenne and Sioux scalps to the log poles. He took all of Mahan's possessions and placed them on the platform with the chief's body. His mustang horse was tied to the scaffold and had its throat cut, as was the custom. Mahan would need all of his weapons, charms, and medicine bags in the next life along with his horse. Gabe made sure that everything was in order before the group left the meadow. Pitani had cut her hair, slit her wrists, and pulled her bone piercings out in mourning of her grandfather. She had also chopped off her small finger on her left hand at the first knuckle to show her gratitude for her grandfather's life for hers. She mourned and chanted her death songs as Davey tended to her wounds.

Haley stood by as witness to all the proceedings. She could not believe she was part of all that had taken place since the wagon raid. She was thankful for Pitani's release and sad for her grandfather's death. For a schoolteacher from the east, Haley had lived a nightmare in real life. She would have stories to tell her children and grandchildren for another eighty years. The impressions of these events were permanently engraved on her mind. Haley asked Gabe if she might rest for an hour before they moved on. Gabe quickly made a comfortable place for Haley on the edge of the meadow and put a campfire in motion.

One of the Pawnees had some venison, and the scout Indians started cooking meat and boiling coffee. Davey carried Pitani over near the fire and placed her on a buffalo robe that one of the mules carried in its pack. She was too weak to walk from the loss of blood and shock to her system. She lay there softly mumbling her songs of mourning as Davey applied medicine to her. He gave both of the women some Ojibwa Indian tea made from four special herbs held sacred by the Indian nations as a healing element to body shock and trauma. Davey applied a compress to the woman's wounds made of biennial wormwood, wild ginger leaves, and mockernut hickory bark. This wound dressing had powerful effects on an open wound and would usually heal them within several days. The principles and remedies that Davey used were taught to him by his Choctaw elders. Haley sipped the tea and was surprised to find it fairly pleasant-tasting. She was handed a stick of cooked meat and ate her fill of the hot morsel. Both women rested and napped while the scouts made plans for their next trail.

Gabe walked over to where Old Smoke had fallen. The big horse laid sprawled out on the meadow grass and seemed quite peaceful with his eyes closed. Gabe thought about all the good times they had together and felt great remorse in his heart. Old Smoke had been his companion for the last eight years through wind, rain, fire, and war. They had weathered not only the elements but countless hours of starvation and thirst out on the plains. Never once had the big grey failed his master. Gabe caught a tear in his right eye on the cuff of his buckskin shirt sleeve. He knelt down to pay homage to the fallen warrior and put his hand out and touched the great horse's side.

Davey walked over to Gabe's side and put his hand on the shoulder of his friend. Davey knew how close the man and horse had been and that nothing could separate the two except death. Gabe said a prayer out loud for all to hear: "Please, God, take this precious spirit into your folds and allow him the rest and peace he deserves. He was kind and gentle to his owner and required little in the way of keep. Place him among the other great horses that have served mankind with distinction and allow us to be together again."

Gabe had no sooner finished the last sentence when Davey exclaimed, "The great one has not yet passed over to the other side."

"What are you talking about?" exclaimed Gabe.

"He's got a bullet in his neck and he's bled out."

Davey put his head on the fallen horse's rib cage and told Gabe to listen. "Listen here. His heart still beats," Davey said as the two scouts put ears to the horse's side and listened for a sign of life.

Gabe raised his head and said, “Well, he’s as good as dead. I owe it to him that he shouldn’t suffer any longer.” Gabe stood and pulled his colt revolver and cocked the pistol in his hand.

Davey said, “Wait, I’ve seen this thing before, and it has puzzled me in the past. When a horse is wounded, most of the time they will lie down and give up the fight. Sometimes they are not mortally wounded, but they have given up in their minds and lie until starvation or predators come and kill them.”

Davey shouted for the Pawnees to come to his assistance. With all the men gathered Davey had one of the Pawnees cover Old Smoke’s head with a leather hide. He instructed Gabe to climb on the horse's neck and hold him down should he try to move. The other Indians would try and hold down the horse while Davey could see if he might remove the bullet lodged in the neck of the horse. The Choctaw had seen this method in his youth many times. He poured some of the trader’s whiskey over his knife and hands and started probing with the knife tip. The big grey horse never opened his eyes.

Finally, Davey reached into the wound with his fingers and located and removed the ball. The ball had only penetrated several inches because it hit the bridle thong before entering the horse’s neck. The wound was superficial when compared to the size of the horse’s enormous neck muscles. All of the men stood, and the cover was removed from the horse's head. Old Smoke lay motionless and appeared to have given up the ghost.

Davey signed for one of the Pawnees to make the death fire. Gabe stood by helplessly as the Indians started a small fire near the belly of the beast. Davey explained that the horse would either realize it’s not so bad off and jump to his feet to get away from the heat on his belly or he would succumb in his mind and accept death. Suddenly, the great war horse sprang to his feet and started kicking at everything in sight. He nearly kicked Gabe's head off as he ran from the scene of the fire and over to where the other horses were tied. Gabe ran after the horse, and upon approaching him, he put out his hand to calm the big grey animal. Smoke put his head down and smelled his master's scent and relaxed.

"Well, I'll be damned, you old son of a bitch. You were faking the whole time," Gabe talked to his old friend. "Here I was praying and fretting over you like a schoolboy who had just lost his favorite dog, and you were napping the whole time. Of all the times to lie down on the trail, this one beats them all. Even the mules' got better sense than to lie down and wait for the buzzards. A small nick in the neck, and you quit the war trail faster than a scared rabbit. I ought to make you carry the mules load for the rest of this trail just to teach you a lesson. I had given up on you, and all the while you were in dreamland stretched out in the meadow clover resting while we fought off those thieving Cheyenne. It's a good thing you came to your senses, because I nearly put you under for good you old cayuse. Some lucky Indian might have come along and been wearing your tail on his war club for decoration."

Davey laughed out loud at the sight of the horse and master being reunited as the afternoon sky turned red with sunset. Gabe and Davey nursed the wound on Old Smoke and fed him bunches of pack oats and cut meadow grass. The whole time Gabe kept talking to the horse like he was his long lost friend. Davey could see the love and admiration Gabe processed for the great war horse, and he reveled in the closeness of such a relationship.

Gabe gave his old friend a complete rub down with his leather gloves and combed the mane and tail of the warrior horse.

The scouts decided to make a night camp since the women were fast asleep and needed their rest. The Pawnees unsaddled the stock horses and pack mules while Gabe started cooking some of his famous prairie stew. The stew became famous while on a scouting excursion with the Pawnee Battalion down on the Republican River. Gabe had volunteered to cook an evening meal for the troopers. While out scouting one day, he gathered some seasonings for a rabbit stew. Upon returning to camp, he proceeded to make a delicious stew of prairie turnips, rabbit meat, and wild mushrooms.

When the stew was finished, the men heartily licked the concoction up to the last drop and crowned Gabe the greatest cook on the prairie. Everyone lit their pipes, and the stories started around the campfires. Along about midnight, the troopers fell restless, and one by one the soldiers crawled out of their pup tents and ran out onto the prairie and bare all to the world. With a handful of sage in one hand and the other hand trying to keep them upright, the entire squad of Indian fighters painted the entire western plains with the remains of the famous stew.

Along about morning, the weary-eyed and grumbling men confronted Gabe only to find the scout also engaged in a Mona Lisa portrait painting of the nearby buffalo grasses. Later in the day Gabe realized the error of his way when one of the Pawnees Indians told him he thought he used way too much bitter bark[5] for seasoning. Gabe's popularity took many days to regain its former status among his fellow troopers.

The camp was a comfortable one, and the scouts made everything as pleasant as could be afforded in the Wyoming

---

[5] Bitter Bark was a popular seasoning among the early settlers of the American West. It was also used in larger doses as a laxative by the Native American Indians.

wilderness. A larger than normal fire was made for the women with plenty of venison stew and hardtack on hand to fill the stomachs of the hungry. Haley and Pitani hung close to one another in the fires dim light. Their prayers had been answered, and the former thoughts of their ordeal were starting to fade with the new world they found themselves a part of. It was decided that the scouting party would ride back down the back trail and try to meet up with Dewey and the army patrol. This would make the trip back to Fort Laramie a safer one than going alone.

As plans were discussed and the weary travelers settled in for the night, Haley occasionally looked at Gabe and admired the handsome scout. Gabe was larger than most men of the era, standing a little over six feet tall. He had green eyes and dark hair, and his overall appearance seemed to be European. He had a softness to him that had come from his mother. He was concerned for the safety of all around and would come to the aid of anyone in need. He was long and lean from many days without proper food and nutrition. His face was hardened and appeared much older than he really was. The sun and wind had cut into his skin, and he had the look of a weathered veteran of the plains.

As Gabe would notice Haley, his eyes would take in her beauty. He didn't want her to catch him looking at her, so he averted his eyes until just the right moments. Once or twice in the firelight, the two traveler's eyes would meet, and Gabe would break with a smile. Haley would return the gesture, and the scout would feel uneasy inside his stomach. Gabe had never been smitten by anything or anyone like Haley Johnson. He looked forward to the day this trail was over, and he could return to his normal feeling self. As soon as Haley was returned to the Mormons, Gabe would be finished with her, and the debt he owed her would be square. These thoughts and many more filled the head of the scout as he was roused from his bed for the night guard.

During the night, the horses became restless several times, and Gabe suspected a bear or mountain cat was prowling around. He figured the Indian fighting was over for now and that both the Cheyenne and Sioux had returned to their lodges. It would be another two weeks to Fort Laramie and another month to Fort Bridger. Gabe wasn't sure how far the Mormon wagon train had traveled. The early fall weather had made crossing the Platte a risky business, and Gabe wasn't sure whether Otis would try it or wait it out until late spring. Gabe would take Haley down to the fort and follow the Mormon trail. Davey had volunteered to escort Pitani back to her people. He would stay there until Otis and his brother Tim made their way back to Omaha for another wagon train. Gabe would get the word to Otis about the location of Davey.

Plans had been made, and if the good Lord was willing, Gabe would carry them out. All through the night, as Gabe sat perched on a rock, listening for sounds, his mind was filled with thoughts of Haley Johnson. He couldn't shake the feeling he had for her, and by morning's early light, he had succumbed to the idea that he might tell her about his feelings. He wrestled with this decision because he didn't want to put a hardship on her and him. Finally, he got up enough nerve and approached where she lay. He tapped her on the arm, and as she rose, he asked if he might have a moment of her time alone to talk. She quickly made herself ready and wrapped a fur skin around her shoulder as she followed Gabe back to his place of concealment. Haley felt completely safe in the hands of her rescuer and she looked forward to hearing what Gabe had to say.

The weary scout sat her down on the rock beside him and started to pour out his life and how he had come to this junction with her. Gabe laid it all out and put his heart in Haley's hands. He didn't hold anything back and told her how he felt about her, but he wasn't sure where all his feelings would lead. Finally, after Gabe had exhausted himself with words and sentences, Haley put her index finger to his lips and said that would be enough. She put her hand around the back of Gabe's neck and kissed him full and long on the mouth. As she pulled her head softly away, she said that his life story didn't matter to her. She had only known him for a short time, and in that time she had seen a man she wanted to live with for the rest of her life. Haley told Gabe the all-important words in any relationship: "I love you and I want to be with you." Gabe nearly fell over backward on the rock he was sitting on when hearing Haley's comments.

Now his heart was history. He would never be the same again. He put his arms around her and held her tight as the morning sun started to peer through the lodgepole pines of the Wyoming forest. Finally, Gabe stood and pulled Haley to him. He bent down and kissed her again as she kissed him back. He could feel the softness of her body and sweetness of her kiss. Gabe had never held a woman this close, and the fragrance of her woman smells made him yearn for more. He finally came to his senses and softened his grip on her. She looked up at him with welcome eyes that would stand the test of time. Gabe had finally found his purpose in life. Gabe's thoughts were flowing like the late autumn leaves from the trees. He would need to think this situation through, and several days on the trail were just what the doctor ordered. The two of them rejoined the others back at camp as the Pawnees prepared some breakfast.

After a satisfying meal of boiled venison and sego lilies, the party decided it was time to break camp and go find the army patrol. As the horses were being prepared and the mules packed, Gabe noticed the two Pawnee scouts having a hard time lifting some saddlebags that had been on the horse Haley was riding. He walked over to the Indians and asked what the trouble was. The Pawnees made a joke and laughed at the white man needing so many bullets that his horse couldn't carry his weight into battle. Gabe was confused, so he hefted the leather saddlebags with one hand,

and he could barely raise the packs off the ground. As he undid the leather windings opened on one side, he could see the bags contained small leather pouches about twice the size of a man's fist. He pulled one of the bags free from the saddle bags and held it in his hand. Are these bullets? Gabe thought. He immediately pulled his knife out and cut the leather tie strings that fastened the pouch closed at the top.

The pouch was nearly more weight than he could bear with his wrist. Gabe opened the pouch and peered inside to see the contents. By this time, Davey and Haley had gathered around and everyone was curious about the pouch. Gabe froze in silence as his brain registered the sight his eyes beheld. He couldn't speak or move a muscle. There in the pouch were hundreds of bright yellow gold nuggets. The pouch was filled with pieces of solid gold. Davey asked if the pouch contained musket balls, and the Indian scouts broke out in laughter again. Even Haley joined in the laughter as the party of scouts was having a joyous time of it. Gabe leaned forward on one knee and partially turned to face the crowd. As he did, this he poured the contents of the pouch out onto the ground for all to see.

The scene went completely silent as the trail weary travelers inspected the bright yellow gold nuggets lying on the ground before them. Gabe looked at Davey and Haley with a puzzled look. He knew that this must be the Frenchman's trade goods from the Indians. Gabe grabbed the saddlebags and with the help of the others, he cut open the bags and displayed the contents to all who witnessed it. There before them were twelve pouches all filled to the brim with pure gold nuggets. Gabe sat back on his hind end and gasped out loud for all to hear. Even the Pawnees knew the importance of the yellow rock and its value to the white man. Haley and Davey just stared at the fortune, unable to find words to describe how they felt. Finally, Gabe stood up and said, "I guess the Frenchman won't have a need for this gold where he's going. We might as well pack it up and take it with us. I'm sure we can put it to good use."

Carefully the gold was packed and loaded on two of the mules. Gabe inspected the packs several times in the process to make sure the gold was not recognizable and the weight of the ore could not be detected by someone looking at the mules' packs. He knew well that just the thought of this treasure would bring out the worst in mankind. A plan was discussed between the scouts. It was decided that they would keep the gold a secret and that they would split up the treasure among themselves. The Pawnee scouts didn't want anything to do with the gold because of their superstitions, for the yellow rock had always brought bad medicine to their people. Gabe felt like they were being taken advantage of, so he proposed that the Pawnees would take the Spencer rifle and war weapons of Black Tongue and his Henry rifle for their silence.

A pipe was smoked in council, and it was agreed upon by all concerned. The day had barely begun, and a new twist in the trail had developed for Gabe. The scout knew that the odds of getting to Fort Laramie with all the gold and the women in one piece would be difficult at best. If the secret of the treasure got out, their lives would be worth nothing on the open prairie. Every back shooting, dry gulchin, cutthroat, and highwayman on the plains would be out on the hunt for the gold pouches. Hell, even the army couldn't be trusted with this treasure, he thought. Gabe needed a plan and he needed it quick.

As the Pawnees prepared for the trail, Davey, Haley, and Gabe discussed their future plans. Pitani was off to herself and still in mourning, so the group thought it better to leave her out of the discussion. Gabe suggested that they take the gold as far as they could with them to Fort Laramie, and then when they found a good spot without prying eyes, they would bury the gold and take the women on to the fort.

Gabe could cut the back trail later and retrieve the gold when everything settled down and the women were safe. Davey thought it was a good idea and he agreed. Davey asked Gabe how much he thought the gold might bring and Gabe paused for a minute and said, “Enough money that none of us would ever want for again." That was a lot for the mind of the young Choctaw as Davey went to attend to Pitani’s needs. Haley looked into the eyes of Gabe, and she could see the concern that had returned to his expression. She knew that they were not out of danger, and this new threat could cost them their lives. Gabe grasped Haley’s hand and reassured her that everything would be okay.

It was time to hit the saddle and get moving toward the fort. Gabe lifted Haley into the saddle and made sure she was properly seated. He gave her hand one last squeeze on the hand and a smile for comfort. He looked over his shoulder as he put his foot in the stirrup on one of the mustangs. The meadow was silent, and the resting place for Mahan would allow the mighty warrior to rest in peace. Pulling the lead rope up tight, he looked at Old Smoke standing there without packs or saddle on with a bandage around his neck and said, “You gonna milk it all the way to Laramie or are you gonna pull your weight? I just thought I’d ask."

On to the timbered trail, Gabe led his horse with the others following in single file. The Pawnees had taken the trail earlier toward the army patrol. The morning sun was full in the sky, and the day had the makings of a cool one. As the weary horsemen reached the edge of the canyon rim, they turned in their saddles and they looked west.

POST-NOVEL

In a windswept canyon along Wyoming's eastern border sits a winding canyon. Cedar trees and rock formations choke the canyon walls. A small stream of water brings life to the wildlife that surrounds the canyon area. Still visible are the winding cut trails used hundreds of years ago by indigenous Native American tribes as they frequented the canyon for water, game, and shelter from the Wyoming winter winds. The canyon has a ghostly feel as one explores its recesses and hidden areas. In this second novel of the series, They Looked West; we find Gabe Tanner and Haley Johnson making their way through the wilds of Wyoming. Gabe will do his best to return Haley to the Mormon wagon train. Many dangers and adventures await the young couple. Together they form a bond that will be tested by the winds of time.

ABOUT THE AUTHOR

Grady Southwick was born in 1952 in the old Lehi, Utah, hospital. He was raised in a farming community by his parents, Ray and Bonnie Southwick. His father was a steel mill worker, and his mother was a homemaker. They were devout Mormons, and Grady was raised in this environment at an early age. Grady lived next door to his grandparents, who worked a beef cattle operation. From a young tender age, Grady was hired by his grandfather to help with the daily chores and operations of the cattle farm. Grady would feed and care for the various animals that were present on the farm. He was indoctrinated to horses at a very young age and took to riding and caring for horses his entire life. Grady received the rank of Eagle Scout at the young age of fourteen. Upon graduation from high school in 1970, Grady enlisted in the army reserves. He served honorably and was discharged from the army in 1976. Grady entered Brigham Young University majoring in Business. He met and married his lifelong companion Patty Christensen in 1972. The couple had four children, three daughters and one son. Grady started his own business in 1986 and continued with its operation for over thirty years. During their lives, Grady and Patty raised their family and became the proud grandparents of six granddaughters and six grandsons. The couple relish time spent with their family. Grady has spent most of his free time in riding and packing his horses and mules along the vast wildernesses of Utah, Wyoming, and Montana. He enjoys fishing and hunting in the mountains, and relaxes with a round a golf or two with his son and wife. Grady has spent a great deal of time in the western recesses and canyons of the vast Rocky Mountains. He frequents these areas on a yearly basis. On any given day, you can find him riding along on his favorite big grey horse named Big Smoke, taking in the beautiful surroundings that God has blessed him with.

Register your book by visiting

www.TheyLookedWest.com

Look for more books by Grady Southwick by visiting

amazon.com/author/gradysouthwick

Follow Grady on Facebook & Twitter

https://www.facebook.com/theylookedwest

https://twitter.com/theylookedwest

www.ingramcontent.com/pod-product-compliance
Lightning Source LLC
Chambersburg PA
CBHW060545310726
48982CB00009B/1380/J

* 9 7 8 1 6 1 9 8 4 7 6 4 4 *